UNFORGIVING
SHADOWS

UNFORGIVING SHADOWS

RAY FLYNT

Five Star • Waterville, Maine

First Edition
First Printing: August 2005

Published in 2005 in conjunction with Tekno Books and Ed Gorman.

Set in 11 pt. Plantin by Minnie B. Raven.

Printed in the United States on permanent paper.

Library of Congress Cataloging-in-Publication Data

Flynt, Ray.
　　Unforgiving shadows / by Ray Flynt.—1st ed.
　　　p. cm.
　　ISBN 1-59414-315-3 (hc : alk. paper)
　　1. Private investigators—Pennsylvania—
Philadelphia—Fiction.　2. Executions and
executioners—Fiction.　3. Murder victims' families—
Fiction.　4. Philadelphia (Pa.)—Fiction.　I. Title.
PS3606.L96U54 2005
　　813´.6—dc22　　　　　　　　　　　　2005007905

For Rebecca

ACKNOWLEDGMENTS

In spite of long solitary hours typing at the computer keyboard, the journey from I-think-I'd-like-to-write-a-mystery to seeing a completed novel in print requires the support of many people.

First, my thanks goes to John Helfers at Tekno Books who believed in *Unforgiving Shadows* and brought it to Five Star Publishing. I am indebted to Hugh Abramson, my editor, whose trained eye and fresh perspectives added immeasurably to the final version.

To members of my writers' group: Janet Benrey, Bert Brun, Christiane Carlson-Thies, Mary Ellen Hughes, Trish Marshall, Sherriel Mattingly, and Marcia Talley, thanks for all the "tough love" and for valuable edits and suggestions as the story came to life one chapter at a time.

I am grateful for the many people who read the completed manuscript and asked questions or offered comments; they include Charles Corritore, Eleanor Logan, Bob Martin, Michael Oring, and Michael Rouse. And for the countless individuals—family, friends, and associates who listened patiently as I recounted Brad Frame's journey as well as my own, and who sustained my hopes of publishing with their supportive words.

And finally, to Rebecca, for her friendship, love, and encouragement, especially during those times when the dream seemed out of reach.

CHAPTER 1

In ninety minutes, Wilkie would die.

Brad Frame's leg muscles ached as he stepped from the car onto the gravel driveway. He needed to stretch after the four-hour drive from Philadelphia, so he placed his hands against the car's body, and braced his legs on the solid ground until he felt his hamstring go taut.

After a moment, the warmth he had retained from the heated leather seats of the Mercedes quickly dissipated into the brisk March night. He zipped up his parka, exhaled, and watched as his breath, visible in the sodium vapor lights at the perimeter of the prison, wafted slowly into space. Standing by the open car door his gaze moved outward from the floodlit stone walls to the grays of distant hills silhouetted against a black sky. It all seemed so peaceful until the rising chants of nearby demonstrators, with their conflicting death penalty messages, reminded him why he stood next to his car on a godforsaken spot in the middle of Pennsylvania.

A few minutes earlier as his car approached the base of the hill on which the prison stood, anti–death penalty protestors had rushed him. They leered at him with angry faces, shaking their hand-painted signs in an unreadable blur, and pounded the windows while shouting obscenities. Their fury surprised and angered him, and he stared back at them in disbelief. He couldn't understand how they could embrace the life of a man who had brought so much pain and suffering to his family. Brad felt his heart racing and his jaw tighten. Words took shape in his mind: *Do you know what this man did to my family?* Before he could shout back the State Police had cleared the roadway, and Brad had continued his journey up the hill.

Brad glanced at his watch—almost 10 p.m. He slammed the car door and reminded himself that it wasn't too late to back out. Frank Wilkie had invited him to the Rockview Correctional facility for the execution. Wilkie, who, eleven years earlier, had kidnapped his mother and sister from their Main Line home in Philadelphia. A week after the kidnapping they were found brutally murdered. Brad zapped the remote to lock his car, then turned toward the chain link fence.

Approaching the gate of the death house, located on the grounds of the prison in a former field hospital, Brad stared up at the v-shape brackets at the top connected by barbed wire into which coils of razor wire had been cradled. Wicked looking stuff. The guards must have seen him coming, because the gate opened with a soft whir and he continued walking toward a thick security window at the building's entrance. A uniformed officer behind the glass muttered, "ID," into the intercom, and Frame flashed his driver's license. A few seconds later a deep buzzer sounded followed by the clank of metal as the door ground open. Another Corrections officer waited on the other side.

"I'm Tom Hardesty." The officer extended his hand. "We've been expecting you, Mr. Frame. You're the last to arrive."

"Call me Brad," he said matching Hardesty's vigorous handshake.

"I see you made it past the demonstrators. Sorry you had to go through that, but they got their First Amendment rights." Hardesty laughed. "The other witnesses are in a holding room, Mr. Frame . . . Brad. You'll be going into the execution chamber shortly. Follow me."

Brad shivered. Hardesty said *execution chamber* as easily as he might say *art gallery*.

Hardesty led him back a short fluorescent-lit hallway on a circuitous route. Brad followed the click of Hardesty's hard-soled shoes down the tiled hallway, past rest rooms, a water fountain, and unmarked doors toward a stout, mustachioed man who waited for them near an open doorway. Hardesty stopped and turned smartly. "This is Mr. Frame," he announced, then turned back and said, "Superintendent Henry Dolewski."

Brad grasped Dolewski's hand, and noticed the superintendent sized him up as if *he* were a new tenant for the cellblock. Force of habit, he surmised.

"It's good to meet you," Brad said. "I was surprised to get your call the other day."

"After twenty seven years in this business nothing surprises me," Dolewski said, adding, "Would you believe I had to scrounge up another witness this afternoon? The condemned man's *other* witness bailed out on us. You can wait in here, Mr. Frame." Dolewski put his hand on Brad's back guiding him through the door. Perhaps a dozen others, gathered in small clusters throughout the room, snapped their heads noting the new arrival.

When the Superintendent had called three days earlier with the news that Frank Wilkie wanted Frame to serve as a witness to his execution, Brad's first instinct was *no way*. But Sharon Porter, an associate in his detective agency had convinced him. She said it might help bring "closure," and that maybe Wilkie wanted the chance to apologize. Brad doubted it. Besides, Brad was an agnostic on the death penalty, not quite understanding how another death would ease the pain he'd felt for the past eleven years.

11

"You might be interested in the briefing materials, Mr. Frame," Henry Dolewski said, pointing at a nearby table. "Now if you'll excuse me, I have important matters to attend to."

Brad grabbed a portfolio, and figured he should introduce himself to the other witnesses. It was easy to spot the government's witnesses; they all wore suits—must have gotten the same memo. A retired police officer, a warden from a nearby county prison, a policy analyst from the State Corrections Department, and a Deputy State Attorney General offered short greetings and polite handshakes. Then a man in a tight-fitting black suit with narrow lapels and wearing a goofy string tie described himself as an "interested citizen" and firmly grasped Brad's hand for an overly long time until Frame finally disengaged.

The media were easy to identify too, clumped in two groups at the far end of the room. The ones wearing denim and casual shirts were all print journalists, Brad surmised, while he recognized one of the two guys in dark blazers, pale blue shirts, fashionable ties, and Reeboks from Channel 6 in Philadelphia. They both looked primed for remote TV broadcasts when the execution was concluded. Brad approached the reporters and quickly introduced himself. He also recognized Paula Thompson from *The Philadelphia Inquirer*, who had interviewed him once as an expert in her coverage of a missing persons case. Thompson started to ask a question, but Brad turned and beat a path to the water cooler, managing to avoid her.

Except for Thompson, all the witnesses were men. What an eclectic group, he thought, with no more in common than if they were all vacationing on the same cruise ship.

10:17 p.m. Brad retreated to a quiet corner of the conference room and thumbed through the Corrections Department briefing kit—undoubtedly prepared for the benefit of the media—detailing the evening's sequence of events. It described death by lethal injection in the clinical language of the law: "Death shall be inflicted by injecting the convict with a continuous, intravenous administration of a lethal quantity of an ultrashort-acting barbiturate in combination with a chemical paralytic agent . . . until death is pronounced by a licensed physician."

"You ever see an execution?" The question rose above the murmur of scattered conversations.

Brad glanced up from the briefing materials and saw the *Pittsburgh Post-Gazette* reporter staring at him.

"I did," the reporter continued, "in Texas, when I worked for the *Dallas Morning News*. They used lethal injection too. Stuck the needle in a muscle, instead of a blood vessel. It took that poor son-of-a-bitch forty minutes to die. I thought I'd never get out of there."

Brad noticed that the policy analyst grimaced at the man's story, while others turned away. Brad, unsure if he wanted to remain for the execution, headed toward the exit.

Paula Thompson blocked his path. In addition to her denim fashion statement, her bedraggled hair made a plea for a fresh shampoo. She reminded Brad of a cobra; its neck flattened and prepared to spit venom. She didn't even count to ten before firing her question at him: "So you weren't content to get the man convicted, you had to come see him die?"

The room grew eerily quiet. Without looking Brad could tell that all eyes were focused on him. He cleared his throat and hoped he wouldn't sound as anxious as he felt. "I take no pleasure at witnessing this execution, Ms. Thompson. I'm here at Frank Wilkie's request, but I'm also confident that justice is being done."

"What do you mean?" the Philadelphia TV reporter asked. "Are you saying Wilkie asked you to attend his execution?" Thompson had broken the dam and questions came flying, even from non-reporters: "Did you meet with him?" "What does he want?" "Did he ask you to petition the Governor for clemency?"

Brad raised both hands in a gesture of surrender. "Look, I haven't seen Frank Wilkie since his trial ten years ago. I haven't got a clue why he wants me here."

Thompson persisted. "What about all the appeals? Didn't you testify?"

"No. I did not testify." Brad met her gaze directly. "Appeals are used to argue law, not facts. The facts are that Frank Wilkie and Eddie Baker took the lives of two innocent people—my mother and sister. That's never been in dispute. The only thing that has, is whether the jury's death mandate should be carried out."

Paula Thompson blinked her brown eyes, then turned and preached to the other witnesses. "A guy sits on death row for ten years. He's already paid a big chunk of debt to society, and then they do this." She shook her head, as if in disbelief.

"It's not my fault the courts can't provide swift justice," Brad countered. "Every time the State was ready to take Wilkie's life, the appeals process kept extending it—first for weeks, then months and years. Judge MacIntee, who tried the original case, died a couple years later. And you know what?" Brad asked rhetorically, realizing a bitter tone had crept into his voice. "That gave some attorney another reason to file an appeal." He drew a quick breath. "Get this! Based on not being able to probe the Judge's state of mind when he sentenced Wilkie to death."

"Do you believe the death penalty deters murder?"

Thompson asked. Brad noticed she was scribbling his comments in her notebook.

"I know Frank Wilkie will never commit another murder." Brad stared at her, as if daring her to dismantle that logic.

"When they start broadcasting executions," Thompson said, "they'll put an end to this barbarism."

Brad walked away from her. He wished he had never come to the prison. Not only wouldn't he find closure that night, but also he faced the prospect of seeing his own words distorted and smeared across the pages of *The Philadelphia Inquirer*.

"Wasn't there another guy convicted of this same crime?" a reporter asked to no one in particular.

"Eddie Baker," the retired police officer answered. "He hung himself in his prison cell a couple years ago. He saved the taxpayers a few bucks, at least."

10:46 p.m. The seconds chugged by. And with each passing minute, the conference room grew more claustrophobic. Each witness managed to find a few square feet of space and paced off the minutes. Brad listened to the idle musings of his fellow witnesses.

Hank, the interested citizen, chimed in, "I don't know how what we're gonna see is any different than what that so-called 'Suicide Doctor' was doin' up in Michigan. This is more humane than the electric chair."

A couple of witnesses nodded their heads. Brad remained stoic, not wishing to get drawn into any debates.

"If you want to see something barbaric, we could bring back public hanging," the county prison's warden wryly offered. "The last public hanging in Pennsylvania was in my county in 1913. Back then each county was responsible for its own executions. Our county commissioners—ever

15

mindful of the public tax dollars—paid an executioner who promised he wouldn't have to spend a lot of money building an expensive wooden scaffold. The guy rigged up this system which used counterweights to hoist the poor man into the air instead of goin' through a drop like a conventional hanging. After a half-hour of prayers and speeches, they strung the man up in the courtyard of the jail. It took him twenty minutes to choke to death, instead of getting his neck broke if they'd've rigged a regular drop." The man paused, then seeming to draw energy from the rapt interest of his listeners continued, "Of course the public was admitted as witnesses along with any unsuspecting drunk and disorderly who happened to be confined the previous night. They considered it therapeutic for the other prisoners to watch the hangings."

Brad felt a headache coming on and massaged his forehead.

Officer Hardesty materialized in the doorway. "Gentlemen, and, ah, lady, if you'll follow me, they're ready for you."

According to the briefing book, Frame was witness number six. The witnesses lined up in order and proceeded single file, in hushed silence, down a narrow corridor until Hardesty stopped, opened a door and directed them into the room where they would view the execution. His was the last seat in the front row, a sturdy wooden chair. The Deputy Attorney General sat next to him, and Frame noticed that Paula Thompson slid into a chair in the back row on the opposite end of the observation room. Officer Hardesty backed out of the metal door and it clanged shut. Soon the only sound Brad heard was the breathing of his fellow witnesses.

There was no question where they were supposed to

look. Three glass panels in front of them offered a full view of the death chamber. Brad was surprised how close they were to where the prisoner would meet his fate. If not for the glass, he could have touched the gurney. He was kept further back watching an oil change at the Mercedes dealership.

The execution room was a modest-sized, windowless, concrete block space painted a pale shade of green. On the right side of the room, next to the only door, a black phone hung silently on the wall. On the left, a small one-way-mirrored window concealed the place where Brad presumed the executioners could observe the prisoner. The briefing materials described a process involving two persons activating separate switches, only one of which actually released the deadly fluid. Like giving one member of a firing squad blank cartridges, he surmised the procedure provided emotional cover just in case one of the executioners later developed pangs of conscience. A coiled plastic tube extended from a slot beside their observation window. It would convey the drugs: Sodium Thiopental, producing nearly immediate anesthesia followed by brain death; Potassium Chloride, paralyzing the heart; and just to make sure, a third chemical, Pavulon, to impede the functioning of the lungs.

Brad's eyes focused on the sheet-covered gurney in the center of the room—the condemned man's deathbed. Behind it stood a white-coated technician with a tray of intravenous needles and plastic tubing, alongside a heart-monitoring machine. He noticed the man wore surgical gloves.

11:02 p.m. Brad began to wonder if the Governor had granted a last minute reprieve. Every once in a while a witness would sigh.

Then Brad saw the door on the opposite side of the execution room swing open, and a uniformed corrections officer held it back. First in the lineup to enter was Superintendent Dolewski who positioned himself behind the gurney.

". . . He leadeth me beside the still waters; he restoreth my soul. He leadeth me in paths of righteousness for his name's sake. Yea, though I walk through the valley of the shadow of death . . ." A wiry black man in his mid-forties dressed in a gray jacket, black shirt, and wearing a clerical collar preceded the condemned man. His words drifted to the witnesses through metal grills above the windows in the partition wall, which gave every sound a muffled echo.

Brad had read in the briefing materials that George Haines was the prison's Protestant chaplain. Continuing to recite the 23rd Psalm from memory, the chaplain moved into position to the left of the gurney.

Four guards escorted Frank Wilkie. Brad barely recognized him, having not seen him for ten years. Back then he'd been a cocky jerk in his late-twenties with a full head of brown hair. Now with thinning hair and a pasty complexion he was dressed in a light blue jumpsuit and already looked sapped of life. Wires connected to sensors taped to his chest protruded through grommets sewn into the suit, enabling prison officials to monitor his heart during the procedure. Brad noticed Wilkie clutched a book in his hands even as his wrists were secured with leather restraints. He glanced at the gurney and then toward the superintendent who remained taut lipped and alert. Two of the guards boosted the prisoner to a seated position on the gurney. Almost immediately, the other officers lifted and turned Wilkie's feet so that he had to lie down. More officers entered the room, each with a task to perform. The prisoner was quickly bound to the table with thick leather straps. With military precision those guards withdrew, and two of the officers who had escorted him removed the leather wrist restraint attached to his belt. They re-secured Wilkie's right arm to an armrest extending from the right side of the gurney, dislodging the book he carried. The book fell to the floor. Brad leaned forward until his forehead touched the glass and could make out that it was a Bible Wilkie had dropped.

Frank Wilkie let out a mournful groan, and flailed about, trying in vain to reach his Bible. The prisoner extended his still-free hand, but two guards jammed his left shoulder back toward the thin padding on the gurney, and the left arm restraint was quickly applied.

"My Bible!" Wilkie thundered. His words echoed through the chamber, destroying the calm atmosphere that had prevailed up to that point.

It seemed to Brad that the prisoner's eyes pleaded with Chaplain Haines. As the guards double-checked the straps securing Wilkie to the table, the chaplain bent down to retrieve Wilkie's Bible.

"I want you to take it, like we talked," the condemned man said. His words were softly spoken, yet loud enough to carry through the grillwork in to the hushed witness chamber. Haines clasped Wilkie's arm and bowed his head in silent prayer. Frank Wilkie squeezed his eyes shut, then opened them as the chaplain withdrew to his appointed station.

Tilting his head to the right, Wilkie showed no emotion as he stared toward the glass of the witness booth. Unlike the death chamber, which was bathed in fluorescent light, the witness observation room was dimly lit, and Brad wondered if Wilkie could see him. The condemned man's eyes

darted anxiously back and forth across the bank of witnesses, all of whom seemed to be holding their breath. Brad
wanted the ordeal to end. Wished he had never come to the
prison. It all felt surreal, like a nightmare from which he
hoped he would soon awaken.

As the prison's physician entered the execution room, all
others withdrew except for two guards, the chaplain, medical technician and the superintendent. One of the remaining guards closed and locked the door from the inside.

The superintendent looked about the chamber, appeared
to spot something on the floor and bent down to retrieve it.
The wall below the windows obstructed Brad's view, but
when the warden stood up he could see it was a single sheet
of paper. The superintendent glanced at it briefly before
folding it and slipping it into his inside coat pocket.

Dolewski surveyed the chamber one last time as if to see
if all was in readiness, then spoke the words Brad thought
might provide the explanation for his invitation. "Does the
prisoner have any final words before sentence is carried
out?"

Wilkie remained impassive. His eyelids fluttered closed,
and then he shook his head from side to side.

Dolewski nodded to the technician who, under the
watchful eye of the physician, inserted a needle into a vein
in the condemned man's arm. Wilkie's body tensed then relaxed. The technician extended the coil of intravenous
tubing—conveying at first only a saline solution according
to the briefing materials—and affixed the tube to the recep-
tacle at the end of the needle now lodged in the prisoner's
arm. The wires attached to his chest were connected to the
heart monitor. The doctor inspected the intravenous line
and pronounced it ready.

Prison staff took their positions at the perimeter of the

room, while the superintendent stood about three feet away from the prisoner. Prompted by a 3" by 5" card held in his left hand, Dolewski repeated the required words advising Wilkie that the death sentence was about to be carried out. The warden looked up from the card, and to unseen personnel behind the one-way mirror he said, "You may begin the execution."

The sound startled Brad—like the pop-whoosh a tire makes when it's separated from the rim—and his body tensed. He recalled the briefing materials had reminded them that the execution used the latest mechanical process, buttons pushed, pre-measured poison sped on its way, starting with anesthesia.

Seconds later, Frank Wilkie lay unconscious on the table.

Witnesses watched in silence. Brad heard the noise again—the second chemical starting its journey. But he didn't jump that time, and found himself questioning his own humanity, since it had only taken once for him to get used to the sound of an execution machine.

Wilkie's breathing became more labored. Longer and longer intervals passed between the natural rising and falling of his chest. The wait seemed interminable. If lethal injection was intended to sanitize an execution, Brad thought, it didn't make it any easier to watch. A gunshot to the head would have been messy, but he would have been out of the stifling confines of the witness chamber a lot sooner.

Brad couldn't pretend he hadn't thought about this moment many times during the last ten years—ever since he'd stood in court and offered a victim's impact statement just before the judge pronounced sentence on Wilkie.

Brad stared in Wilkie's direction, but he wasn't really looking at him. His mind drifted back to happier times:

"Brad!" He heard his mother's voice calling to him as he stood at the kitchen window. He pictured her shouldering a large blue canvas bag, wearing the floppy straw hat that she always used to shield the sun when gardening, and carrying a box. "Lucy and I are planting some flowers along the path," she shouted. "We could use your help clearing out the underbrush." Moments later he'd joined them in what she called her "secret garden." She'd had Brad's dad build a set of steps down the steep slope at the back of their Bryn Mawr home and clear a place for a wooden bench. In that secluded spot it felt like they were miles from anyone, in fact, looking back up the hill Brad couldn't even see the roof of their house. "What are you staring at?" his sister Lucy had asked, as she sat cross-legged in the dirt sorting flower bulbs. "You can't even tell there are houses around here," he'd said. Brad smiled as he recalled his younger sister, her face smudged with dirt as she wiped a few strands of hair out of her eyes and glanced back toward their house to see what he was talking about. "What are you planting, Mom?" he had inquired. "I'll give you three guesses," she said, with a twinkle in her eyes. But he only needed one— *Daffodils*—her favorite flower.

The steady alarm on the prisoner's heart monitor shook Brad from his thoughts, and then he noticed the green flat line. An aide reached over and turned off the alarm, while the physician consulted his watch. The doctor extracted a stethoscope from his jacket pocket, hooked it on his ears, and listened to the prisoner's chest. After several more agonizing minutes and a second check with the stethoscope, the doctor finally signaled that Wilkie was dead. The technician drew a sheet over the body. The door to the cubicle opened and witnesses were invited to leave.

Nobody declined.

Brad, closest to the door, hurried out of the room hoping to elude further inquiries from the media.

11:35 p.m. Outside the prison the chilly temperature felt curiously refreshing after the longest half-hour Brad had ever spent, lending a tinge of reality to the evening, as did the presence, immediately outside, of an ambulance standing ready to remove Wilkie's body. For an instant, Brad thought he heard the muffled shouts of prisoners behind the cellblock walls. Maybe they were protesting—in vain—the loss of one of their comrades. The yellowish tint of the sodium vapor lighting in the prison compound made the fog appear eerie as it rolled in from the valley below.

"Mr. Frame!" a voice shouted from behind.

Brad cringed, then stopped and turned around.

Chaplain George Haines had caught up with him just as he approached the exit gate.

"Mr. Frame, I have something for you," the Chaplain said. "Wilkie wanted me to give you this."

He thrust Wilkie's Bible into Brad's hands.

CHAPTER 2

"I don't understand." Brad grasped the Bible by the spine, noting the gilded lettering *Placed by the Gideons.*

The chaplain, who had to run to catch up with him, gasped for air—signaling for patience with one finger held aloft. "I had specific instructions," he said, in an accent Brad thought might have been from Mississippi. "Earlier this evening, I spent about an hour with Frank. Before I left, he showed me the Bible. He said, 'There's somebody I want to have this. When it's over.' He was very insistent. Then gave me your name. I asked how was I supposed to get the book to you, and he said he'd invited you and hoped you would come. Superintendent Dolewski pointed you out."

Brad leafed through a few pages of the Bible. A chill came over him. He wasn't sure if it was from the cold March night or from handling the Bible, a personal possession of the man who had decimated his family. "Look," Brad said, feeling agitated and waving the Bible in his hand, "could we go someplace to talk?"

Chaplain Haines glanced back toward the wall, behind which the execution had taken place. "I suppose so. I'm through for the evening." He pointed toward the main prison complex. "There's a vending machine over by the commissary, and a couple—"

Brad cut him off. "Not here. Is there a place nearby where we can go?" He didn't want to spend another minute on the grounds of the prison.

The chaplain squinted and tucked his tongue into the

corner of his mouth. "Emma's Tavern is open till 2 o'clock. It's just four miles up the road." He pointed north.

Brad nodded. "Emma's Tavern. I'll meet you there."

Once outside the prison Brad rushed to his car, unlocked the door, and slid behind the wheel. He laid the Bible on the passenger seat, then sank into the leather upholstery and leaned his head against the headrest, still shaken from the experience of watching a man die. Brad couldn't understand why Wilkie wanted him to have the Bible. He turned on the ignition, jacked up the heat controls to take away the chill, and buckled his seatbelt. He closed his eyes and replayed the chaplain's words, then his mind fast-forwarded over the events of the evening—the demonstrators, the confrontation with Paula Thompson, Wilkie led onto the lethal injection room gurney, and his mournful cry when the Bible flew from his hands. Brad's eyes blinked open and he glanced at the Bible on the seat next to him.

Brad fished his cell phone from the center console, flipped it open, and turned it on. He concluded she would still be awake, so he speed-dialed Sharon Porter, hoping she could help him sort things out. The call went into her voice mail, and he left a message: "Hi Sharon, it's Brad." Glancing at his watch, he said, "It's just before midnight. The execution is over. But there's a new development. The prison chaplain just handed me Wilkie's Bible. I'm hoping to find out what that's all about. I guess I'll see you in the morning."

Frame guided his car down the hill wanting to avoid another confrontation with demonstrators who were rapidly dispersing. Activists on both sides of the death penalty debate wandered down the road toward their cars in straggly lines, carrying placards, now held at their sides. One sign read: "Spare an innocent life." *Innocent,* Brad thought, clearly that person had never experienced the pleasure of coming face-to-face with Frank Wilkie. Another sign hand-lettered in orange Day-Glo paint read: "Only God can take a life." Brad wished Wilkie had seen that sign twelve years earlier.

Television vans from all the major networks—their satellite dishes hoisted toward the sky—lined the road at the base of the hill. As Brad neared the intersection with the main highway, he recognized one of the reporters who had witnessed the execution, now bathed in video lights from the waist up, his Reeboks hidden from the camera's view. A gaggle of demonstrators stood nearby seemingly mesmerized as they watched the reporter. Brad avoided further notoriety by turning his Mercedes left at the base of the hill and opening it up to cruising speed as he headed north toward Emma's Tavern.

A few miles later Brad noticed red neon lights on the right hand side of the road piercing the gathering fog. He slowed to confirm he'd arrived at Emma's then dropped into second gear and turned onto the unpaved parking lot, swerving to dodge a few mud holes. He passed four pick-up trucks and a beat-up sedan before parking in a secluded spot between a tree and split rail fence. He grabbed Wilkie's Bible, made sure the car was locked, and headed for the entrance.

Emma's had no claim to style. *You're still in Pennsylvania,* Brad reminded himself. How different this part of the state seemed to him, and for an instant contemplated whether the roadside hangout had indoor plumbing. The tavern boasted a ten-stool bar, and seven tables with mismatched chairs crammed into a narrow space alongside a billiard table at the rear. The stale odor of beer—mingled with the smell of burnt popcorn—permeated the joint. Cigarette smoke haze hung in the air. Two men sat at the bar drinking beer and watching a Celtics-Lakers game, while two more played a game of pool.

Brad noticed the others staring and realized his wool slacks and chocolate-colored turtleneck weren't part of the usual dress code. He gravitated toward a gold-speckled Formica table in the corner, and watched as the bartender traipsed over to take his order. Lean of body and expression, his salt and pepper hair slicked back, the bartender sprouted a couple of day's growth of beard.

"What'll-ya-have?" the bartender asked, pencil poised above a scratch pad.

Brad studied the place mat, which doubled as the printed menu, and noticed a damp ring from the glass of a previous customer. "A western omelet."

"Kitchen closed at eleven."

"I'll just have an order of dry wheat toast."

"I told ya the kitchen closed at eleven," the bartender grumbled.

Brad knew he would test the limits with his next question. "Do you have any imported beers?"

"Nope." The bartender began tapping his pencil on the order pad.

Brad glanced at the place mat again—hoping for inspiration—but only saw the wet ring. He frowned. "Just bring a pitcher of beer—your choice—and two glasses," Brad said. "Someone will be joining me."

"Good enough." The bartender ripped a copy of the order slip from his pad, and laid it face down on the edge of the table before ambling back to the bar.

Brad propped his elbows on the table, put his chin in his hands, and took in the sights and smells of the tavern. It'd be a long time before Emma's would earn four diamonds.

He gave it three cockroaches. Brad felt a tap on his shoulder and heard the chaplain, "Is it alright if I join you? You look deep in thought."

"I was just wondering where Emma was," Brad said, then gestured to the empty chair across from him.

Chaplain Haines, still wearing his black shirt and gray coat but minus his clerical collar, sat down.

"I wasn't sure if you drank, but I ordered a pitcher of beer and two glasses," Brad said.

"It's okay, I'm from a liberal denomination." The Chaplain leaned closer, "Besides, I don't have to worry about any of *my* parishioners finding me here."

They both laughed. A tense silence followed before Brad offered, "I'm sorry if I was curt back at the prison."

The Chaplain gave a wave of his hand. "That's okay. It's a terrible business." He rolled his shoulders, as if trying to shake the tensions of the night.

"Was this your first execution?" Brad asked.

"My third. After the first one, I thought it might get easier," he said, patting his chest and taking a deep breath. "So far it hasn't. The first time I was just plain scared. Now, I find myself conflicted about the death penalty and what purpose it serves."

Brad shrugged. "An eye for an eye," he said matter-of-factly before sliding Wilkie's Bible toward the middle of the table. "Tell me about this."

The chaplain glanced at the Bible then back at Brad, with an expression at once benevolent and penetrating. "Like I said, Frank asked me to give it to you."

"Did he say why?"

"No. Just insisted I get the Bible to you."

The bartender arrived and deposited a water-spotted glass pitcher brimming with an amber liquid and two glasses. "This a friend of yours, George?" he asked.

"Just doin' some business, Jack," the chaplain replied.

The bartender hung around the table, looking first at Chaplain Haines then Frame. Finally Brad said, "Run a tab."

Brad poured each of them a beer. "I never thought of Frank Wilkie as a religious man."

"The prospect of facing the Lord makes even the strongest man rethink his life," the chaplain said. "Ever since they moved him up here for the execution I've been trying to get Frank to pray, but he wouldn't do it. Then about three weeks ago he asked if I could get him a Bible. I told him no problem—the prison gets them donated. I offered to read it with him. He said no, but every once in a while he asked for my help in understanding the words."

Interested in that detail, Brad leaned forward. "What words?"

The chaplain rubbed the base of his neck as he thought for a few seconds. "Like Thessalonians. He wanted to know how to say it and what it meant. I explained they were a group of people the Apostle Paul had written a letter to."

The chaplain was long on details and short on answers, Brad thought as he took a sip from his glass, still not understanding why Wilkie wanted him to have the Bible.

"Every time I saw him after that," the chaplain continued, "he had his head in the Scriptures."

"I didn't know he could read," Brad said, recalling that Wilkie's attorney had argued illiteracy as a mitigating factor to keep his client from a death sentence.

The chaplain smiled. "I didn't say he was *reading*. In fact, I asked him questions, about the parables, and I could tell he didn't understand."

"Do you conduct services for the inmates on death

row?" Brad asked, glancing at his watch and thinking about the long trip home.

The chaplain shook his head. "Not really. We visit a couple times each week, providing spiritual counseling for those who want it. Death row isn't exactly a huge congregation. The State transports the prisoners here shortly before the scheduled execution date. They moved Frank up from Pittsburgh right after Thanksgiving, because his execution was originally scheduled for early last December. Then there was an unexpected stay." The chaplain shrugged, "They just kept him here instead of sending him back like they usually did if an execution got postponed."

As the chaplain spoke Brad thumbed through the pages of the Bible. At the bottom of one page he spotted the word *eddie* scrawled in pencil, the name of Wilkie's accomplice in the kidnapping and murder. "Did Frank Wilkie ask you for spiritual counseling?" Brad asked, just to keep the conversation going while he thought about the significance of the word Eddie popping up in Wilkie's Bible.

"He didn't even want to *talk* until a month ago. But by then he knew all his appeals had been exhausted. His attorney drove up to give him the bad news. Right after that visit, Wilkie asked me for the Bible."

The chaplain kept glancing over Brad's shoulder.

"Am I keeping you from something?" Brad asked.

Chaplain Haines looked embarrassed. "No . . . I, ah . . . just tryin' to see the score of the game. Looks like the Lakers are losing their edge."

Brad felt like he was losing his edge too, as he stared at the flyspecked wallpaper and frowned. "Who was Wilkie's attorney?"

"Ronald something. Young guy from Philadelphia. Allessi! That's it. Ronald Allessi."

The name didn't ring a bell for Brad, and he knew most of the prominent attorneys in Philadelphia. "Probably a public defender."

"Sure didn't act like a public defender," the chaplain said.

"What do you mean?"

"I spent ten years as a chaplain with the county prison before I started working here," George Haines explained over the shouts of the drunks at the bar cheering on the Celtics as they tied up the game. "I've seen a lot of public defenders. This guy didn't dress like any public defender I've ever seen."

Brad thumbed through a few more pages of the Bible, and tried to imagine how Wilkie could afford an attorney other than a public defender. "Can you tell me what Frank talked about tonight? You know, during the time you spent with him before . . ." Brad let his voice trail off.

"Sure," the chaplain replied. "It wasn't a confessional or anything like that. Frank rambled a lot. Talked about being a kid, growing up in Philadelphia. He spent a few summers with relatives in Kentucky, and mentioned fishing in a pond out there. I asked him about Christmases when he was a child, and he said his mother always made sure that he and his brother and sister had a Christmas tree with white lights on it, even though his family wasn't very religious. I inquired about his dad, and Frank told me he never knew his father. Apparently the jerk ran out on his family when Frank was a baby." Chaplain Haines took a sip of his beer then added, "Did you know Frank got committed to his first juvenile institution when he was nine?"

The chaplain stared at Brad, apparently trying to gauge his reaction. Brad knew Frank's rap sheet well, including his juvenile record, and remained stoic.

"Frank was childlike tonight. No bravado. No false defiance. Guess what?" Haines said before answering his own question. "He asked me if it was going to hurt when he died."

"What did you say?"

"I assured him it wouldn't." George gulped his beer, and with foam stuck to his upper lip, added, "But how do I know?"

Brad recalled that Wilkie had a brother and sister, just like he did until Wilkie took his sister away from him. Maybe they would know why Wilkie had left him the Bible. "Did he talk with anyone in his family?" Brad asked, as he returned the Bible to the table.

The chaplain pursed his lips. "He didn't have any family left. His mother died two years ago. He told me his brother was killed in a gang fight, and that his sister overdosed on heroin."

An all-American family, Brad thought, unable to check his bitterness.

"When I asked Frank if he wanted me to contact anyone, he said just to make sure you got the Bible."

"God, why me?" Brad muttered, hitching his fingers behind his head. After all, that's why he had driven to this stink-hole of a bar, hoping to get some answers. He couldn't say *closure*.

The chaplain shrugged, then emptied the rest of the pitcher into his glass. His third glass of the evening, Brad noted. Remembering the drive home, Brad had only finished one glass of beer and pretended to nurse a second.

Brad picked up the Bible again, opened it to Psalms, and slowly turned pages. Each page of Wilkie's Bible was printed in two columns. Suddenly, in the margin between the columns he spotted another penciled word—*sorry*.

Sharon had suggested Wilkie might want to apologize. At that moment Brad knew he had to get back to Philadelphia. He'd had enough of Emma's Tavern, and he wanted answers.

Brad looked up and saw the chaplain leaning in to him and staring. Brad slammed the Bible on the table and shouted, "I don't get it, George. The guy's not content to wipe out half my family. Now he leaves me with a religious memento. What the hell is he trying to do? Rough up my conscience?"

The guys at the bar yelled for quiet. Brad noticed the bartender scowl in his direction before placating the bar jockeys by jacking up the volume on the television.

Chaplain Haines gawked at him, his eyes opened wide. "You saw the words, didn't you?"

"Yes," Brad whispered, wary and intrigued by what the chaplain might know. "Why didn't you say anything?"

"I wasn't sure," the chaplain explained. "Wilkie was so insistent about getting you that Bible. I thought that maybe he'd written a note. I quickly leafed through it and spotted a couple of words in the margins. No doubt he wrote them—the Bible was brand new when I gave it to him. But I don't know what it means."

"That makes two of us." Brad stood, pulled a twenty out of his wallet, and tossed the bill on the table. "That'll cover the tab. Are you stickin' around?"

The chaplain stood and clasped Brad's hand. "Thanks! Yes, I'm gonna stay. There'll be guys getting off shift soon from the prison and stopping by. I'll have plenty of company."

"I'd better be going," Brad said, loosening his grip and retrieving the Bible from the table. "I have a long drive ahead of me."

"I'll pray for you." The chaplain patted him on the shoulder.

I'll need it, Brad thought. He could barely see his own hands, bathed in the orange-red neon of Emma's sign, as he inched his way back to his car on that fog-shrouded night.

CHAPTER 3

Brad gradually eased his car into fifth gear, punched up a CD of Camille Saint-Saens' Organ Symphony No. 3, and sped down the highway. The further Brad traveled from the tavern the easier he could breathe. Picturing Chaplain Haines and a few of his buddies unwinding at Emma's after a day working in a State Correctional facility gave him the willies, conjuring up an oppressive picture of gloom after a day of doom.

Within twenty miles the fog had lifted—from the roads—if not Brad's head. The dramatic crescendo of the Organ Symphony's finale couldn't drown out the competing thoughts swirling through his brain. Wilkie's Bible and what information it might hold nagged at him. But he kept coming back to the question of what had lured him to the execution in the first place. Hell, he turned down hundreds of invitations a year, most of them to swankier places than the Rockview penitentiary. What made him accept Wilkie's request? In spite of what Sharon had said, Brad knew he wouldn't find closure. Nothing could close the black hole that had ripped through his soul when his mother and sister died. His brother Andrew, the take-charge son, had tracked Brad down in Miami Beach and broke the news of their kidnapping. The prodigal son flew home to help Andrew support their father through ransom demands, hopeful phone messages, and FBI red tape. All the while hoping for a successful reunion with their loved ones, but when their bodies were found, Brad helped support his dad through the funerals. The journey reshaped Brad's life, creating not just a new chapter but a whole new volume on the bookshelf of his existence, sitting next to tomes labeled childhood, teen years, college, and a ten-year odyssey called *finding himself.* Brad knew when this current book—label it *transformation*—began: eleven years ago March 12th. He wondered if Wilkie's execution was the last chapter. Had that drawn him to the death chamber at Rockview? Maybe, he thought, pushing the repeat button on the CD and jacking up the volume.

Brad's car hugged the curves of the road as it followed the meandering flow of the Susquehanna River around the bedrock of the mountain. In the light of a partial moon Brad spotted the engine of a CSX freight train crossing a bridge heading for his side of the river. A train aficionado, he recognized the engine as General Motors, circa 1980. For half-a-mile he raced to catch up with the locomotive exceeding the posted speed by at least twenty miles per hour, but with the train barely making forty it was hardly a contest. Still, in the wee hours of the morning the competition fueled his imagination, made the trip go faster, and helped him stay awake. A few minutes later the skyline of Harrisburg, the state capital, loomed in the distance. Amazing, he thought, how all those tax dollars made a small city look big. With two more hours to drive, Brad welcomed the sight of the Turnpike entrance. Home was a four-lane straight shot.

Brad rumbled over the cobblestones on the curved driveway of his Bryn Mawr mansion shortly before five a.m. Spotting lights on inside, he feared Aunt Harriet—on one of her periodic visits from New York—was afoot, maybe fixing an early morning pick-me-up in the Butler's pantry. He stepped from the car and inhaled, savoring the fresh air. He detected the lingering odor of burnt logs from one of his neighbor's chimneys, and noting a light breeze from the north, figured the Mackenzies must have had a roaring blaze in their fireplace the previous evening. Brad glanced up at the starry black heavens with Venus shining back at him near the horizon. He remembered Wilkie's Bible and grabbed it from the passenger seat. Approaching the front door, he gingerly turned the key in the lock, hoping to tip-toe across the foyer and up the stairs to his bedroom before Harriet knew he was home.

Brad closed the door and spotted Sharon Porter waiting for him in the doorway to the kitchen, dressed in jeans, a Gap sweatshirt and flip-flops; her smiling freckled face a welcome sight after his stress-filled night.

Pointing at his watch, Brad said, "What are you doing up so early?"

"I got your message—sorry I didn't answer, but Mark and I were at that new Jazz Café over by the mall. I figured you'd be home about now and might want some company. I set my alarm."

He felt a tear well in his eye, a delayed reaction after a night of dreary reflection. "I'm glad . . . you did," he said, the words momentarily catching in his throat.

Sharon was the right arm in his detective business, having joined the agency three years earlier. His equal in analytical ability and detection skills—though he seldom admitted that to her. Nick Argostino, a Philadelphia police detective and Brad's mentor, had urged him to hire Sharon. Her father, a detective who worked for Nick, had taken his own life. Sharon had lived with her father and needed a place to stay and a chance to rebuild her life after the tragedy. Nick suggested letting her stay in the apartment above the garage once used by his family's live-in groundskeeper. In the early days of his detective agency, the apartment had functioned as his office, where he and Nick had many meetings. Brad reluctantly acceded to Nick's request, but had no regrets.

Sharon was also a hugger. She ran over and threw her arms around him. "Oh, Brad, I watched the news reports. I'm sorry." As she squeezed tight, he realized that Sharon had gradually become family, like the sister he no longer had.

She pushed him back and wrinkled up her nose. "You stink!"

"Yeah, it's great to be home, thanks!" Brad sniffed at the shoulder of his jacket as remnants of stale beer, cigarette smoke, and burnt popcorn leeched from the fabric. "Jeez, I smell like a skid row bar," he said, surprised he hadn't noticed earlier.

Sharon nodded. "Where have you been?"

"Come here." Brad ignored her question; he could regale her with tales of Emma's later, and beckoned her over to the kitchen counter where he opened Wilkie's Bible. In the quiet of his kitchen Brad noticed the cracking sound of the book's spine as he opened it to Psalms, and flipped through pages until he found the word *sorry*. Handing it to Sharon, he said, "Take a look at this. In another place, I can't remember exactly, I found the word *eddie*. I'm gonna go grab a shower and change clothes. See what else you can find."

"I made coffee," Sharon shouted after him as he took the steps on the curved staircase in the foyer two at a time.

"Thanks," Brad called back, adding, "I knew there was a reason I hired you."

Twenty minutes later, in fresh clothes and smelling much more agreeable, Brad found Sharon sitting in the breakfast nook. She was thumbing through the pages of the

Bible with her left hand, while a pencil in her right hand hovered over a tablet. He poured himself a fresh cup, and waved the half-full pot in front of her.

"In a minute." She looked up. "I've found fifteen words so far. I'm in the Book of Thessalonians. Oh, here's the word *eddie*." Sharon made a notation on the tablet.

She continued, "I found another reference to Eddie back in . . . let's see, here it is—actually two words—*and eddie* in Ezekiel. The printing's in pencil, so it's kinda hard to make out, and I'd take long odds that Wilkie never won any prizes for penmanship."

Brad stared at the list over Sharon's shoulder. Sharon had numbered each word in the order in which she had found it in the Bible, along with the page number from the Bible. The word *sorry* appeared once, while a variation of *kill* made the list three times so far. "It doesn't look like an apology to me."

Sharon flashed him a hold your horses look, pulled the paper closer, and blocked his view with her arm.

"Here's another word, *get* in the Book of Ephesians," she announced. "You sure the Chaplain had no idea what this was all about?"

Brad shook his head. "He convinced me he didn't. I wouldn't want to play poker with him if he did." Brad slid into the seat across from her and took a long, grateful sip of the dark brew.

"Here's Revelations," Sharon said, poking the page with her finger.

"Wilkie went to a lot of trouble to send me a message," Brad said, trying to act calm as Sharon neared the end of the Bible. "Maybe it has something to do with the prison."

"I found another one." Sharon jotted the number 18 on her pad and next to it the word *real,* and the Bible's page

number 1159. She turned the remaining pages, then announced, "That's all of them."

Sharon turned the notepad sideways so they both could
study the list, and Brad hitched his fingers together behind
his head and leaned forward.

1. big	7. and eddie	13. guy
2. i	8. not	14. killer
3. talked	9. he	15. me
4. paid	10. kill	16. eddie
5. sorry	11. find	17. get
6. killed	12. money	18. real

Brad read the words aloud in order, then read them
backwards. Wilkie had kept the words simple, most one syllable. Brad looked at Sharon and asked, "Can you make any
sense out of this?" But he could see by her blank expression
that the message was a mystery to her too.

"Eighteen words," Brad muttered to himself.

"That's like a bazillion possible combinations," Sharon
said. "Maybe a few less if you apply the rules of grammar."

Grammar? Brad looked quizzically across the table. Yes,
there were too many combinations, with or without
grammar . . . eighteen times seventeen times sixteen times
. . . like Sharon said, a bazillion of them. His spirits sank,
and for the first time during the long night exhaustion over-
came him. Brad felt a headache forming behind his forehead. Outside he noticed the glimmer of first light.

"My answer is in the last two words, 'get real'," Sharon

said, and then in a move that startled Brad she picked up the Bible, held it upside down, and fanned through the pages.

"What are you doing?" Brad asked.

"I thought maybe he left some kind of a key."

"Of course!" Brad pounded the table with his fist, startling Sharon. He suddenly remembered the paper that Superintendent Dolewski retrieved from the floor of the execution chamber. It must have fallen out of Wilkie's Bible, and would be the key to Wilkie's message. Brad described the scene for Sharon, adding, "I'll call Dolewski tomorrow." Brad glanced at his watch and corrected himself, "I mean later today."

CHAPTER 4

"Good morning, Aunt Harriet."

Brad waved to his aunt from the marble tiled foyer, intending to offer a quick greeting before getting on with his work. The silver-haired dowager of the Frame family—Harriet Frame Beecham, his dad's younger sister—commanded attention, whether holding court with her neighbors in New York's Gramercy Park or selecting salmon fillets at the South Street market. Like an ocean liner steaming for port, the sleek and fast boats knew to steer clear of her wake, and Brad was no exception.

"Oh, Bradford," Harriet cooed, easing herself up from the drawing room sofa, "I didn't hear you coming. Last night must have been horrid for you. I was just reading about the execution in the paper. You poor dear." He stopped near the archway to the drawing room. She looked regal in her navy blue suit, white blouse and trademark pearl earrings, he thought, as she chugged in his direction, brandishing a copy of *The Philadelphia Inquirer*.

Harriet planted a peck on his cheek then shoved the newspaper into his hands. "You'll want to read this." Brad tucked the *Inquirer* under his arm, figuring that as an eyewitness he needn't read a second-hand account.

Aunt Harriet aimed her finger at him. "Bradford, this mansion is a mausoleum! You've got to pump some life back into it."

"It's good to see you so peppy this morning." He laughed, and gave her a quick hug to placate her. Remembering he'd only had two hours of sleep, he added, "Did you rest well?"

"Don't change the subject," she scolded. "You need to find a woman who can make this place over." Harriet made a sweeping gesture with her arm and groaned. "All this cut velvet fabric on the sofas, the gold color, and the worn, faded rugs. It looks like Lyndon and Lady Bird just moved out."

Brad forced a smile. He tried to think of a rejoinder, when Sharon rushed in carrying a newspaper. "You might want to take a look at this," she said, handing him a second copy of the *Inquirer*. Sharon had piqued his curiosity, but the musings of the fourth estate would have to wait; her newspaper joined his aunt's under his arm.

"Hold that thought, Aunt Harriet," Brad said, gesturing with his open palm, "I need to confer with Sharon."

Brad guided Sharon toward the middle of the foyer and in hushed tones asked, "Any messages? I phoned Superintendent Dolewski's office early this morning and asked that he call me."

Sharon shook her head. "Nothing yet. But I'm heading over there now. I'll let you know if he calls."

"Thanks," Brad said, turning back to his aunt.

Harriet kept Sharon in her sights, calling after her. "Wait just a minute, Sharon. Don't you think Bradford needs someone to spruce up this old house?"

Brad winked at Sharon. "Aunt Harriet, are you saying I need a decorator?"

Sharon played along, as he hoped she would. "I heard there's a new interior design shop opening in Haverford."

"No, not a decorator." Harriet aimed her piercing eyes at Brad, and he could tell she saw through their impromptu performance. "I'm saying that you need a *wife*."

Brad didn't feel like he had to detail his social life to his aunt. There had been plenty of women, young, beautiful, exciting, but nothing ever lasted. And over the last decade he'd met too many gold diggers, or women whose biological clocks were racing, or those who seemed to enjoy the museum's gala more than his company.

The grandfather clock came to life and Westminster chimes echoed through the foyer. Brad noted it was eleven forty-five, and watched as Sharon ducked behind the curved stairway to a doorway that led to the office in the west wing.

"What time does your train leave, Aunt Harriet?" he asked.

His aunt puckered her mouth, furrowed her brow, and straightened her shoulders. "You'll be rid of me soon enough, Bradford." Pointing toward her leather satchel and matching make-up case neatly piled next to the front door, she said, "I've already called for a cab. I know how to take care of myself."

"I'm forty-three years old, Aunt Harriet," he said, with growing impatience. "Please don't lecture me. I can take care of *myself*."

Harriet drew in a breath and peeked at him over the top of reading glasses perched low on the bridge of her nose. "You cannot recapture the past by turning this house into a shrine."

"Aunt Harriet, it's still Dad's house."

"And when is he coming back here to live?" she snapped.

He knew she was right. Another one of Wilkie's victims, his father would spend the rest of his days at the assisted living center. The first stroke was barely six months after the kidnapping. The doctors attributed it to acute stress. Then additional strokes, each progressively more debilitating until his dad required round-the-clock nursing care.

Harriet asked, "When did you last see your father?"

"A few days ago. Just before you arrived. I try to visit him at least twice a week." Brad feared he sounded defensive.

A pained expression crept onto Harriet's face. "Joe's breathing seemed more shallow this time."

"It's been that way for a couple weeks," Brad explained. "The doctors are concerned about his kidney function. They were doing blood tests yesterday. I'll let you know when I get the results."

Harriet extended a delicate arm, pulling him toward her, kissing his forehead. "Your father would want you to live your life in the present, Bradford—not in the past."

Brad gave her a big hug, and leaned down to whisper in her ear: "I always appreciate your advice, Aunt Harriet," adding, "But it's still *his* place."

Harriet turned and walked toward the window, alternately looking out onto the cobblestone drive and checking her diamond-studded watch. "Humph, I wonder if the cab driver even knows how to get here?"

"Give the driver a few more minutes." Brad patted the seat of an Empire-style settee situated in the nook formed by the curved stairs. "Come sit with me, Aunt Harriet," he beckoned, reassuringly. "I'll wait with you until your cab comes."

She sat next to Brad, a quiet truce between them. Brad noticed that Harriet rocked back and forth in her seat, absently tapping the arm of the sofa with her hand. Brad recalled all the times he had seen her on that same seat as she waited patiently for a cab to come at the end of her visits to Philadelphia. Widowed before the age of fifty, and with no children, his family was the only family Harriet had left.

"Do you remember your grandfather Frame?" she asked, breaking the silence.

"Sure, I was sixteen when he died."

"Your grandfather never wanted me to leave Philadelphia. Fifty-one years ago I met my future husband in a saloon in Hell's Kitchen. I was only seventeen, and had taken a bus to New York City with three friends from Palmer school. If our parents only knew what we did that weekend!" She giggled and her voice trailed off. Uncle Oscar had been dead for more than twenty years, but Brad couldn't picture him *or* his aunt in a saloon.

"I gave Oscar my address that weekend and he later wrote to me. We carried on a long-distance romance. I used to tell your grandpa that I was spending the weekend with a friend, when I was really visiting Oscar in New York."

Brad covered his mouth and gasped in mock outrage at her story.

Harriet blushed. "Don't I sound awful? Eventually my father—your grandfather—found out, and one Sunday night he met my train at 30th Street Station. He forbade me from any more trips to New York, but by that time Oscar and I already knew that we wanted to get married. I was almost eighteen and I told your grandfather that it was my life, not his. That's why I'm telling you to live your life, don't let the shadows from that horrible tragedy—or even your devotion to your father—prevent you from enjoying your *own* life."

"You've convinced me," Brad said, leaning over and gently kissing her on the cheek. "I'm gonna sell this house and move to New York, maybe search for a place in Hell's Kitchen."

"That wasn't my point, and you know it," she grumbled, pulling away from him and checking her watch again. "At least in New York when I call for a cab it comes."

"Aunt Harriet," Brad said, as he stood. "I'd like to hear more about your saloon-going days. I'll drive you to the train station."

Aunt Harriet beamed. "Oh, Bradford, would you? You're a dear."

Pacing behind his desk, Brad paused periodically to glance down at *The Philadelphia Inquirer*, open to the front page of the local section with Paula Thompson's by-lined article about Wilkie's execution. *Damn her.* The story began harmlessly, and even had a few facts in the first paragraph:

ROCKVIEW, PA *Frank Wilkie, 39, under sentence of death for the last ten years, and with all his appeals exhausted, was executed late last night at the State Correctional Institution in Rockview, Centre County. L. Bradford Frame watched impassively as Frank Wilkie, the kidnapper and killer of his mother and sister, was put to death. Wilkie was the fourth man executed since Pennsylvania abandoned its electric chair in favor of death-by-lethal-injection.*

The Governor rejected last minute pleas for clemency from attorneys representing Wilkie, and from interest groups charging the death penalty was cruel and unusual punishment. Dozens of demonstrators stood vigil on the fog shrouded road leading to the prison, singing hymns and heckling State Police dispatched to maintain order. At 9:23 p.m. the State Supreme Court lifted a temporary stay granted by a Commonwealth Court Judge, and the Philadelphia-based Third Circuit Court of Appeals refused to hear any further appeals in the Wilkie case, clearing the way for the 11 p.m. execution.

Led into the State's death chamber, his eyes glistening with apprehension, Wilkie remained composed until a Bible he clutched in his hands was thrown to the floor by one of the guards. After screaming for the Bible's return, Wilkie declined the warden's offer to make a final public statement. The warden then signaled two Corrections officers, who reportedly volunteered to serve as executioners, located behind a one-way mirror in the chemical injection room. Once the intravenous administration of lethal chemicals began, it took nearly ten minutes for the condemned man to die. Wilkie's chest heaved repeatedly and his body convulsed in spasms before he lapsed into unconsciousness.

"The execution went as planned," Warden Henry Dolewski announced to a small group of reporters waiting outside the prison. "Frank Alan Wilkie died at 11:32 p.m." An ambulance sped from the prison grounds carrying Wilkie's body to an undisclosed location for an autopsy.

L. Bradford Frame, heir to Joseph Frame's immense fortune, and who operates a private detective agency from his Bryn Mawr mansion, was one of twelve witnesses to the execution. Often grist for gossip when seen in the company of prominent Main Line socialites, Frame said he was glad Wilkie "will never commit another murder." Asked whether the appeals process had been fair to Wilkie, Frame asserted he never "argue(d) the law, only the facts." One witness summed up the feeling of the others, uneasy at Brad Frame's presence, "I hope it makes him feel better to see Wilkie die, I don't think I could be here if it was one of my family he killed."

Wilkie's attorneys were reportedly handling funeral arrangements, which will be private.

What bothered Brad most was the continuation reference at the bottom of the page—*See Brad Frame, 8B.* Forget about Wilkie, the slug insinuated, enticing people to turn the pages and read more about him. Unfortunately, as he well knew, the death of a criminal wouldn't sell newspapers, but maligning prominent Main Line families could. *Damn her!*

Wind rattled the three sets of French doors leading to his office patio. Turning his head, Brad saw a funnel of dried leaves swirling above the rubberized canvas covering the in-ground swimming pool. Aware of a chill, he grabbed both copies of the *Inquirer* and headed for the fireplace at the opposite end of the office. After stacking seasoned hickory logs on the wrought-iron grate, he gathered a large sheet of newsprint into a mass between his hands, gave it a quick twist, and jammed it between the logs. Instant kindling. Brad found the process so therapeutic that he yanked a second sheet from the pile, imagining his hands around a certain reporter's neck.

Taking his words out of context, Thompson had implied that he didn't give a whit about the law and saw the execution as his own private vendetta. Brad continued wringing the paper, wishing he could as easily squeeze her half-truths and innuendo off the page. Thompson didn't seem to have enough ink to mention his community service with several non-profit organizations on whose Boards of Directors he served, but found space to mention the gossip whenever he was spotted with an attractive woman.

"Damn her," he cursed aloud, and bruised his knuckles as he shoved another wad of paper between the logs. *Ouch.*

Brad opened the damper and touched a flame from a butane lighter to the crumpled wads, watching as the paper burst into bright yellow flames. A confetti of newspaper ash curled up the flue. If only his anger would dissipate as easily.

He knelt in front of the stone hearth until the wood blazed on its own and the scent of burning hickory wafted into the room. The office was the one place where Brad felt completely at home. Built to his specifications and designed to look like an old carriage house; a covered breezeway connected it to a hallway behind the kitchen. He had taken pains to match the brick of his parents' home, and placed dormers along the second floor roof to mirror the third floor of the Georgian-style main house.

Brad padded back across the thick green wool carpet and paused, resting his hand on the corner of the massive oak partner's desk, large enough for two people to work—one on either side, facing each other. Originally his father's, the desk brought back memories of his childhood when their mother took him and Andrew into Philadelphia's center city to visit their dad's office. Dad's partner would reach deep into the bottom drawer on her side of the desk and produce Tootsie Roll Pops for them. Aunt Gertie, as they used to call her, served Brad first. But she always gave extra candy to his older brother, which caused more than a few tussles between them on the way home in the back seat of his dad's old Buick. Brad pulled open the bottom drawer, half expecting to find an errant Tootsie Roll Pop. He chuckled to himself wondering what he would have done had he found one.

Brad returned to his seat behind the desk as Sharon bounded into the office with her cell phone glued to her ear. "What are you up to?" Sharon asked, adding, "I'm on hold."

"I've been cremating the *Inquirer*," Brad said. Spotting the sports section still on his desk, he flung the paper in her direction. "You're on your feet. Take care of this, if you would please."

"I have an idea," Sharon said, as she pushed back the fireplace screen and tossed the crumpled paper on to the fire. "Why don't you just buy the publishing company?"

Brad ignored her suggestion, and pointed toward her cell phone. "Who are you on hold for?"

"I'm chasing down a lead on David."

Brad nodded as he thought about the runaway teen that they'd been hired to find.

"I went by his school yesterday and talked with his nerdy friend Lou." Sharon plopped down on the leather sofa. "Lou said David chatted regularly with a girl on the Internet. She lives in Colorado, and Lou figures he's heading that way. I'm on hold while Lou tries to locate the girl's screen name."

The phone rang.

Sharon picked up the extension on a table near her end of the sofa. Brad grimaced at the sight of her holding the receiver at her right ear and the cell phone at her left. "Brad Frame Agency," she answered with the authority of a switchboard operator at a Fortune 500 company. Sharon held the receiver against her chest and whispered, "It's Superintendent Dolewski."

Brad signaled for Sharon to listen on the extension.

He picked up the phone on his desk. "Superintendent, thanks for getting back to me."

"No problem, Mr. Frame. What can I do for you?"

"What I have to ask may sound a little unusual," Brad began.

"In my line of work hardly anything sounds unusual." Dolewski laughed huskily.

"I bet. I was wondering if . . . as you gathered Frank

Wilkie's personal effects . . . if you found any Biblical references?"

Dolewski responded, "You mean like a list of Bible verses?"

"Yes." Brad looked hopefully toward Sharon, and noticed her glancing at her cell phone, grimacing, and folding it shut.

"As a matter of fact, yes," Dolewski replied. "I realized it must have fallen out of Wilkie's Bible. It was a sheet of paper with chapters and verses from the Bible scribbled in pencil. I don't remember them exactly."

Brad ran his fingers through the hair on his left temple, sure that the list of verses would help make sense of the words Wilkie had written in the Bible. "I wonder if I might get a copy of that list?"

"Well, Mr. Frame, there's a slight complication." Dolewski's voice seemed to turn more formal. "I had a visitor within the last hour. Mr. Wilkie's attorney, Ronald Allessi, came to retrieve Frank Wilkie's personal property. We had boxed up the prisoner's stuff, like we always do, just in case anyone called for them. I put that list of Bible verses in the box."

"I see," Brad said, trying not to sound too disappointed. "I was just curious . . ."

"I should warn you, Mr. Frame," Dolewski continued, "Mr. Allessi is looking for you. Allessi asked me about an article in today's *Philadelphia Inquirer*. We don't get the *Inquirer* out here in the boonies, but I gathered that the newspaper reported Wilkie having a Bible at the execution. Mr. Allessi specifically asked about it because there wasn't any Bible in a box of the prisoner's possessions. So I phoned the Chaplain. He told me that he gave Wilkie's Bible to you. Based on the fireworks Mr. Allessi put on while he was here, I'm guessing he's calling directory assistance right about now for your phone number."

Brad glanced over at Wilkie's Bible, sitting safely on the edge of his desk.

"I appreciate the heads up," Brad said. "And thanks for the information about the list."

"I figure it can't be a coincidence what with that lawyer looking for Wilkie's Bible and you asking about a list of Bible verses." The superintendent paused, and Brad weighed whether to share more information about the words written in Wilkie's Bible, when he heard, "I made a photocopy of the list, Mr. Frame, if you'd still like to have it."

"That would be great," Brad said, trying not to sound too excited. "Here's my fax number—"

"Unfortunately," Dolewski interrupted, "our fax machine is broken. But I can mail it to you."

"Don't you have a Kinko's or another store where you could use a fax machine?" Brad asked.

He could hear Dolewski sigh on the other end of the line.

"There's a place about eight miles from here," Dolewski said. "It's on my way home, so I'll fax it to you tonight."

Brad thanked Dolewski and gave the superintendent his fax number before turning to Sharon and saying, "Too bad we have to wait, but that list should help us figure out what Wilkie was trying to tell us."

CHAPTER 5

Brad found a visitor's parking spot near the entrance to the Bairnes Care Center, a one-story brick building once home to an elementary school. He leaned momentarily against the trunk of his car and surveyed the tranquil setting, admiring the mature maple and elm trees, lush manicured lawns, and freshly tilled flowerbeds. He opened his trunk and retrieved two flats of daffodils he had bought at a nearby greenhouse, each planted in a small clay pot wrapped with green gingham fabric and tied with a yellow bow. He juggled them in his arms and pushed the trunk closed with his right elbow.

Tawana, the regular receptionist, wearing a pink pantsuit that matched the blush on her cheeks beamed when she saw him coming. She nudged a co-worker exclaiming, "Look what Mr. Frame's brought for us today."

"My mom always liked daffodils," Brad explained. "I thought these would give everyone a taste of spring."

"Now aren't you sweet," she said, lightly stroking the petals of one of the flowers.

"Make sure you keep one for yourself, Tawana," Brad said, scooping up a pot. "I'll take this one for Dad."

After a short jaunt down the brightly-lit carpeted corridor, Brad arrived at room 117, where he pushed on the handle with his free hand.

"Hi, Dad! Look what I brought." Brad placed the daffodil on the nightstand next to his father's hospital-style bed, with the head elevated. All the other furnishings in the room were from their Bryn Mawr home, including a green

54

and gold brocade chair that had always been his dad's favorite.

His father lay silently, his thick gray hair combed straight back, and a blanket pulled up midway on his chest. His skin seemed more jaundiced, Brad thought, his cheeks sunken, and his eyes cloudy as they aimed at the ceiling.

Brad pulled up a chair next to the bed. He stroked his father's hand where a needle inserted near his wrist connected him to a plastic bag of dextrose suspended from a rod attached to the bed. He grabbed his father's other hand and gave it a light squeeze, but on this visit his dad didn't squeeze back. It had always been his dad's signal that he could hear, after he lost the ability to speak.

Brad spoke. "They spread fertilizer on the lawn the other day, Dad. The grass will soon need mowing twice a week. Oh, and that pear tree you planted out back of the kitchen is in full bloom." Still no return squeezes so Brad released his dad's hand and sank back into his chair.

Noting how thin he'd become it was hard to imagine his father charging down the gridiron, a junior letterman tackle. A football scholarship was how he'd put himself through college and got the education he needed, which eventually led to his successful business. Brad smiled as he remembered what an Eagles' fan his father had become, bundling the family up on a crisp fall Sunday and taking them to his box at the old Veteran's Stadium. His sister Lucy never cared for football, but she loved the attention she got from her dad at the games. As a child she had sat on his lap as he showed her off to friends in the adjoining boxes on the Club level. And he had doted on her, lavishing hot chocolate and cookie treats on his darling daughter. *God, how Dad loved Lucy.*

Late afternoon sun streamed through a sliding glass door

opening onto a patio seating area. The steam-heated room felt warm and stuffy, and Brad got up and pushed a panel back allowing a rush of cool air into the room

Turning back, Brad spotted the Picasso hanging on the wall behind the bed, and another flood of memories came over him. The original had hung in his dad's office, before he donated it to the Philadelphia Museum of Art. This was a reproduction. His dad called it a conversation opener, since visitors to his office couldn't resist asking about it. Over the years, the story of how he acquired it got embellished, with his dad ultimately claiming he'd purchased it from Picasso himself—at his Paris studio. Brad's mother had once shared the real story. They had seen Picasso in Paris during their honeymoon, from a distance of about fifty yards. A crowd had gathered across the street from their hotel at a small café, and when his dad inquired what caused the commotion, the hotel's doorman explained, "C'est Picasso." When his dad hadn't understood, his mother clarified, "Pablo Picasso, the famous artist." Later, during a business trip to New York, his dad purchased the signed print at a Fifth Avenue gallery as a birthday present for Brad's mother. But she hated Picasso's work, claiming it didn't fit with her décor, so it ended up in his dad's office.

With the room aired out, Brad closed the sliding glass door, returning to his dad's bedside. Brad heard a hollow breathy sound as his dad exhaled from a half-opened mouth. Aunt Harriet had remarked about the shallow breathing, and it wasn't getting any better, which worried him.

Studying the profile of his dad's face, Brad thought about what Harriet had told him. His dad had led a full life. The family's tragedy had struck as his dad approached retirement, whereas Brad was barely in his thirties at the time of the kidnapping. In some ways, his life seemed more focused since then. He'd developed a career to help bring justice and peace of mind to other people struck by tragedy, but that same peace eluded him. Like the trains that Brad loved so much, it often seemed as if his career sped along the Main Line, while his life had switched to a seldom-used siding. He thought about Aunt Harriet's advice to live his own life, and about the twists and turns he had taken over the last eleven years. He knew she was right. *But what should he do about it?*

The door swung open and a nurse entered. "I'm sorry, I didn't know you were here, Mr. Frame," she said. "I was going to give him a sponge bath. I'll come back later."

She turned to leave, but Brad stopped her. "That's all right, Karen. I was just about to leave. I'll come back again on Friday."

Brad stood beside the bed, and held his dad's hand again. He bowed his head. Religion wasn't a part of his life now, but he still believed in a Higher Power, and knew that his prayer—drawn from youthful experiences in church— would be heard. He wasn't asking God for much—pain-free days for his dad and tranquility for himself. "I love you, Dad," Brad said before gently placing his dad's hand back on the bed, covering it with the blanket.

"Thanks for coming, Mr. Frame. I know he appreciates your visits." Karen put her hand on his shoulder, but he was so choked up he couldn't respond. As he returned to the hallway, he swiped the tears from his eyes.

CHAPTER 6

Brad punched the button on the answering machine and replayed the message that he first heard an hour earlier. Mr. Frame, this is Ron Allessi. I'm with Blankenship, Trawler and Ivanic. I plan to stop by your office at 1 p.m. today to pick up Mr. Wilkie's Bible. In even tones, Mr. Allessi hadn't asked if he could pay a visit; he was practically on his way.

An all-day soaker had invaded Philadelphia, creating the kind of day when the chill seemed to start from the inside and work its way out. Brad relished the warmth from the fire blazing in his office fireplace. Glancing up at the Regulator on his wall he realized it was about time for Allessi's visit. He straightened a few papers on his desk, and centered Wilkie's Bible on the leather writing pad in front of him.

Inching along using half steps, Sharon staggered into the office balancing an antique silver urn, about a fourth her size, on a tray in front of her.

"Here, let me help you with that," Brad said, relieving her of the heavy silver tray and positioned the hot, coffee-laden urn on a table between two leather recliners.

Bringing the silver service was Sharon's idea; she wanted to impress their guest. Brad, who didn't feel hospitable, couldn't have cared less. Sharon had already dragged out cups and saucers along with a matching creamer and sugar bowl from his mother's Haviland collection. She lit a can of Sterno and placed it under the urn. Brad looked at Sharon, rolled his eyes, and asked, "Couldn't he just stop at Starbucks?"

Sharon clicked her tongue. "Now . . . now."

"By the way, Sharon, I plan to offer Mr. Allessi a seat near the fire."

"Ah, the old hot seat?" she said with an evil grin.

"No," Brad explained as he slipped Wilkie's Bible into the top drawer of his desk, "I want to keep him as far away from this Bible as possible."

Sharon nodded before heading back to the main foyer. She had volunteered to wait by the front door and greet Mr. Allessi, but Brad knew she wanted a head start in sizing him up.

Brad heard a car door slam, recognizing a solid sound indicative of luxury engineering. He looked out a front window of the office and spotted the tail end of a Lexus in his driveway. Less than a minute later Ronald Allessi abruptly entered the office ahead of Sharon. He slipped off his still-dripping Burberry raincoat, handing it to Sharon who held the coat at a distance to avoid getting wet and hung it on the office coat tree.

"Mr. Frame," Allessi recited in professional tones, "I'm Ron Allessi," as he headed toward Brad with an arm extended. Brad grasped his hand, felt an extra firm grip, and determined not to try and match his physical strength. Allessi had dark hair and an olive complexion. Impeccably groomed, Allessi sported the latest in fashion neckwear, a Cashmere coat, and a one-inch scar above his left eyebrow.

Their handshake ended, Allessi retrieved an engraved silver case from his inside breast pocket, and handed Brad a business card. Brad glanced at the card before laying it on his desk.

"Would you care for a cup of coffee?" Brad winked at Sharon as he asked. He directed the attorney—who he judged to be mid-thirties—to the leather chair nearest the fireplace.

"Yes, thank you, with cream," Allessi said.

Brad grabbed an empty cup, but Sharon snatched it from his hands and soon delivered the cup and saucer to Mr. Allessi. Brad sat in the other leather chair, while Sharon sat opposite them in her usual spot on the sofa. The picture of civility, Brad thought, the three of them clustered by a roaring fire, savoring aromatic logs, sipping coffee, and fighting off the dampness.

Allessi eyed his watch. "If you don't mind," he began, "I'd like to get right to the purpose of my visit. I'm here to retrieve Frank Wilkie's Bible."

Brad and Sharon exchanged glances. They knew as much from the attorney's brief phone message.

"Giving me his Bible was Wilkie's dying wish," Brad said. "You can speak with the prison's chaplain for confirmation."

"I've done that," Allessi said. "But neither the chaplain nor Mr. Wilkie had the legal right to dispose of property that Mr. Wilkie had already assigned to his legal team."

"When?" Brad asked.

"About six weeks ago."

"You *negotiated*," Brad emphasized the word, "a property agreement with Frank?"

"Let's say I presented it to him . . ."

"Convenient," Brad murmured.

". . . And made certain he understood what it was," Allessi concluded.

"What was the reason for having such an agreement with Frank?"

"I don't have to go into that with you, Mr. Frame. You're not a party at interest."

"Oh, I'm *very* interested." Brad found Allessi cold and off-putting beneath all the sartorial splendor and profes-

60

sional demeanor. He figured it was time for a good offense, as he stood and walked over to his desk. He fingered the attorney's ivory-colored business card on the desk in front of him. "Blankenship, Trawler and Ivanic," Brad read from the card. "Why is a firm that specializes in corporate law handling public defender duty for a condemned murderer?"

Allessi glanced at the floor, and sighed. "We're not his public defender. He dismissed his court-appointed attorney two years ago. That's when I took on the case." Allessi tugged at the cuff link on his left sleeve, showing off his French cuffs.

Sharon got up from her seat and crossed over to the smoldering fire, adding another log. Passing Allessi she remarked, "Another reason for delaying Wilkie's appeals."

Allessi shrugged.

Allessi's cockiness angered him, and with his voice rising Brad asked, "Did you have a written agreement with Wilkie two years ago?"

"We had . . . understandings."

Brad tried to soften his tone. "Did these *understandings,* by any chance, have anything to do with the $500,000 ransom my father paid for the safe return of my mother and sister?"

"I'm afraid we're getting off track," Allessi said, shifting in his chair. It seemed to Brad as though the question may have cracked Allessi's façade.

Brad pointed a finger at the attorney. "We're not off track at all."

The newest log on the fire burst into full blaze with a whoosh that made Allessi jump.

Allessi pulled his monogrammed briefcase onto his lap, and rolled the combination lock into proper sequence before snapping open the case and shuffling through papers.

Brad kept on the pressure. "What's wrong with this picture? Your firm began representing Wilkie two years ago. I can check the record to be sure, but that coincides with the Governor's first signing of his death warrant. You represented Wilkie *without* any formal agreement until six weeks ago when he signed over rights to his estate including any personal effects from his stay in prison, which probably only includes a few magazines, a dime-store watch, maybe a Zippo lighter . . . it hardly seems worth the trouble. Unless . . ." Brad practically shouted the word, and paused before repeating it more softly. "Unless you know where Wilkie stashed his share of the ransom."

Sharon chimed in. "Then, two weeks later you told Wilkie his appeals were exhausted. Bye, bye, Frank." Sharon waggled her fingers. "We got your signed agreement. Have a great life, what's left of it."

Allessi seemed flustered. "My firm knows nothing about any, uh, ransom money." He retrieved a legal-sized sheet of paper from his opened briefcase. "Look, here's a copy of Mr. Wilkie's signed and witnessed statement authorizing our firm to take possession of his personal effects." He waved the document in the air. "You have his Bible, and we want it."

Brad reached in his desk drawer and removed Wilkie's Bible. Holding the bound volume tightly, he walked over to where Allessi was seated and brought it within his grasp.

The lawyer's eyes got big, as if he had seen the Holy Grail.

"What's so special about this?" Brad drew the Bible back and thumbed casually through its pages. "I don't see anything extraordinary. It's not rare. Placed by the Gideons—there's got to be millions of those," he said, with all the sarcasm he could muster. "There's nothing missing. Starts with Genesis and concludes with Revelation. The Revised Standard Version—more austere than the King James, I have to admit, still I've always found it more poetic than some of the newer versions."

Once again the attorney shifted uncomfortably in his chair. "Don't play with me, Mr. Frame." The now roaring fire hadn't melted the ice in his voice. "I'm not some wet-behind-the-ears kid just out of law school. I didn't spend my life in a cocoon. I grew up in Camden. I saw two of my older brothers buried before I was in second grade. When I was eleven, I joined a gang—to survive. When I was thirteen, I got this." Allessi pointed to the scar over his left eye. "The guy who gave it to me wasn't so lucky." He shrugged. "Thanks to our parish priest, my parents got a stipend to send me away to a private school." He loosened his silk tie. "If I hadn't gone, the courts would have found someplace for me. At St. Ignatius Academy, Sister Mary Paul changed my life. I knew *how* to survive; she made me want to survive. I don't need sarcasm from you for trying to do my job."

"I'm glad you told me that story," Brad said, "because you just proved you can understand what it was like to be in Wilkie's shoes."

"Frank doesn't have any shoes. We have them," Allessi responded coldly.

Brad returned to his desk, feeling Allessi's gaze glued on the Bible. Brad laid it on the corner of the desktop then returned to his chair and waited silently until Allessi's gaze finally met his. "Did you ever play poker in Camden?" Brad asked.

"Sure," Allessi replied. "I don't see what that's got—"

"Before I hand you all the chips, I'd like to see more cards. You come here boasting about your agreement with

63

Frank Wilkie—an agreement that predates his possession of the Bible. You turn over one ace, and expect me to just hand over the Bible?"

"As a licensed detective, you wouldn't want to violate a legal agreement," the attorney said. "If you don't want to cooperate, we can always get a court order."

Brad shook his head. "You've got to do better than that. What does Wilkie's property agreement have to do with the missing ransom money?"

Allessi pursed his lips, looking exasperated. "Nothing."

"Then tell me why you need this Bible . . . this *particular* Bible."

Allessi closed his briefcase and crossed his arms in front of him. "I'm . . . I'm not authorized to provide that information."

"Then who is?" In their verbal poker game Brad decided to raise him one and call. "Get him over here. I'm willing to cooperate with you, but not before I get some answers."

Silence. Allessi stroked his index finger across his upper lip, apparently thinking, but then Sharon laughed. Brad didn't know why. Maybe a release of nervous energy, but nothing incenses a guy more than thinking a woman is laughing *at* him. Brad could almost feel the heat behind the stare Allessi flashed in Sharon's direction. Finally, Allessi said, "I can't give you specifics, but it has something to do with a book deal."

Brad felt the anger rising in him. He wanted to shout, but managed to keep it to a growl. "Are you serious? A book about Wilkie?" Brad slammed his fist on the table between them, rattling the cups and saucers and prompting a distressed look from Sharon. "Damn it." Brad jumped up from his seat and paced in front of Allessi. "Only the book won't be about him as much as about his crimes. And that means it'll be about *my* family. I asked you to show me your cards and you just turned over a couple of jokers."

"Mr. Frame, I cannot confirm—"

"Let me lay *my* cards on the table." Brad leaned into him as he spoke, and balled his right hand into a fist.

"Brad!"

At the sound of Sharon's voice he relaxed his hand, but continued questioning Allessi. "You were scheduled to witness the execution. Why didn't you?"

"Who said I was supposed to be there?" Sounding innocent, Brad knew Allessi was toying with him.

"The warden told me *another* of Wilkie's witnesses had cancelled. All his family is dead. Who else but you? You hadn't been to visit Frank in over a month."

"Something came up."

Sharon jumped into the fray. "What might that have been? Another prison property agreement." Sharon happily mocked him, but Brad suspected she wanted to give him time to cool down.

Brad didn't want to cool down and fired his own question. "If you're gonna write a book about Frank Wilkie, you should've been there to research the final chapter. What do the people who pull your strings think of the list of Bible verses Frank left? Have they figured out Frank's code?"

"Forget it!" Allessi came roaring out of his chair. Brad sensed that his question had hit close to the mark. "I'm tired of playing games, and getting shit on for my trouble." His Camden upbringing showed. "I came here—politely I might add—to get Frank's Bible. If you won't give it to me voluntarily, then I'll see you in court." Ron Allessi took a quick survey of the room, as if fixing his bearings for the exit. "Now, if you'll get my coat."

Sharon pointed at the coat tree. Allessi snatched his coat

and threw it over his arm, then raced down the hall. Sharon ran out of the office to catch up with him.

"He's gone," Sharon announced when she'd returned to the office. "He jumped into his Lexus, a midnight blue sedan, and left you a few rubber streaks on the cobblestones."

Brad nodded as he stood in front of the fireplace, with his back to her. "I heard the squealing tires." He stared down at the glowing embers in the fireplace grate, upset with himself for losing control in their meeting. Brad had shouted at people before, and would do so again, but always for calculated effect. It usually only took him a split-second to decide whether fawning or fury would get him the response he wanted from a client, suspect, or witness. Brad had lost it with Allessi. Nothing calculated about it.

"Brad." Sharon called his name.

He closed his eyes, and tightened the muscles in his face.

"Brad?" she repeated, this time with an edge to her voice.

He sucked in a big breath, before turning to face her. Deep concern lined Sharon's face. Brad painted a soft smile on his own face before saying, "I don't think we've heard the last of the Camden con-man."

CHAPTER 7

Shortly after seven Brad walked into the kitchen to the aroma of freshly brewed coffee.

"Oh, good morning," Sharon said, with a wide-eyed glance in his direction.

"You're up early." He headed straight for the coffee maker, double-checking the time on the kitchen wall clock. It wasn't out of character for Sharon to be awake at that hour, but she usually ate her breakfast in her apartment, located above the garage, just east of the mansion. Brad filled his favorite ceramic mug, one he'd earned two years earlier on a weekend Habitat for Humanity building project, and stirred in a half-teaspoon of sugar. The variation in her morning routine was only a minor mystery, he concluded, and she would undoubtedly explain over breakfast. Out of the corner of his eye Brad thought he saw her slide something off the table and onto the bench beside her. He dropped an English muffin in the toaster.

"Did you and Mark get together last night?

"No."

A concise answer? How *that* was out of character, a question about Mark often produced a five-minute response. "Everything okay?" Brad rummaged through the refrigerator door bins in search of apricot jam.

"Uh huh . . ." Sharon said, prompting Brad to stare at her. "What?" she said, with an open-mouthed gape. "Everything's fine. Mark had class last night."

"Ah!" Brad wondered why it took so long to elicit that bit of non-classified information.

Toting his cup, Brad placed it opposite Sharon on the cloth covered breakfast table, near a bay window with views of his backyard. "Be right back. I'm gonna get the *Inquirer*."

He took two steps before Sharon said, "It's not there. I looked earlier."

"Hmmm, it's usually here by now." The second mystery of the morning, Brad mused, as he continued toward the foyer, but Sharon stopped him.

"Come and eat your breakfast while it's warm!"

"Yes, Aunt Harriet."

"I'll check again when I get up." Sharon smiled sweetly before bringing a glass of orange juice to her lips.

Brad didn't feel like arguing and returned to his seat.

"Remember the letter we got last week from the guy in Pittsburgh wanting you to investigate his wife's disappearance?" Sharon asked.

Brad nodded as he savored the taste of homemade brandied-apricot preserves on his muffin.

"I think you were hasty in turning him down," she said. "His wife has family in Chicago and, I was thinking . . . you know? Maybe we could fly to Chicago and at least speak with her family, see if they've heard from her."

Brad dabbed a napkin at the corner of his mouth. "She's dead."

"What?"

"Police found her body yesterday afternoon, at the edge of a playground a few miles from her home. They've already arrested the husband for her murder."

"How do you know all this?"

"I saw a story on the eleven o'clock news last night."

Sharon gasped. "A Pittsburgh murder on *our* local news! Did the police connect you to the case . . . you know, say the killer had tried to hire you?"

68

Brad shook his head. "It made national news because of the unusual way in which they solved the case. It seems the wife wasn't completely dead when he dumped her body in the playground, and she had time to write his name in the dirt before she died."

"Wow!" Sharon appeared relieved. "So asking you to get involved was a diversionary tactic on his part?"

"Yeah, the complete story's probably in today's *Inquirer*," Brad said. "Relax and enjoy your breakfast and I'll go see if the paper's here yet."

"No. Wait!" Sharon tried to get up, jostled the table, and her juice glass tipped over and made a mess.

"Shit," she muttered, pulling up the tablecloth and dabbing the growing wet spot with the dry edge of the cloth.

Brad threw his napkin on top of the spill to help sop up the liquid.

Sharon wriggled toward the window on her side of the table, trying to avoid a rivulet of orange juice careening over the edge. When Brad heard a recognizable thump beneath the table, he looked over at Sharon who had frozen in position. She gazed back at him with a deer-caught-in-the-headlights expression.

"Did I just hear this morning's *Inquirer* fall on the floor?" he asked.

"Yes," she said softly, pouting, as if in defeat.

"Hand me the paper."

"Not while you're eating," she implored.

With calm intensity, Brad said, "Sharon, give me the paper, please!"

"Okay," she said. "But don't say I didn't warn you." Sharon reached under the table and retrieved the morning paper, handing it to him.

Brad got up from the soggy table, which Sharon

promptly began to clear, and placed the newspaper on the nearby counter. Below the fold of the front page he saw the article that Sharon had tried to keep from him. Paula Thompson had struck again.

KILLER LEAVES CRYPTIC MESSAGE

The Bible Frank Wilkie carried with him to his execution may have contained a final message, according to speculation by officials at the Rockview State Correctional Institution in Central Pennsylvania. The Bible was mistakenly given to Brad Frame when he attended the execution of the condemned killer.

Frame's mother and sister, Edith and Lucy Frame, were kidnapped eleven years ago and their ravaged and dismembered bodies were subsequently discovered in a boat docked in Fairmount Park.

Brad swallowed, hoping to digest the angry lump forming in his throat, then continued reading.

Following a three-month-long investigation, in which Brad Frame personally participated, aided by reward money from his family's fortune, Frank Wilkie and Eddie Baker were arrested and charged with the crime. Both men were convicted on two counts of first-degree murder and kidnapping, and sentenced to death. Baker died two and one-half years ago at the Graterford Correctional facility in Montgomery County. His death was ruled a suicide, although human rights advocates later questioned the ruling. Wilkie was executed on Tuesday at Rockview, which has housed the State's execution chamber since 1913. Pennsylvania changed its method of execution from the electric chair to lethal injection in 1990.

According to sources at the state penitentiary, Chaplain George Haines, 47, of Bellefonte, acted contrary to established Corrections Department policy when he turned over Frank Wilkie's Bible to Brad Frame during a secret meeting at an area tavern following the execution. Late yesterday afternoon officials were reportedly eyeing disciplinary action against Haines, a nine-year veteran of the chaplain's office, but have declined further comment pending the outcome of their investigation.

"It's customary to turn over personal effects to the next of kin," a Corrections Department spokesman in Harrisburg explained. "A Bible is one of the most personal of an inmate's possessions. I'm sure we can count on Mr. Frame's cooperation to see to its safe return." *See Killer's Message, A19*

Folding the paper open to the continuation of the article, Brad wasn't so sure about *Mr. Frame's cooperation.* He couldn't help notice that Sharon kept glancing in his direction as she scurried between the table and the counter cleaning up the breakfast dishes. She wadded up the soiled tablecloth and tossed it in the laundry room. He rescued his mug before she could put it in the dishwasher, and continued reading.

Ronald Allessi, of Blankenship, Trawler and Ivanic, visited with Wilkie just days before the execution and echoed the sentiments of the prison's spokesman. "I'm sure we all appreciate the dreadful pain Brad Frame and his family have endured during the last several years, but we're anxious to tie up the loose ends of Mr. Wilkie's life as well." Asked if he expected Frame's cooperation, Allessi asserted, "I'm confident he will cooperate. After all, he's a licensed detective, sworn to uphold the law."

Brad Frame was unavailable for comment.

Brad left the paper lying open on the counter and returned to the breakfast nook. He clasped his hands together in front of his face, propped his elbows on the table and gazed out the window. Brad exchanged glances with a wary-eyed sparrow, perched on the sill of the angled bay window, until it flew away. The morning sun cast deep shadows across the dew-covered grass, and beyond he saw men from the landscaping service spreading fresh mulch around the budding trees. The tranquility of his backyard belied the turmoil he felt within.

"I'm sorry," Sharon said, sliding into the booth across from him.

Brad avoided her gaze, continuing to stare out the window. He imagined her hangdog expression; he'd seen it before. He could understand why Sharon would think the article might upset him, but why had she hidden the newspaper? They had worked together for three years, survived hairy situations with criminals. They'd become a good team. She often acted on impulse where he usually weighed all of the possible options. He'd learned to trust her instincts—maybe he should now.

Brad turned to Sharon. "Apology accepted." She grinned broadly. "On the condition," he continued, "that you explain why you hid the newspaper from me." Her smile faded.

"I'm worried about you," she began. "You lost control during your meeting with Allessi. You're too emotionally wrapped up in Wilkie's case, even if it has been eleven years."

She'd nailed him on that, Brad thought, embarrassed.

Sharon continued, "After yesterday I figured you should just give Allessi back the Bible and get on with your life. Wilkie's Bible can't give you back your mother and sister. And an apology from Wilkie, even if it's written in code, won't mean much."

Brad agreed with her. "But?"

"Then this morning I saw the article. It seems like Allessi is in overdrive trying to get the Bible back. Even though I can share your pain, I think I still have an unbiased perspective. So I keep asking myself what we have overlooked?"

She made sense, he thought. "And the answer is?"

"Well," Sharon said, then took in a deep breath. "At first I thought you hit the nail on the head when you confronted Allessi about the ransom money. The article doesn't mention the ransom, maybe because Allessi doesn't want people to focus on it. If he thinks there's a message in that Bible that will point him toward missing ransom money . . ." Sharon didn't finish her thought, but kept talking. "Allessi knows that Wilkie wanted you to have his Bible; you told him that, and I bet he heard the same thing at the prison. We keep asking ourselves why Wilkie wanted you to have it, and that's the same question they're asking down at Blankenship, Trawler and Ivanic. They've got the list of Bible verses and you have the Bible. Their list doesn't make any sense without what you've got."

"And vice versa," Brad reminded her.

"But the warden is sending *you* the list—so in the next day or two you'll know—but they won't. Look, even Thompson stumbled on it. Allessi managed to set up the reporter on a story about you getting the Bible after the execution, but somebody at the prison spilled the beans about the list of scripture references."

"Sharon, you've seen the words Wilkie wrote in his Bible. How are words like *kill* and *eddie* going to point anyone to hidden ransom money?"

Sharon shrugged. "Maybe the numbers in the list of chapters and verses do. Like coordinates on a map."

Brad scowled. "Wilkie wasn't a codebreaker for the CIA for Christ's sake, he was a middle-school dropout with an IQ slightly more than . . . that squirrel." Brad pointed at the furry creature scampering up the tree outside his window.

"See!" Sharon pointed a finger at him across the table accompanied by a stern expression. "This is exactly why I didn't want you to see that newspaper article. You are on edge—no better than you were at the end of your meeting with Allessi. Now if you'll be quiet I'll give you the rest of my theory."

Chastened, Brad leaned back and folded his arms across his chest prepared to listen.

"Okay, follow this," Sharon said. "If you didn't know anything about Wilkie and the murders, et cetera, and you just read that article, who would your sympathies be with—you or Wilkie's family?"

"Wilkie, I guess."

"Let's take Allessi at his word, that getting the Bible relates to a book deal. Allessi worked with Wilkie for two years. If Wilkie wanted to, he had a lot of time to tell Allessi where they stashed the ransom. But a true crime story featuring the most infamous crime of the last decade and one of Philadelphia's most prominent families could reap a bonanza. Remember, Allessi came over here to play nice after he picked up Wilkie's personal effects, after he got a list of the Scripture references, and *after* he learned you had Wilkie's Bible. The Bible closes the circle between Wilkie and your family. I think this morning's article is aimed at: A) Putting pressure on you to get the Bible back, and B) Generating publicity to increase demand for the future book."

Sharon made the picture look easy, but Brad couldn't fit together all the pieces of the puzzle. She must have noticed the skepticism on his face.

"Allessi is the only named source for the article," Sharon said, holding up one finger. "Pity the poor chaplain with all these bureaucrats coming down on him for granting the last wish of a dying man. From his law firm Allessi could have easily put pressure on State Corrections officials. And if he read Thompson's article on the morning after the execution, he knew what her bias would be if he planted another story with her."

The phone rang.

Sharon jumped to answer it. "Hello."

She tugged at the phone's extension cord to unravel its kinks.

"This is Sharon Porter, I'm Mr. Frame's associate." She sounded very businesslike *and* protective, Brad thought. "Oh, yes, Superintendent Dolewski, I'll get Brad for you he's—" Sharon had moved in Brad's direction, but stopped abruptly. "Sure I can take a message, but he's sitting right—" Sharon listened, and furrowed her eyebrows.

"Yes, Mr. Dolewski. I know about the list of Scripture references."

As Sharon held the receiver to her ear Brad saw her face sag.

"Yes, Superintendent," she said. "I'll make sure Brad gets the message."

Sharon hung up the phone handset and exhaled.

"What did he say?" Brad asked.

"Dolewski worked late last night, and forgot all about faxing you the list," Sharon announced. "And as of this morning he has been *requested*—that's the word he used—not to forward you a copy of Wilkie's scripture verses."

Brad felt his shoulders slump. "So it's a stalemate. We're never going to find out what Wilkie's message means, but I'll be damned if I'm turning that Bible over to them."

Sharon sat opposite him once again, deep lines forming between her eyebrows. Brad clutched his mug like it was a hand railing on the deck of a rolling ship. He looked at Sharon and could only shake his head.

"You have any assignments for me today?" she asked.

Brad shook his head. "Any more news on that missing kid?"

"Yeah, I got the screen name of the girl he's been chatting with—L-i-t-l-e-B-i-t-s-c-h." Sharon spelled the girl's Internet handle, adding, "I bet if she could spell she'd be dangerous. Her profile confirms she lives in Colorado. By this afternoon I hope to have an address."

"Good work," Brad said.

"If you don't need me for anything special, I'm going out for a while," Sharon said before she got up from the table and rushed out of the kitchen.

Brad sat watching the landscapers work in his backyard, and he thought about what Sharon had said about Wilkie's Bible.

CHAPTER 8

Brad remained in the kitchen after Sharon left, watching the landscapers as they prepared to mow his lawn, and reflecting on her analysis. She had given him an idea, and he decided to take action. Only when he headed for his office forty-five minutes later did he think to question why Sharon had left so abruptly. What was she up to? She sure knew how to push his buttons. Unlike the many cases he had handled for clients, it bothered him to feel so out of control, unable to shape events affecting his own life.

He settled into the comfortable chair behind his desk long enough to check e-mail, then extracted Wilkie's Bible from the drawer. Approaching his desktop copier, he realized he couldn't lay the Bible flat in his machine, so he decided to visit a Kinko's within five miles of his Bryn Mawr home. He opened the desk drawer once again; this time to get the copy of Sharon's list, since it noted the Bible pages where he could find Wilkie's words.

Traveling west along Route 30 in the direction of Paoli, Brad passed St. Matthew's Episcopal Church where he had faithfully attended with his family until heading off to college. There he'd drifted away from formal religion, describing himself to friends as spiritual but not religious. In truth, Brad had ventured into a few churches over the years, but found the experience smothering. One could no longer duck into a pew and enjoy the worship service—singing the hymns, listening to the organ, having the occasional sermon strike his soul like a note affects a tuning fork. No, one had to pass the sign of the peace and endure questions from parishioners once they spotted a stranger in their midst. Making his way to shake hands with the minister after Sunday services too often felt like running a gauntlet: *Are you new in town? What church were you baptized in? Won't you join us for tea in the first floor parlor?* Ironic, he thought, that a man who everyone knew professionally as an extrovert could be so introverted in social situations—including church. St. Matthews, for all its cold gothic architectural details, gray granite walls, pewter candelabras, and ice-blue stained-glass windows, evoked a warm family memory for him. Glimpsing the Bible on the seat next to him, Brad saw further irony that a killer's Bible had stirred his reflections about church versus spirituality.

At Kinko's, a clerk behind the counter directed him to the self-service copy machines, and as he ambled that way Brad congratulated himself on not staring too intently at the man's facial piercings. Bible in hand, Brad lifted the cover on the copier and studied how best to position the book for copying on regular sized paper. Brad opened the Bible to page 41, the site of Wilkie's first word, and placed the Bible face down on the glass. He inspected the control panel, which looked more complicated than the machine he was used to at home, and selected the proper paper size, collating and enlargement settings then pushed the start button. Nothing happened.

"You gotta stick a credit card in here," a young lady at the next machine said, tapping a small box mounted on a pole next to the machine. She wore a baggy Villanova sweatshirt, and it looked like she was copying a thick term paper. Her long blonde hair was pulled into a ponytail, and her piercing limited to a diamond stud on the left side of her nose.

"Thanks," Brad said, as he pulled out his wallet and retrieved his American Express card, inserting it into the machine's card reader. He realized it had been awhile since his days spent in a copy shop, back when the staff recorded page counter numbers on each machine before and after each use. In his college years he'd never thought of a copy center as a place to meet girls, and glancing again at the young woman next to him, for a fleeting second wished he were twenty years younger.

Brad pressed the start button. The machine whirred to life, and out popped a perfect copy of Genesis, Chapter 42, with *big* written in pencil next to verse 28. He studied the copy and decided it looked fine.

"Are you like a minister or something?" his Villanova copying-neighbor asked.

Brad smiled back at her, grateful for her help. "Something," he replied, hoping she wouldn't ask any more questions.

Ten minutes and less than two dollars later, Brad inserted the freshly copied pages into the Bible and returned to his car. On the trip home he passed St. Matthew's Cemetery, on the opposite side of the road from the cathedral, and he decided to stop.

Brad couldn't remember when he'd last visited his mother's and sister's grave. He drove his Mercedes along the winding narrow road toward the northwest corner. His family was among the first to be buried in the newly opened section eleven years ago, but now he found the downward sloping hillside dotted with headstones. Brad parked the car and walked in the direction he recalled as their gravesite. Clouds blocked the sun and a brisk wind swept up the hill, but Brad didn't feel cold. He spotted the mahogany-colored marble marker with FRAME chiseled into its shiny surface. The plot had room for four graves and at the foot of two of them were flat stones engraved with his mother's and sister's names—Edith Lucille and Lucille Harriet—along with their birth and death dates. He had forgotten Lucy was named after his mother and Aunt Harriet. He wondered, sadly, how soon it would be before his father would be laid to rest next to his mother.

Brad eyed the fourth grave in the plot, and decided he wasn't ready to think about how it might be filled.

Brad knelt down and pulled a few weeds that had sprouted near the edge of his mother's stone, and vowed to return and plant some flowers on their graves. A flat shiny stone, perfect for skimming across a pond, lay just above Lucy's name. He wondered if a lawnmower had kicked it up on the surface of the marker, or if someone had placed it there—a sorority sister or maybe an old boyfriend? If so, he felt guilty that someone else visited more frequently than he did.

The last seventy-two hours had focused his mind on shortcomings and failures, Brad realized. He could do with a little introspection, Brad knew, but now the press questioned his reputation and motives as a detective. Stirring his emotional pot had resurrected old doubts and surfaced new challenges. As he stared down at the graves, Brad understood he couldn't turn back the calendar and undo what Wilkie had done to his family, but God, how he wished he had never gone to Wilkie's execution.

CHAPTER 9

Brad went for a long drive after he left the cemetery, hoping to sweeten his sour mood and make sense of Allessi's demand for the Bible. He did his best thinking in the car with the sunroof open, fresh air pouring over him, and the radio tuned to his favorite classic music station. At dinnertime, after running a few local errands, he returned to his office. He laid Wilkie's Bible on his desk and searched through it one more time, the eraser end of a pencil in hand.

Brad carried the photocopied pages from the Bible to his bedroom, the master suite that his parents had used when they lived there. His dad had installed a safe in the wall above the dresser. Brad swung open a hinged painting and dialed the safe's combination, two in a clockwise direction and two more counter-clockwise, until the door snapped open. Like his dad, Brad didn't keep much in the safe, except for a passport, a list of credit cards, and a copy of his will, preferring to use a bank's safe deposit vault for truly valuable items. He remembered how his dad used to joke that if a robber ever ordered him at gunpoint to open the safe, the look on *his* face would be matched by the robber's once he saw how little there was to steal. Brad placed the copied pages from Wilkie's Bible in the safe and closed the door. He twirled the locking mechanism, a lucky spin his dad used to call it, and replaced the picture.

A half-hour later, while rinsing off under the shower, Brad thought he heard the sharp-pitched squeal of his security alarm. He quickly turned off the water, and listened. Then he jumped out of the shower and grabbed a towel as he ran to check the security panel in his bedroom. A liquid crystal display alerted him that 911 had been called. Since Brad hadn't activated the intruder security system, he knew the automatic activation meant a fire. Brad jumped into the pair of pants he had worn earlier and yanked on a sweater. He raced down the stairs barefoot. He didn't smell smoke when he reached the foyer, so he dashed into the kitchen and down the back hall toward his office. A smoky odor greeted him near the office door, and he couldn't recall lighting the fireplace that day. He groped for his keys in his pocket, fit the proper one into the lock, then felt to see if the door was hot before opening it.

Flames leapt up to the left of his desk, and a large area of carpet seemed fully engulfed, as the room filled rapidly with smoke. Brad noticed an odor other than smoke—petro-leum-based he thought—which triggered his suspicion of arson. Glancing toward the French doors he saw a broken pane of glass above the lock in the middle set of doors. Though the heat intensified as he approached his desk, Brad opened a drawer and retrieved several disks of back-up computer files, shoving them in his pocket. Then he no-ticed the Bible missing from his desktop, and a clearer pic-ture of the crime emerged in his mind.

Yellow-orange flames lapped at the office ceiling from beside his desk, and with each breath he inhaled more smoke and less breathable air. Brad made his way to the French doors gasping for breath. He spotted shards of broken glass on the floor, and paused to inspect the door's locking mechanism. Brad reached for his handkerchief to cover his nose and mouth. He found it harder to see as the smoke filled the room. His chest felt suddenly heavy and Brad knew that if he didn't leave the office soon they'd find him collapsed on the floor.

He pushed on the handle of one of the French doors and stumbled onto the patio. Sirens warbled on the driveway side of his office and the rumble of truck engines sounded near. "Back here," Brad shouted before sputtering into a cough and falling on his knees. Three men rounded the corner axes in hand and toting fire hoses. They ignored him and began fighting the fire, though he thought he heard one of the firemen call *civilian down* on his radio.

Brad couldn't recall how much later, but he realized he was lying on a stretcher laid on the ground. Two emergency workers knelt beside him. He felt woozy and his eyes weren't focusing clearly. "I'm okay," he muttered, coughing and straining to catch his breath. He drew a hand to his chest.

Brad heard a man's voice say, "We're going to put this on your face." Then they slipped a mask over his nose and mouth. He inhaled, at first savoring the fresh oxygen, then sputtered as his lungs expelled noxious air. Brad struggled to sit upright.

"It's okay," a woman said. "Relax and breathe normally."

A few minutes later Brad pulled the mask off his face. "I think I'm okay," he said standing up. Though he felt a little wobbly, he tried not to let it show. More aware of his surroundings, Brad watched as the firemen aimed their hoses at the persistent flames. Light gray smoke wafted from all three wide-open French doors. Brad thanked the medical personnel before one of the firemen barked at him, "We need you outta here, buddy, so we can work."

Barefooted, Brad meandered gingerly around to the front of his house. He sat on the stone curb beneath one of the ornamental gaslights, which lit the driveway. He noticed the gray stone and white trim on his mansion pulsating pink

from the lights of the fire trucks and ambulance. An unmarked police car, sporting a portable flashing dome light
on the driver's side, pulled into the driveway.

The warbling sirens had attracted a crowd. Brad's neighborhood consisted of over-sized estates in a variety of styles,
each on several acres of land, shielded from curious eyes by
manicured barriers of trees and shrubs. Children didn't understand the concept of privacy that their parents had paid
landscapers to secure. They cut pathways through the
bushes to facilitate playing with the neighbors' kids. Via
these informal footpaths neighbors approached the chaotic
scene.

Brad's neighbors had given names like Fletcher and
Haywood, and the fire in Frame's office was the biggest
news to hit the neighborhood since the New York Stock Exchange extended its trading day. They clustered in small
groups on the cobblestone drive swapping rumors and
hoping for news from fire personnel scurrying between their
trucks and the mansion's west wing.

A moment later he saw his neighbor Gertrude Lindstrom
rolling toward him in her wheelchair, with her husband Emerson walking briskly to keep up.

"Are you alright?" Gertie asked, looking rather grim.

Emerson offered him a clean handkerchief, and Brad realized his face must look awful. He swiped the cloth across
his forehead removing a grimy film of soot, then folded the
cloth to a clean spot before wiping his cheeks.

"Check in my purse, Em," Gertie pleaded. "I usually
carry an ammonia capsule in my purse."

"I'm fine, Gertie," Brad said. Over her shoulder Brad
noticed Emerson pointing at his chin, and Brad dabbed the
handkerchief, once more removing dirt from his face.
Gertie still stared at him apprehensively. Brad remembered

his hair. He had run directly from the shower to the office, and imagined how bad it must look. Touching his still damp head confirmed his worst fears, and he reached into his pocket for a comb.

"There, Gertie, do I look more presentable?"

She cocked her head, asking, "Don't you think you ought to lie down?" As usual she favored the left side of her mouth when she spoke. Her right hand lay motionless on a blanket in her lap, and her winter-white complexion stood out beneath a dark, thinning pageboy-style haircut.

"Now, Gertie," her husband cautioned, "he knows how to take care of himself."

"I'm sorry if I tried to take over," Gertie said, as Emerson tucked a shawl around his wife's shoulders.

"Some people intrude," Emerson Lindstrom intoned, pausing like a veteran stand-up comic, "My wife Gertrudes."

Emerson might have expected a drum roll and rim shot, but Brad didn't react. Gertie appeared unaffected by his sarcasm, acting as if she didn't hear her husband. Emerson pursed his lips like a little boy who'd been caught eating candy before dinner, and winked in Brad's direction. A few years had passed since Brad had seen him, and Emerson's rugged face seemed etched more deeply around the eyes and mouth. Tiny blood vessels were visible on his nose and cheeks, and white hair covered his head.

"We called 911 on my mobile phone," Gertie explained, nodding toward the zippered pack slung on the left side of her motorized wheelchair. "Em was taking me for a walk, and I told him I thought I smelled smoke, and then we saw a big black puff of it coming from your place. At first, Em thought you had a fire in the fireplace. But then agreed it looked suspicious and we called 911 on my mobile phone."

"You already told him that," Emerson said, for which she scowled at him.

She continued, "Then we came over here to see if you were okay."

"We weren't sure if you were home," Emerson said, gesturing toward the estate, "but we heard the fire trucks coming right after we—"

Gertrude interrupted him. "It didn't take us that long to get here. I was sitting in our garden, when Em came back from tinkering on his Hudson. He promised me a walk this evening, but then he went off to work on that old car, and I'd just about given up on the idea since it was almost dark, but Em insisted."

A chilly breeze laden with the smell of smoke swept across the cobblestone driveway. Gertrude Lindstrom tried to use her good arm to pull the blanket down around her legs, but Emerson jumped in to help her.

Brad saw an old Ford circa should-have-been-in-the-dump-by-now pull into his driveway. With fire trucks and emergency vehicles filling the drive, the car backed into a service truck parking area near the entrance. Brad watched as Sharon jumped out of the car. Sharon slammed her car door so hard that Brad winced wondering if it could remain on its hinges. Her boyfriend Mark emerged from the driver's side.

A fireman, rolling up a hose, yelled at her as she ran toward Brad. "Hey lady, stay back behind the truck."

"I live here!" Sharon shouted, trying to be heard over the rumble of the fire truck motor.

"I don't care if you're the Pope," the man pointed, "go around the other side of the trucks."

She obeyed and a few seconds later Brad saw her approaching him and the Lindstroms from a different direction. Sharon Porter screamed, "What's going on? I just got back. Are you okay?"

"I'm fine," he assured her. "Somebody set fire to the office."

Her mouth gaped.

Mark Bertolet caught up with her. An easy-going character in his late 20's, his occupation appeared to be perpetual student. If he got a job, Brad thought, at least he could afford a new car.

Brad introduced Sharon and Mark to the Lindstroms, and recapped for them how he discovered the fire.

"Is that your '67 Fairlane?" Emerson asked Mark.

"Yeah, pretty cool don't you think?" Mark beamed at the prospect of discovering a fellow car enthusiast.

"You sure you weren't hurt," Sharon asked, eyeing his hair and possibly a few remaining smudges on his face.

Brad shook his head.

"Mr. Frame," a police officer called out as he approached.

Brad stood up to greet him. "Yes."

"I'm Lieutenant Norton," the investigator crisply identified himself. "The fire department is almost finished. They'll keep a man posted outside your gate overnight in case the fire should flare up. Arson is a definite possibility. We suspect an accelerant was used. We'll cordon off the area with crime scene tape, and come back in the morning when we can sift the ashes for clues."

Brad nodded. "I smelled something suspicious when I first noticed the fire."

"I'm afraid I'll have to ask you to stay out of that building, Mr. Frame, until we've finished. It was your office?"

"Right," Brad responded, concerned because the officer

had used past tense to describe the office. "I don't think there's any reason why I need to get in there before tomorrow."

"If you don't mind, I'd like to ask you a couple questions." The Lieutenant scanned the group assembled in the driveway, adding, "I'd be happy to question you privately."

"No. There's no problem." Brad pointed at his neighbors. "Lieutenant, do you know the Lindstroms, Gertrude and Emerson?" The officer smiled and tipped his hat. "And this is my associate Sharon Porter and her friend Mark Bertolet."

"Perhaps we should head home, Gertie," Emerson offered.

Gertie flashed her husband an unmistakable I'd-really-like-to-stay-and-hear-this look.

"There's no need for you to leave," Brad said. "Go ahead with your questions, officer."

"Do you have any idea who may have wanted to do this to you?" Officer Norton asked.

Brad scratched his eyebrow as he thought about the question. "You know I'm a private detective?"

Norton nodded.

"Over the years I've made a lot of enemies. There might be someone who'd like to get even."

"How about a case you're working on now?" the officer probed.

Brad shook his head.

"There's been some controversial publicity about you, Mr. Frame."

"So?" Brad snapped, and he felt Sharon's hand on his shoulder. Maybe he should let her answer the questions. He knew Thompson's articles would come back to haunt him.

"Could this incident be related to that?" Norton asked in even tones.

Recovering from his momentary defensiveness, Brad responded, "I really couldn't say." Though he knew, based on what he'd seen in the office, the arson had everything to do with the publicity surrounding Wilkie's Bible.

The investigator was the epitome of professionalism and courtesy, but Brad could see the officer wouldn't buy a non-response even if he delivered it courteously. "This morning's *Inquirer* mentioned a Bible. There's apparently some dispute about it. Could this incident be related to that Bible?"

Gertrude Lindstrom maneuvered her wheelchair closer to the officer, apparently straining to hear, while her husband rocked on his heels acting like he didn't know her.

Brad responded, "It's possible. The Bible was in the office. The fire . . . How much destruction was there?"

"About two-thirds of the office sustained damage," Norton responded.

"It's gone," Brad said.

Sharon brought her hands in front of her face as she gasped, a fact the officer seemed to note.

"Could I speak with you privately, Mr. Frame?" Brad nodded and followed Officer Norton closer to the front door of his mansion. Out of earshot from the others Norton merely reiterated that he'd return in the morning, and for Brad to expect more questions at that time.

Brad returned to find Sharon comforting Gertrude Lindstrom. Tears welled in Gertie's eyes as she said, "I gave that Bible to your parents forty years ago. When they first moved into the house. A family Bible to record important events, use at baptism . . ."

Brad knelt down beside the wheelchair. "Your gift is still safe, Gertie. I have that Bible in my bedroom. It's not the same Bible."

"There was a story in this morning's paper," Emerson said, joining in calming his wife. "It's a prison Bible."

"I never saw the paper," she snapped, embarrassment turning to anger over jumping to the wrong conclusion.

Gertrude swiveled her motorized wheelchair on the cobblestone drive, apparently deciding to leave. "If we can do anything for you, Brad, please call."

The wheelchair surged forward then abruptly stopped as she turned back toward him. "How's your dad?"

The question brought Brad back to the emotionally charged subject of his family. "He's . . . he's not doing very well. But I'll tell him you were asking."

"Thanks again for your help," Brad called after them, watching as the Lindstroms returned down the path toward their home.

"That old guy looks like a mortician," Sharon said.

"You're in the ballpark." Brad grinned. "Em's a retired investment banker. He knows where to bury your money."

"What about her? Did she have a stroke?" Sharon asked.

Brad shook his head. "Gertie developed a tumor on her spinal column seven years ago. The doctors recommended surgery, which she had, but she's been partially paralyzed ever since. Without surgery, Gertie wouldn't have survived."

"She's a feisty old bird," Sharon commented.

"Her mind seems as sharp as ever. Dad used to think she was overly meticulous and annoying when she was younger. She used to drive him crazy with questions about the smallest issues."

"Humph," Sharon sniffed. "That's back when all men thought any woman in the business world was annoying."

"No. It's thanks to her that my dad started Joedco, his business, and they were partners for nearly thirty years.

Gertrude Lindstrom inherited this land along with a fortune when her father died. She bankrolled Dad's idea, and became the company's Vice President for Finance. About that same time, Gertie sold twelve acres of land to my dad and he built this house."

Sharon linked her arm in his saying, "I know you've never worked with any annoying females."

Mark walked behind them, and Brad heard him chuckle.

Sharon tried to steer him toward the front door of the mansion.

Brad resisted, saying, "Let's go this way."

He led Sharon and Mark around back to survey the office. A broad strip of yellow crime scene tape hung across the French doors leading to the office. Black soot clung to the exterior siding above the entryway. Burned furniture dragged onto the patio still dripped evidence of the firemen's hoses, and an acrid smoky odor defied the wind, refusing to leave. The three of them peered through the open holes of glass smashed out of the French doors, viewing the damage with the benefit of the low-level landscape lighting around the patio.

"This side of the desk doesn't look good," Brad said.

"It's the biggest desk I've ever seen," Mark said.

"My mother got Dad that partners' desk when he started his business. So huge, but he always seemed to need every square inch of it for his piles of paper." Brad put his hands up to the window to shield his view, straining to see the extent of the damage. He hoped to salvage the desk. "I remember Mom bringing us kids to visit Dad's office. Dad would take us into the lunchroom and get us whatever we wanted from the vending machines. I always wanted a Coke, which was dispensed in those old-fashioned green bottles. I think they only cost fifteen cents back then, maybe twenty. We'd come back to the office and Dad would sit Lucy on top of the desk and play patty cake with her, while Andy and I would always play in the cavernous area underneath."

Brad closed his eyes. In his imagination he could picture his sister's legs dangling over the edge as he and his brother played pirate or caveman below. Then a Tootsie Roll Pop appeared from Gertie's side of the desk and they forgot what they were playing to enjoy the treat. Maybe that was Gertie's plan all along, to stop the two of them from careening back and forth disturbing her work. Brad smiled.

He felt Sharon's hand on his shoulder again. "I'm sorry about the Bible, Brad."

Brad stood, hands on his hips, staring at the arson scene. "It's gone," he mumbled.

"You'll be able to make repairs," Sharon said, trying to comfort him.

"No," Brad shook his head. "I mean the Bible's missing. Whoever did this took the Bible and set the fire to cover his tracks."

"What?" Sharon looked shocked. "Now we'll never figure out Wilkie's final message."

"I have good news," he said. "I made a photocopy of all the relevant pages in Wilkie's Bible this morning, then I erased the original entries. I figured if Allessi got a court order for the return of the Bible, I should be ready to return it on short notice. If we ever get a list of scripture verses from Dolewski, we'll be able to put it all together."

CHAPTER 10

Brad looked out his bedroom window at eight-thirty Saturday morning and spotted the arson investigator's car, a beige American-made model with municipal plates. He wondered what they might find.

A half-hour later Brad walked out to the patio carrying a plate of freshly baked cinnamon rolls courtesy of Pillsbury. "Would you guys like some sweet rolls?" Brad shouted through the open doors, just as he spotted a camera flash inside his office.

"Thanks, Mr. Frame," Lieutenant Norton said. "Put it down over there, and we'll get it."

Brad set the plate on the glass patio table. He noticed the buds dotting the trees, figuring they only needed a few more sunny days before they'd be donning their spring leaves.

"You find anything?" he asked, easing into a patio chair. The office looked dark behind the sun-drenched patio, and Brad realized he would have trouble seeing any details at that distance.

"Get a shot of the ceiling right above the desk, Skip," Norton ordered his partner. "Hey, there's rolls out here too." The Lieutenant walked toward him. "We're just collecting evidence, Mr. Frame."

"You can call me Brad."

The second officer rolled a wheelbarrow full of charred debris through the French doors and dumped it onto an empty spot on the patio. Brad watched as the officer knelt down on the stone surface and transferred bits of the debris into plain metal cans then sealed and labeled them. He'd seen similar cans at the crime lab.

"I didn't know you guys did demolition work," Brad said.

Norton flashed him a fake smile. "Just collecting evidence. We'll be able to determine what accelerant was used to start the fire—but you already know that. Skip thinks it's some kind of paint thinner. I'd trust his nose."

Brad got up and moved closer to the open doorway for a better whiff.

"You got a sniffer like a bloodhound's, don't you, Skip?" Norton laughed. "Did you get a sample from the left side of the desk?" he asked, as his partner sealed up two more cans of evidence. "There's a lot of charring there."

"I'm on that right now, Jim."

Brad saw that the floor had burned through to the joists in several places and a chunk of drywall from the ceiling had collapsed near his desk.

"Step back a little further from the door, Brad," Norton ordered.

"You guys need anything?"

The Lieutenant shook his head. "We're almost through. We should have the lab results within a week. We'll most likely be back. If your insurance agent has any questions, tell him to call us."

"When you're done, can I get back in my office?" Brad asked.

"Sure," Norton nodded. "Oh, Brad?"

"Yes," he answered, wary of the tone in Norton's voice.

"That Bible we talked about last night, was it bound in leather?"

"No. Why?"

"Unless a fire is very bad, you can usually tell a charred

book after the fire. The outer edges might be burnt, but the inner pages can even be readable—but you already know that." The Lieutenant glared at him. Brad was experienced enough as a private detective to know he was under suspicion, and matched the officer's glare with a penetrating gaze of his own. "In any event," Norton continued, "we didn't find any Bible. We even checked the grate in your fireplace, no Bible. It's missing."

"I thought I told you that last night, Lieutenant," Brad said.

"You implied the Bible was destroyed in the fire."

"Well," Brad said, "I don't know what you heard, but I've got four witnesses who heard me say 'It's gone'. Maybe when you find the missing Bible you'll also have your arsonist—but you already know that."

CHAPTER 11

Brad watched the investigators pack up their equipment and disappear around the corner with several debris-filled cans destined for analysis. He picked up the plate with the remaining cinnamon rolls, and as he turned toward the kitchen he spotted Sharon.

Her mouth crimped in annoyance. "What are you doing?"

"I'm taking these back to the—"

"That's not what I mean. We need Lieutenant Norton on our side. You think baiting him will help?"

"How long were you spying on me?" Brad asked.

"Don't change the subject. Answer my question."

Brad stared at her in icy silence.

She continued to press, and Brad felt his gut tighten. "You could have told Norton about Allessi's visit, about him demanding the Bible, maybe shared your own suspicions about who started the fire."

Brad brushed past her. "I've got work to do."

Brad deposited the plate on the kitchen counter. Wanting to put distance between himself and Sharon, he continued toward the library, which was on the opposite side of the foyer from the drawing room. Until repairs could be made, the library would function as his temporary office. Brad yanked the wooden swivel chair back from the small desk and sat, surrounded by walnut shelves lined with leather-bound volumes and Book-of-the-Month Club best-sellers still in their faded paper jackets. The odor of furniture polish and aging leather hung in the air. Still fuming

after his confrontation with Sharon, Brad opened his laptop
and grabbed a Zip disk; it carried the aroma of the fire in
his office, and Brad was glad he had retrieved it just in time.
He flipped on the computer, and had inserted one of the
disks when Sharon appeared in the doorway. He froze,
shutting his eyes, hoping she might just glower at him for a
moment and then move on.

"You didn't shave this morning," she said.

Brad ignored her, inspecting the list of file names on the
disk. He frowned as he popped out that Zip and inserted a
new one.

"In the last three years I've never seen you unshaven.
Hell, you freak out over a five-o'clock shadow." Sharon
tramped to the edge of his desk and stood with her arms
crossed.

"Don't crowd me," Brad muttered. Brad scanned the
computer files looking for the contact information of the
contractor who had built his office. *Damn.* It was frustrating
not finding the information he wanted *and* watching Sharon
take a seat in front of him. He ejected the second disk and
tried a third.

"Your Aunt Harriet is right," Sharon said. "This house
could use a makeover. These chairs look and feel like they
came from a monastery garage sale. And what is it with all
those porcelain vases?"

Brad's anger simmered, but he ignored her. He left the
laptop on, pushed back his chair, and got up to leave.
Sharon caught up with him before he reached the bottom of
the staircase. She turned and practically spat in his face.
"You still keep the Glock in your nightstand?"

Brad nodded, and before he could wonder why she had
asked, Sharon dashed up the stairs. Brad seized the opportunity to return to the quiet refuge of the library, this time

closing the door behind him.

Moments later, Sharon charged through the door with Brad's pistol slung over her shoulder, encased in its black leather holster. Her face flushed as she advanced, trapping Brad against the edge of the desk.

Practically nose-to-nose, she yelled, "Your head hasn't been screwed on straight since you went to that execution. The Brad Frame I signed on to work with is gone. I don't know where he went." She turned to leave, but then she swiveled around at him again. "You shouldn't be near a gun today. You might hurt yourself." She patted the pistol. "I'm hanging on to this for safe keeping."

Sharon, who seemed to be choking back a sob, ran out of the library.

"Go to hell," Brad muttered under his breath as the door slammed behind her.

An hour later Brad was still in the library, staring into space but not focusing on anything in particular. He thought he heard three taps from the doorknocker on his front door, but chose to ignore them.

The pounding on the door continued. Probably a high school kid trying to sell subscriptions, he thought. After a few minutes of silence, Brad figured whoever rapped on his front door had gone their way.

A couple of thuds echoed through the foyer, like the sound of a boot against the kick plate of his front door. He vacillated between ignoring the noise and upbraiding the offender. But as the blows to his door persisted Brad rose from his chair, left the library and marched to the front door. He threw it open, prepared to give holy hell to an overly eager magazine salesman.

Brad first saw Sharon Porter standing on the other side

of the door. For an instant he figured she'd gotten locked out, but then he spotted Nick Argostino. Instead of shouting obscenities at what he thought was a noisy visitor, his mouth hung open.

"Nick . . ." Brad had known Nick for eleven years. As the Philadelphia detective who'd investigated the kidnapping of his mother and sister, Nick guided Brad into the private detective business and served as his mentor.

"Hello Brad. We'd like to talk with you." Nick never showed his badge, but his manner suggested this was more than a social call. With curly dark hair, trimmed close to his scalp, a mustache laced with twisted strands of gray, and a slight paunch over his belt, Nick would look at home behind the meat counter at the Reading Terminal Market.

"I . . . I don't understand. What are you doing here?" Brad flashed a questioning look at Sharon, who stood with her feet planted and a determined expression on her face. He noticed Nick's government-issued sedan in the driveway, as a light breeze carried the sweet fragrance of hyacinth mixed with the pungent aroma of fresh tan bark across the portico.

Brad shouted at Sharon, "You called him, didn't you?"

"Yes. I . . . ah. I . . ."

He glared at her. "Stay out of my personal business."

"Brad," Nick said, with the firm voice of authority, "we need to talk."

Dazed, Brad stood back so they could enter.

"Let's go into the living room," Sharon suggested, pointing toward the archway to the left, and closed the front door behind them.

"Let's not," Brad said, heading for the stairs.

Brad felt Nick's hand pressed against his back. "Give me

a few minutes of your time," Nick said, as he guided him toward an armchair in the corner of the room. Nick and Sharon pulled up straight-back Chippendale side chairs forming a close triangle with him. He felt cornered, and couldn't face them, preferring to stare at the floor.

"Sharon came to see me yesterday," Nick began.

Ha! So that's why she skipped out in a hurry.

"She told me about your meeting with Mr. Allessi and the unexplained message in Wilkie's Bible. Of course, I'd already seen Paula Thompson's articles in the *Inquirer*—"

Brad grunted. "God damn her!"

"Yes, Sharon told me you've been angry lately and moody," Nick said in even and deliberate tones. "She's worried about you."

Brad, who had kept his gaze riveted at the floor, glanced up at Sharon. She sat wringing her hands, anxiety etched on her face.

"And today Sharon told me about the fire in your office and the missing Bible." Nick continued, "You're a strong man, Brad. You've had a lot to cope with in your life, but every one of us has a breaking point—physically and emotionally."

"I don't know . . ." Brad murmured, then got caught up in another swirl of his own thoughts. He'd experienced an encounter like this once before, more than a decade before, when he joined a support group after the murder of his mother and sister. He didn't think he needed another twelve-step program.

"Sharon is worried—justifiably so, based on what I've seen—that you've reached the breaking point. And we'd like to bring you back before you hurt yourself or jeopardize your hard-earned reputation."

Westminster chimes tolled the half-hour. As much as he

resented hearing Nick's words, Brad thought the silence worse.

"You're the most even-keeled man I know," Sharon said, in a husky whisper. "But you've had more moods in the last five days than I've seen in three years. Usually you're so focused . . ." Sharon's voice cracked, and she fought back tears. "But when you get like this. . . ."

Brad tried to stop her. "You don't have to. . . ." Brad ached, partly for himself but mostly for Sharon. They shared a common bond of family tragedy. When she was in fifth grade her younger brother died suddenly of a brain aneurysm. Her mother died of pancreatic cancer when Sharon was in high school. And then three years ago, her father, a decorated Philadelphia police officer, had committed suicide. That's when Nick first approached Brad and told him about Sharon. Would Brad take her on as an assistant, Nick had asked. They had talked about her family quite a few times during the past three years, and each time Brad played the role of consoler. How many times had he handed her his handkerchief to dry her eyes?

"We love you, Brad." Sharon said through her tears. "And we want to see you get past this."

"But I don't need . . ." Brad started the sentence without knowing where it ended. *What didn't he need? People who cared for him? Of course, he did. What couldn't he express?* Brad raised both hands to the top of his head.

"We're here today to offer our support," Nick said. "Whatever you need, we want to help."

Sharon added, "You don't have to bear the burden alone. That's why we're here. That's why I got Nick involved."

Brad shifted uneasily in his seat, and he coughed.

Sharon left the room returning moments later with a

glass of water. She placed it on the table next to Brad. He nodded to her in thanks and took a gulp, hoping it would clear the lump from his throat.

"I'm sorry I encouraged you to go to the execution," Sharon said. "I honestly hoped something good might come of the experience. I never intended to open up old wounds."

The silence grew as they let him mull his thoughts.

Nick leaned forward. "Look, Brad, I know what you're going through. I was there eleven years ago. I had to pull you back from the edge then, too. Remember?"

Brad nodded. He knew exactly what Nick meant—it had been a turning point that could have propelled his life into a completely different orbit.

"In my line of work I deal with tragedy all the time. Two weeks ago I had to pay a visit to the wife of one of my officers and tell her that she was a widow. A scumbag, high on crack, opened fire on her husband with an assault rifle. And you know what he was doing? Sitting in his patrol car eating his lunch. The toughest part of that assignment was seeing her two little boys—maybe three and four years old. They've got their whole lives ahead of them, but that family is gonna face the same kind of choices as you. They can let the bitterness infect them for the rest of their days, or they can move on. Ten years ago *you* were able to get past your hostility, and I'd regret seeing you stung again. You may need professional help to get through this. But we're not going to let you travel this emotional valley by yourself."

Brad buried his head in his hands. Their voices fell silent and Brad could only hear the rhythmic ticking of the grandfather clock in the front hall. He realized he had a choice of confronting his fears or letting them dominate him. Thinking back to the night of the execution, he wondered what it was about the experience that had brought him to this confrontation with mentor and colleague? He had witnessed far worse in his life. Pick it apart, he thought. Images of Wilkie, Paula Thompson, and Ron Allessi formed in his mind.

Emotional release started slowly. Brad looked up, first at Nick, then Sharon. His face flushed, and he gasped for air, his entire body heaving. Tears flowed down his cheeks, and he moaned, wailing, "Oh . . . oh."

Sharon sprang from her chair, but Nick's arm shot out, preventing her from crossing the room. She sat back down.

The quiet Brad had craved an hour earlier—in the sanctuary of the library—now seemed like torment. He knew he had to express his concerns and allay their fears, and he considered what he would say.

The grandfather clock chimed the hour.

Brad reached into his back pocket and retrieved a handkerchief. He blew his nose. He took a deep breath, cleared his throat and spoke. "This past week has dredged up so many bad memories. Dad has taken a turn for the worse, and I don't know how much time he has left. I've struggled with all the garbage that Wilkie's execution stirred up—all the conflicting emotions. But I didn't realize until this afternoon how it affected my work, or how the people I care about see me." He looked at Sharon through moist eyes, and noticed the tears welling in hers. "I'm sorry, Sharon."

"What bothers me most," Brad continued, "are the questions I can't answer: What was Wilkie trying to tell me? How can I stop an ambitious lawyer hell-bent on publishing a book that can only defame my family? And what gives with a reporter whose life now seems devoted to tarnishing mine? I don't know where to start."

"Oh, Brad." Sharon rushed over and threw her arms

around him as he sat in the chair.

Sharon squeezed him hard. "I think you could cut back to two days a week with your fitness trainer," Brad quipped. If anything, Sharon seemed to tighten her grip.

When Sharon finally unclenched, Nick said, "If a client came to you with these same questions, you'd develop a game plan, wouldn't you?"

"Yes," Brad nodded.

"The most important thing is to stay focused," Nick said. "You can't answer all these questions immediately, and you can't do it all yourself. Remember the saying about a lawyer who defends himself has a fool for a client. The same is true for private detectives."

Brad smiled. He felt his equilibrium returning. "When did you make that up?"

"Just now," Nick replied, not missing a beat. "You're too wrapped up in this mystery, and you know it. You can stay involved, but let us help. What's the first thing we need to do?"

Brad glanced at Sharon. "Get the list of Bible verses," she said, "so we can figure out what Wilkie wanted Brad to know."

"Did Dolewski say who asked him not to send you a copy?" Nick inquired.

"No," Brad explained, "he said that he had been requested not to forward the list."

Nick scribbled notes in a small black notebook. "Okay, I have a few connections in the Corrections Department." He winked at Brad. "Let me contact them and see what I can find out."

CHAPTER 12

After midnight Brad retreated to the attic of his Bryn Mawr estate. He stood on an elevated platform in the middle of the room. Several electrical transformers hummed in front of him and he eagerly fingered the controls on two of them. Brad adjusted the engineer's cap on his head, before turning the rheostat to launch a model vintage steam engine along a section of track wending its way through miniature re-creations of the suburban villages on the Main Line. In the farthest corner of the attic stood a reproduction of 30th Street Station before a backdrop skyline of Philadelphia. He heard Sharon's muffled voice calling him from below.

"I'm up here," Brad shouted, his baritone voice echoing down the wooden stairwell.

Brad heard clomping feet, then silence and a long pause before a white handkerchief tied to a long-handled barbecue fork was thrust into the room. Brad laughed.

"Truce?" Sharon asked sheepishly, lowering her flag and peeking over the top of the wooden planks that formed the platform.

"Sure," Brad said. "C'mon in."

"I figured I better find out if you were still speaking with me. You know, after this afternoon," Sharon said.

"I needed a good kick in the ass." Brad dimmed the overhead lights, and with the push of another button transformed the scene from dusk into nightfall, as thousands of tiny lights illuminated the display.

"You wanna beer?" Brad offered.

Sharon nodded.

"Help yourself. There's a mini-fridge under the platform." Brad pointed. "I don't have any glasses though."

"That's okay. I've survived a few frat parties without a glass." Sharon laughed as she grabbed a can of Michelob from the refrigerator and popped the metal tab.

"I tried to call you earlier this evening," Brad said, as he maneuvered the steam engine onto an abandoned siding. On a different circuit he connected a two-engine tandem to a string of freight cars for a trip into the hills of his layout.

"Mark and I went out to dinner and a movie, and didn't get back until late. When I walked Mark to his car I saw the lights on in the dormers and figured you were playing." Sharon took a swig of her beer and stood at the edge of the train platform. "You've added quite a few new displays. I don't remember the cable car."

"I keep tinkering. Check this out." Brad flipped a switch that animated a circus display set in a field of fall foliage.

"Cool." Sharon sipped her beer. "You said you tried to call me. What did you want?"

"I wanted to thank you for contacting Nick, even if I did seem pissed off when I saw the two of you standing at the front door."

"That's my job," Sharon said, beaming and giving him thumbs up.

Brad eased onto a stool in front of the control panel.

"What is it about guys and trains?" Sharon asked, as she circled the layout. "I remember my older brother had a Lionel train, 027 gauge I think, when he was in high school. It wasn't much, only an engine, two cars and caboose, but he was so proud—you would have thought he owned Amtrak."

If he's a taxpayer, he *does,* Brad realized.

"I don't usually tell people about my hobby," Brad said.

"Why not?"

"I guess playing with miniature trains . . ." Brad paused and laughed.

"What's so funny?" Sharon asked.

"I was going to say that playing with trains doesn't mesh with the macho image of a detective, but I wouldn't describe my blubbering performance with you and Nick this afternoon as macho either."

Sharon dismissed his explanation with a wave of her hand. "I worked for you a year before you showed them to me."

"I've been puttering with trains—off and on—for thirty years. I was ten when my parents gave us—my brother and me—the train set. I'll never forget it. For six weeks before the holidays that year, workmen were here in the attic hammering and sawing. My brother and I had strict orders not to come up. We had no idea. On Christmas morning, after we opened our stockings, my parents made us close our eyes as they led us up the stairs. When we opened our eyes, Andy and I were in shock. We spent time every day that winter playing with the trains, and my dad used to come up and help. My brother lost interest in the trains as the warm weather returned and he could play outside, but I managed a few minutes of railroading every day.

"In my college years, I appreciated the trains more and more. It's like your parents, sometimes you don't realize how important they are until they're not around," Brad added ruefully.

"Yeah, I know what you mean." Sharon sipped her beer.

"It was also popular with my fraternity brothers. Every weekend I came home from Princeton, I could always count on a buddy who wanted to come with me to work on the train. I've added to the layout, over the years, which is now three times larger than what my parents gave us." Pointing at the bank of transformers and switches, Brad asked, "Wanna try your hand at the controls?"

"Really?" Sharon asked, stepping up onto the control platform that overlooked Brad's miniature railroad. He pulled a second stool up to the control panel, inviting her to sit.

"Here, try these." Brad pointed to two transformers. The first one controlled an Amtrak replica traversing the Main Line from 30th Street Station, while the second shuttled freight alongside a loading dock.

Sharon took the controls, preferring the Amtrak model. "What are you building over there?" she asked, pointing to a torn-up area of the display.

"I'm gonna add a monorail on the old Chestnut Hill line."

Brad noticed that Sharon took to the controls of model railroading in one easy lesson.

Turning toward him, Sharon said, "I'm sorry to hear your dad has taken a turn for the worse."

Brad pursed his lips, acknowledging her concern, then retrieved a beer from the mini-refrigerator. Holding a can aloft he asked, "Another?"

Sharon shook her head. "Your dad started the family's business, right?"

"Yes, in the 60's. He landed a few defense-related contracts. They even did work for foreign governments, under the watchful eye of the Feds. It was his company's expertise with computer technology that made it a multi-billion dollar industry. In more recent years the firm has diversified into satellite and Internet communications systems." Brad returned to his stool on the control platform.

"What was it like growing up rich?" Sharon looked embarrassed the instant the question passed her lips.

Brad laughed. "I never realized we were rich when I was a kid. We traveled and I saw how other people lived, so I knew we were better off than most. But we never lived an extravagant lifestyle. Even my mother's family, which came from a long line of inherited wealth, always seemed down to earth to me. I went to private schools in the area, and most of my schoolmates came from similar backgrounds. But one thing I'd never confronted as a kid was fear. I led a sheltered life, and wasn't prepared to deal with the seamy side of society when Mom and Lucy were kidnapped."

"Nick told me a little bit, before I came to work for you, but you've never shared the details before," Sharon said. "Wanna talk about it?"

It struck him as odd that she'd never heard the details. For several years afterward, it seemed like he shared the details of the crime with anyone who would listen—relatives, college buddies, support groups, acquaintances, and girlfriends. Even total strangers he encountered at an airport check-in or a super market checkout line had heard the story. He knew they couldn't care less, but he found healing in replaying every grim nuance. The details lived in his mind, like a mutating virus he couldn't kill.

Brad adjusted the rheostat to restore the daytime lighting conditions on the train display.

"It was eleven years ago March 12th," he began. "Andrew tracked me down in Miami Beach and told me that Mom and Lucy had been kidnapped. I made it to the Miami airport in thirty minutes, raced to the first ticket counter I spotted, and got a first-class seat on a direct flight to Philadelphia, arriving home four hours after Andrew's call. My dad had just received a phone call, informing him that Mom and Lucy were safe and that he was to wait for further instructions."

Brad walked around the platform as he talked, and repositioned a boxcar that had jumped the track.

"Andy and I suspected a crank call. Dad must have too, or I don't think he would have waited so long to contact the police. That was life before cell phones, and we were convinced Mom and Lucy might return any minute from shopping. But of course they didn't." Brad took a gulp of his beer.

"The second call came at ten-thirty that night, demanding a million dollars in unmarked, non-sequential bills, none larger than $100. The kidnapper said he would call the next day with directions on where to drop the money. After the ransom demand, Dad contacted the FBI. They told him to sit tight."

"Did your dad recognize the kidnapper's voice?" Sharon asked.

Brad shook his head. "No one did. Either Andy or I listened on the other line whenever a call came through, but the voice was slow and gravely; clearly disguised." Brad sat on the platform stool facing Sharon. "It was four days before Dad heard from the kidnappers again. God, those were an excruciating four days. We couldn't sleep. We worked out a schedule so one of us would be near the phone at all times, but mostly all three of us stood around waiting for it to ring."

"Didn't the FBI tap your phone line?"

"They did. Not only the lines here but at Dad's office. The kidnappers must have anticipated that. One of the secretaries at his office found an envelope marked CONFIDENTIAL for my dad. The note instructed him to go to a pay phone at five o'clock and to call a specific number. Dad never told the FBI about the note. He called—as ordered—and told the kidnapper he couldn't come up with one million, but could pay a ransom of $500,000 dollars. They told him to wait, and he would hear from them.

"We waited an agonizing two days before we heard anything. Another note showed up at Dad's office, providing instructions on where to deliver the money. Andy took the money to the drop spot, where he found another note telling him where we could find my mother and sister. The kidnappers sent him on a wild goose chase to a school parking lot in Lancaster County."

Brad's voice cracked for an instant, and he swigged his beer before resuming his story. "Less than an hour later the police found their bodies in Fairmount Park. They were under a canvas in a rowboat tied up in the Schuylkill River. Mom's throat had been cut. Lucy's neck had been broken, and . . ."

Brad realized anew how long it had been since he had told the story. Years earlier, in forced repetition, he'd managed to recount the gruesome details without flinching. "Lucy had been raped. The police said there were cigarette burns on their bodies, indicative of torture. When the trial came, we learned that Baker had a record of sadistic behavior. As a juvenile—at the age of eleven—he was arrested for torturing animals in his neighborhood." He drew in a breath, pausing to compose himself. "I was thirty-two when all that happened. It was hard for me to imagine that anyone could inflict that kind of pain on another human being. The coroner said they'd been dead for at least three days."

Brad paused, aware of the hum of several trains making their way around the track. He turned off the transformers. "Only about half the details ever made the papers. Speculation kept the story alive for months."

"I remember first hearing about the case when I was in college," Sharon said.

"Dad was never the same. He managed to cope through the funeral, but a big part of him died when they did. Six months later he had a stroke, which left the lower half of his body paralyzed. Dad will be seventy-eight in September."

"This afternoon, what did Nick mean when he said he had to pull you back from the edge once?" Sharon asked.

"It's another long story, if you're game?" Brad asked.

Sharon nodded.

Brad turned off the transformers, and display lighting on his miniature railroad. "I'm hungry. Let's go make a sandwich."

Sharon led the way to the kitchen of Brad's estate, and then slid into a seat at the breakfast nook.

"Want to split a ham and cheese?" Brad asked.

Sharon nodded.

"In the first few weeks after their deaths the police department had three detectives assigned to the case," Brad explained, as he laid a couple slices of wheat bread on a plate. "After a while Nick Argostino was the only one. I was determined to help find their killers, and even took some criminology courses that summer." Brad found packages of deli ham and Swiss cheese in the refrigerator, and heaped the ham onto the bread. "But it took several months before I gained Nick's confidence and he started sharing information with me. The clues the police developed, including tracing the location for the phone booth numbers Dad called, pointed to a West Philadelphia neighborhood as the most likely location of the killers."

Brad felt his jaw tighten.

"You don't have to go into all of this," Sharon said.

"It's okay. I convinced Nick that we should collaborate,

with his experience and detective talent, alongside my money. I started working West Philadelphia and offered money—big money—for details on the killer's identities. Nick gave me tips on persons that I should contact."

Brad remembered that Sharon liked spicy mustard, and found a container of it in the refrigerator. He cut the sandwich in half, applied mustard to Sharon's half and mayonnaise to his own. "I've learned there is no honor among criminals that can't be breached with a few crisp hundred dollar bills. On October 26th a paid informant told me that the killers were holed up in an abandoned house down on Carson Street." Brad handed Sharon her sandwich and sat opposite her. "I called Nick to tell him where they were, and said I'd meet him there. I drove like a wild man.

"I slid the car into the curb about a block ahead of the address, and walked toward their hideout. Right in front of the house, I spotted Frank Wilkie exiting, carrying a garbage bag. We even passed on the sidewalk before he ducked between the buildings to deposit the trash out back; he never recognized me." Brad took the first bite of his sandwich. "I surprised myself how cool I acted passing within a few inches of the man who had murdered half my family. I followed him to the backyard from the other side of the duplex, peered around the corner and watched as he dropped the plastic bag in the garbage can. I pulled my gun out of the holster, released the safety, and slipped my index finger around the trigger. At that moment I had only one thought on my mind: Revenge. The son-of-a-bitch didn't even know I was there."

Brad stared toward the bay window of the breakfast nook, noticing a tree in the corner of his lot bathed in a landscape spotlight. His hand gripped the imaginary weapon while the muscles tightened on his arm and his neck. He extended his arm, as if taking aim. Brad's eyes refocused and he saw his own dim reflection in the glass of the bay window. He lowered his arm.

"I heard a voice whisper, 'Don't do it.' It was Nick. He was right behind me and I never even heard him. Next thing I know Nick shouted at Wilkie, 'You're under arrest.' Nick stepped out from the protection of the house; his service weapon raised, he confronted the killer. Wilkie lifted his hands over his head. I still had a clear shot at him as I crouched at the edge of the house, but an instant later I relaxed my trigger finger. At the same time other officers went through the front door and captured Eddie Baker."

"I don't know how I would have reacted," Sharon said.

"I know you. You'd have done the right thing," Brad said. "The other night at the execution, when I saw Wilkie laying on the gurney, I didn't feel anything for him. The venom was gone. If there was a silver lining in attending Wilkie's execution, it was that realization. Can you understand?"

"Yeah," Sharon said, bobbing her head. "What did Nick say to you after they were arrested?"

"He never mentioned it again. Nick's a good cop. I owe him my life, certainly my career. I've often thought about what would have happened if I had fired that weapon. I surely would have gone to jail for shooting an unarmed man. Pulling the trigger would have put an end to my plans to serve justice. Nick said I had a detective's blood in my veins. I already had earned my undergraduate degree from Princeton, but Nick urged me to go to Penn and pick up a degree in Criminal Justice. Nick said that after I got training, and set up a corporation, he would serve as the licensed private detective for the agency. Later, the County Sheriff took me on as a deputy and after a couple of years I qualified to get my own license. Then I hired you so I barely have to work anymore."

Sharon blushed. "I know your brother is in Houston. How has *he* coped with your family's tragedy?"

"Andy is a workaholic. He took charge of the family business. I guess you could say his first marriage was a victim of the trauma we went through. His oldest son is in the custody of his first wife. He's had two more children with his second wife. Since most of the government contracts now involve the space industry, he moved the corporate headquarters to Clear Lake City, near the Johnson Space Center."

"You ever think of settling down and raising a family?" she asked.

"Now you sound like my mother." Brad laughed. "When I turned thirty Mom pressured me to settle down. I'd been dating Christine for about a year before the kidnapping. We got engaged on Valentine's Day and the wedding was planned for the following Christmas. She was a Main Line socialite—which meant she had good breeding. After everything that happened I guess I became more self-absorbed than she was. After the murders, all of the happiness drained out of my life. She and I . . . Well, our relationship didn't survive either. Call it another casualty of our family's tragedy."

"Must be tough putting those experiences behind you?" Sharon said.

"As our meeting this afternoon demonstrated, I haven't been doing a very good job of that lately. I try to replace the bad memories with good ones."

"Ah, I see. The trains."

Brad smiled. "Yes, I have a lot of great memories."

Sharon covered her mouth, and seemed to stifle a yawn.

"I think I better get some sleep. It's almost two o'clock, and I promised Mark I'd join him for early Mass and then meet his folks for brunch."

"Sharon," Brad wore a grave expression, "I hate to break the bad news, but it's almost three. This is the night we *spring ahead* to Daylight Savings Time. We lose an hour."

"Ahhggghh!" Sharon groaned. "On second thought, maybe I'll skip Mass."

CHAPTER 13

"Nick called. He's on his way." Brad heard Sharon yell as she ran across the patio to where he sat. He winced as she nearly crashed into workmen carrying a stack of eight-foot-long two-by-fours through the open French doors, but she sidestepped them at the last minute. "He has news."

"Great," Brad said, leisurely turning pages of the morning's *Inquirer*.

"You disappeared early this morning," Sharon said, as she seized the sports section from the bottom of the newspaper pile. "I looked out my window at 6:45 a.m. and your car was gone."

Brad only grunted.

With a deep sigh, Sharon slipped into a chair next to him, an idiosyncrasy that usually meant she had news to impart but was holding back for just the right moment. Brad poured her a glass of orange juice.

"Thanks." Sharon fidgeted with the topaz birthstone ring on her right hand, but any significance of that was lost on Brad. He was too busy enjoying a front row seat on the season of renewal. Sun-warmed buds on the trees opened to a tender shade of green and crocuses poked their way out of the damp soil. The grass, still moist from the morning dew, needed its second cut of the week. On the opposite side of the patio a three-man crew was restoring his office. In less than a week they had removed damaged furniture and stripped drywall and floorboards from fire-affected areas. That morning the crew replaced wall studs, applied new drywall, and by week's end the office would be ready for paint and carpet.

Renewal had penetrated Brad's psyche, too. He had taken steps to unravel the conundrum he faced since Wilkie's execution, and felt his emotional equilibrium return. It helped that the *Inquirer* hadn't published anything about him in over a week. Mention of the fire had been relegated to a one-paragraph blurb on page 18 of the local section, reporting fire trucks responding to a blaze at his address, but omitting his name.

Sharon glanced in Brad's direction as she brought the juice glass to her lips, but when their eyes made contact, she quickly averted her gaze. How could he cut through her reticence and find out what was on her mind?

"By the way, I got an e-mail from the mother of that missing kid," Brad said. "She is extremely grateful to us for finding him and persuading him to return home. I told her that I would pass her praise along to you, since you handled the case."

"Thanks," Sharon said, "but it wasn't hard to convince David to return home, especially with his mother's offer to buy his airline ticket. He'd run out of money and spent two nights sleeping on the streets of a strange city—not to mention the embarrassment he suffered. *LitleBitsch*—the love of his Internet life—turned out to be a sixteen-year-old guy pretending to be a seventeen-year-old girl offering to make every one of his raging hormonal dreams come true. I located *LitleBitsch* online, and pretended to be a teenage guy. *She,*" Sharon made quote signs with her fingers, "quickly invited me into a private chat room. It didn't take me long to figure out I was chatting with a guy."

"Dare I ask," Brad said, "what gave the guy away?"

Sharon blushed. "Well, I know women can be graphic, but in short order he used just about every slang word to

118

describe a penis that I've ever heard."

Brad nodded, declining to ask for more specifics.

"After I led him on for ten minutes—all the while he thought he was leading me on—I revealed I was an agent with the State's Attorney General's office and fully prepared to file charges if he didn't cooperate. I said my partner had traced his IP address and we would dispatch an agent to his home in less than five minutes, unless we got his help with a case. He couldn't type cooperation fast enough." Sharon pantomimed her hands typing on a keyboard, and Brad laughed. "I gave him David's screen name and said *he* was the person we were looking for. *LitleBitsch* spilled the whole scam, explaining how he got his kicks from stringing guys along, promising to satisfy their fantasies, and inviting them to Denver. David took the bait. He ran away from home and hopped the first bus for the mile-high city. Their plan called for him to show up at an apartment building at 8 o'clock on Tuesday night, at which time *LitleBitsch* would call his cell phone and tell him what apartment *she* lived in and David could 'come on up'." Sharon struck a pose: back arched, one hand on her hip, and the other behind her head.

"Wait a minute," Brad said, "when we met with David's mother she said he didn't have a cell phone."

"Well, he didn't have one, but there are few obstacles that a horny teen will let stand in the way of sexual fulfillment. He borrowed one from a friend. Talking on the phone with his victims—listening to their voices as they realized they'd been snookered—was how *LitleBitsch* got his kicks. So he wouldn't arrange to meet anyone unless he could call him on his cell phone. Once *LitleBitsch* gave me the cell phone number David was using, I contacted him and arranged for his trip home."

Brad sat shaking his head. "The government should round up a few guys like *LitleBitsch* and channel their creativity toward doublecrossing Al Qaeda. Good work, Sharon! What would I do without you?"

Sharon's face flushed, simultaneous with a pained expression crossing her face. "There's no easy way to say this. I have a job offer," she said meekly.

Brad had anticipated a news bulletin from Sharon, but this one surprised him. He stared at her hoping for details.

"Nick made the offer," Sharon said, in an apologetic tone. "He called me on Monday asking if I'd be interested in a job on the Philadelphia police force. He said they were desperate for qualified women in the department."

"An entry level position?" Brad asked. Now he knew why Nick was on his way. He wanted to tell Brad about the job offer in person. Sharon was a great asset to his business, and he'd hate to lose her, but he had known before he hired her that being a cop was her career goal.

"Yes, I'd be starting as a rookie," Sharon said, adding, "Nick said that with my experience I could move up fairly quickly."

"Sounds like a good opportunity," Brad said, unconvincingly.

"Brad, I think it's in my blood. As you know, my dad was a Philadelphia cop. I've always wanted to follow in his footsteps. As long as I can remember, there was something about a uniform and badge that made my heart skip a beat. I think that's why I married Ken. He was a cop, too. Later, I discovered I was more attracted to the badge than to Ken. After the divorce I moved back with dad until his . . ." the word caught in her throat. ". . . his suicide. It's funny how things work. I hated moving back home, but it drew my dad and me closer. And after he died I was so glad that we'd had that time together for what turned out to be his last few years. And then you gave me the chance to work with you, for which I will always be grateful. When Nick asked me if I'd be interested in a detective position I jumped at the chance. I don't want to turn my back on you—especially with what's been happening lately—but how do I know if an opportunity like this will ever come along again? I'm torn, I really am." Brad could see the conflict in her expression and hear the anguish in her voice. "But I may be jumping the gun," she cautioned, "I've got to be able to meet the physical requirements. The first test is next week."

"You'll pass. I don't have any doubt about it."

Brad's cell phone chirped.

"I'm standing at your front door," Nick Argostino said when Brad picked up, "but no one is answering. I'd hate to have to beat it down."

"We're on the patio, Nick." Brad pocketed his phone, and went to the kitchen to get a mug, returning in time to see Sharon pulling out a chair so Nick could sit.

"What's up?" Brad asked, perching on the edge of his chair, anticipating Nick's apologia for luring Sharon away from his agency.

A self-satisfied look crossed Argostino's face. "I got the list of Scripture references that was in Wilkie's Bible."

"My God! How?"

"Harry Schaeffer, a cop I worked with fifteen years ago, is a shift supervisor at Rockview. I called him and explained the situation and he said he would do some snooping around. He got back to me that everybody in the prison's administration knew about the list, but that it was locked in the Warden's office. He said there was no way he could get in there without raising a lot of suspicion. I told him to forget it." Two birds squawked noisily as they flew from a nearby beech tree, momentarily distracting them. Nick continued, "Then last night he called me back to say he had decided to check Wilkie's file in the main records room. As a supervisor, he has unlimited access to the records area, but he waited until after the secretaries went home, just to be sure. Right on top in Wilkie's file—there's a reason the government does everything in triplicate—was a photocopy of the same list the Warden had. Harry didn't have access codes for the copy machine in the records room, so he hand-copied all the Bible references and faxed it to me this morning. Now all we need are the pages you copied from the Bible and maybe we can figure out the message."

"They're up in my bedroom, I'll go get them." Brad pushed back from the patio table and bounded through the garden toward the kitchen entrance of the mansion. He took the stairs to his bedroom two at a time. Standing in front of the safe, Brad hesitated before his fingers touched the lock. Was he prepared to learn Frank Wilkie's final message to him? Sensing he would soon pass through a gateway from which there was no return, he twirled the lock cylinder in sequence, opened the safe, and retrieved the pages he'd copied from the Bible. Brad rushed back to the patio, stopping by the library to get a tablet and pencil.

Brad handed the tablet to Sharon. "Will you copy down the words as we figure them out?" She nodded. "Okay, Nick, give me the scripture references in the order you've got them and I'll find the corresponding page from Wilkie's Bible."

"The first one is Luke, Chapter 8," Nick said.

Brad sorted through the photocopied pages from Wilkie's Bible several times. Frustrated at not finding it, he said, "I don't have a Luke, Chapter 8."

Nick held his list at arm's length. "A three . . . maybe it's a three instead of an eight."

Brad raised an eyebrow. "Time to visit your eye doctor, Nick." Brad thumbed through the stack again. "Here it is, Luke, Chapter 3." Brad spotted the word scrawled in childlike print between the columns near the bottom of the photocopied page, and announced, "The first word is *'me'*."

The early going was tedious, taking at least five minutes to decipher the first seven words of Wilkie's message.

"All right, what's the eighth verse?" Brad tried not to show his impatience.

"Ezra, Chapter 4," Nick said.

"Where's Ezra in the Bible?" Sharon wondered. "I don't remember that one."

Brad ignored Sharon's question. "Found it. The word is *'kill.'* What's next?"

"Joel, Chapter 2."

As they reached the halfway point, Brad lined up the remaining active pages in front of him like a practiced bingo player, and turned the used ones face down on the table. He found that his eyes could scan all of them in a matter of seconds and lose less time than leafing through the pile. After the seventeenth word—*'i'*—was revealed, Brad turned to Nick. "Is the last scripture reference in Exodus?"

Nick nodded.

"*Sorry* is the final word." And in Exodus, Brad thought. If Wilkie had been a genius, he might have intentionally selected Exodus—symbolizing a journey to a new place—for his final word. Instead, Brad surmised, its location was pure happenstance.

Brad slid the tablet with the completed sequence of words between Sharon and Nick, then stood between them as they studied the words.

me and eddie not big guy paid money kill eddie
talked he get killed find real killer i sorry

"It sure doesn't make much sense without punctuation," Sharon commented.

Nick exhaled. "Unfortunately, that's the best you get with a third grade education."

"We can figure it out." Brad put both elbows on the table as he studied the words. Assuming they were now in the correct order, he began dividing them into phrases. Wilkie's spare syntax made the task difficult.

me and eddie not big
guy paid money kill

Brad glanced at Nick for a nod or other affirmation on the logic of arrangement.

Nick rubbed his chin and sighed. "Too bad this isn't in English. Try moving the word 'guy' to the end of the first line."

Brad rearranged the lines as Nick suggested, then copied the remaining phrases.

me and eddie not big guy
paid money kill
eddie talked he get killed
find real killer
i sorry

"Maybe the word 'eddie' belongs at the end of the second line," Nick wondered aloud. "I always suspected Eddie Baker was killed and didn't commit suicide. But I never thought Wilkie did it."

Brad shook his head. "No. He couldn't have. They weren't housed in the same prison. Wilkie did his time at Pittsburgh. Baker was at Graterford when he died. But this message clearly says Eddie was killed because he talked."

"If Wilkie was in Pittsburgh, how did he learn that Eddie was killed?" Sharon asked.

"The prison system has faster networking than AT&T Broadband," Nick said.

"This is a death bed confession," Sharon said. "The second line means he and Eddie Baker were paid to kill your mother and sister. He's telling you to find the real killer!"

Brad agreed. Why couldn't Wilkie have just given him the name of the "real killer"? Why had he resorted to such a roundabout means of telling him? Couldn't he have blurted out the news on the death gurney? It troubled Brad that a case he thought was closed a week earlier was wide open again, and with more sinister implications.

Nick glanced at his watch. "Sorry, guys, I've got a meeting at headquarters at one o'clock. Let me know how you want to handle this, Brad, and how I can help."

Brad stood up, put one hand on Nick's shoulder and offered a handshake with the other. "Why don't you find out more about the death of Eddie Baker. You've got connections at Graterford, don't you?"

Nick frowned. "Yeah. Most of 'em are guys I sent there to do heavy time. Maybe one of my buddies in the department has a contact. Let me see what I can do."

Sharon volunteered to escort Nick to his car, which reminded Brad that Nick had never said anything about his job offer to Sharon. He'd forgotten about it in his eagerness to learn more about Wilkie's message.

Brad shouted after him, "Tell Ruth I said 'Hi'."

Brad resumed his seat and studied Wilkie's cryptic message. His eyes were riveted on the page, and his lips occasionally mouthed the phrases. When Sharon returned to the poolside patio table, Brad stood and gathered all of the papers in his hands. "Well, Sharon, it looks like we've got to find a killer." Brad added, "I'll need your help."

Sharon hesitated before asking, "Don't you think you ought to let the police handle this one?"

"Like I said, I'll need *your* help."

Sharon looked at him with a sardonic grin. "It'll take a few years before they make me chief of detectives."

"We can count on Nick, I'm sure. But the police aren't going to invest the resources necessary to delve into an eleven-year-old case that's already marked *closed* on their books. Wilkie's message raises more questions than it answers. When I attended Wilkie's execution I didn't expect to find closure, but I'm sure as hell going to get to the meaning of this," Brad said, waving the tablet with Wilkie's message in his hand. "I need time to think. Let's get together first thing tomorrow morning and develop a game plan."

"Sounds good," Sharon said. "Hey, you never told me where you snuck off to this morning?"

Brad shrugged. "I had a date."

Sharon fired questions in rapid succession. "Who with? Do we know her? A breakfast date?"

"Well, appointment would be a better word," Brad explained. "She works evenings most of the time, so breakfast seemed like a good time for us to get together."

Sharon stared at him expectantly. "Aren't you going to tell me who it is?"

Brad leaned back in his seat, and laced his hands behind his head. "I had breakfast with Paula Thompson of *The Philadelphia Inquirer*."

Sharon's jaw dropped.

CHAPTER 14

Brad managed only four hours sleep before he woke pondering Wilkie's message. At four-thirty a.m. he shaved, showered and dressed before heading to the library. The mansion's sole inhabitant, he descended the curved stairs illuminated only by light spilling into the foyer from the flickering gas lamps that lined his driveway. Sharon's room, on the second floor of the garage, had a clear view of the Palladian window above the mansion's entrance, and Brad knew that if she awakened to the sight of the crystal chandelier blazing inside the two-story foyer, Sharon would investigate. He didn't want company; besides he would soon have to learn to manage his business without her.

Sitting at his desk, Brad fired up the laptop, as he pulled the tablet in front of him, mulling Wilkie's message. He typed Wilkie's crudely written phrases into his computer, using a 36-point font, then hit Ctrl + P on the keyboard to print a copy. Brad studied the page, as if visualizing the words larger would clarify their meaning; or even better, suggest what he should do. *Paid money kill:* Brad's eyes focused on those words.

Events from the kidnapping—still vivid after more than a decade—surged in his brain, from the alarming phone call he got from his brother to casting roses on the graves of his mother and sister after their funeral. They had been targeted for the ransom money, because of the family's wealth, or so he thought. *Paid money kill.* Brad struggled to accept this new information that Wilkie and Baker had been paid to kidnap his mother and sister.

First light streamed through the shutters of the library, casting faint shadows on the Oriental rug, where Brad paced a well-worn path reflecting on Wilkie's note and its meaning. *Find real killer.* What did the real killer want? Why had he selected Brad's mother and sister as the target? It could be for reasons other than money, and Brad wondered if he would ever know the answer. He thought about Nick's advice, to break down the case into manageable chunks. Brad knew he had to depend on others, and he needed evidence. When the crime-lab report was completed the police would know what accelerant fueled the fire in his office; it could help nail an arsonist, and Brad had strong suspicions as to who was responsible. Nick promised to ask questions about Eddie Baker's death, because if Baker was killed in prison, maybe they could find a link that knew Baker's secret. *Find real killer.*

Brad leaned back in his chair and rubbed his eyelids. When he opened them, he found himself staring at the family portrait above the library's mantel. He was barely a teen when an unknown artist—whose name his father could not remember and whose scrawled signature provided no help—painted the portrait. The artist had managed to capture Andy's boredom, and Lucy's angelic countenance, while Brad's face evoked his wonder at the portraiture process. His mother looked serene, an incredible talent he realized for a woman with three children between the ages of 9 and 18, and his father stood proudly towering over all of them, the family's bedrock.

My dad—Brad reeled from a gut wrenching thought. Whoever was responsible for ordering the kidnapping and murder of his mother and sister had his dad as their ultimate target. After all, it was *his* wife and daughter, *his* wealth, and *his* business.

Brad looked at his watch—7:10 a.m.—deciding if it was too early to call Gertie Lindstrom. If anyone had insight into his dad's business from eleven years ago it would be her. He knew her phone number was on a Rolodex card that he'd kept in his office desk, but everything in the fire-damaged office had been discarded or moved. Brad called 411, asked for her number, and paid the extra money for the phone company to automatically dial it. He held his breath. She answered on the first ring.

"Good morning, Gertie, this is Brad Frame. I'm sorry to call you so early—"

"I've been awake since five," she said, sounding chipper. "You caught me before my morning swim."

"I'd like to come over to talk with you," he said.

Gertie agreed. She seemed eager for his visit, and Brad suspected she hadn't had many visitors since her surgery. Almost out the door, Brad remembered his nine o'clock meeting with Sharon. He penned a note for her and Scotch-taped it to the library door.

Sharon,

I've got an early meeting with Gertie Lindstrom. Didn't want to disturb you. Working on ideas. Call the Philadelphia Clerk of Court's office and request a transcript from Wilkie and Baker's trial. See if you can put a rush on it. I should be back before noon.

Brad

The Lindstroms lived about three hundred yards beyond the manicured foliage and thick woods that lined Brad's patio. But it was a chilly April morning and he preferred to drive, which turned a three-minute jog into a quarter-hour journey. The heated leather seats of his Mercedes felt good, as Brad turned west onto Route 30 and jostled with morning rush hour traffic. Fortunately, he was headed away from the city, which meant that the traffic moved, as opposed to the two crawling inbound lanes. Two traffic lights later he turned left into the quaintly dubbed Cider Mill Farms. Driving past contemporary estates on a nineteenth-century-style stone driveway, Brad recalled that Gertie's father had once owned nearly five hundred acres of this land, but that except for her family's old homestead, it had all been subdivided or sold to developers. As the Lindstrom's two-hundred-year-old farmhouse came into view at the end of the drive, Brad realized that it had been several years since his last visit.

The rough-cut sandstone house was smaller than Brad's mansion, but still an impressive structure, with thick walls and recessed windows topped with granite lintels. At the front porch a makeshift wooden ramp covered the steps, and at the foot of the ramp sat a white van with license plates designating its use by a person with a disability. Accustomed to the manicured lawn and shrubs of his estate, the Lindstroms' yard looked shabby by comparison, and in need of a "curb appeal" makeover.

Brad parked his Mercedes behind the garage where Emerson Lindstrom was working on his antique car. The two-tone green sedan appeared to swallow him, as Em leaned over the engine fiddling with the carburetor. His white hair stood out in stark contrast to the dark underside of the hood. Grimy jeans, pulled high, accented his paunch, and his T-shirt, yellowed at the armpits, was smeared with automotive grease. The sun spilled into the open garage and gleamed off the polished chrome surfaces.

"Good morning, Em," Brad announced.

Lindstrom jerked upward, banging his head. "I never

heard you coming." Em rubbed the back of his scalp and took a deep breath. "Whew," he whistled, and managed a weak smile. "You gave me a start."

"Cool car," Brad said. "I'm guessing 1953."

"1952 Hudson Hornet," Em said proudly, hiking his pants further over his gut.

"How long have you had it?" Brad asked.

"Too long." Em made a crude laugh by inhaling a gulp of air. "She'll get on the road one of these days. I bought it ten years ago. Been fixin' it ever since."

"You'll probably get run off the road in that car," Brad commented as he thought about the morning rush hour traffic.

"Not this baby," Em said, confidently. "She's got a first-rate six cylinder engine. She can still challenge most of what's sold today. This model won a lot of stock car races in her day."

Brad ventured closer to the car and noticed Em rolling nuts and bolts, reminiscent of Captain Queeg's marbles, inside an oil soaked rag in his hand. Em laid the clean items in a cardboard tray perched on the car's fender.

"Don't get too close." Em barked. "Sorry, but I just polished those fenders. I don't need fingerprints all over them."

"I understand," Brad said, as he aimed toward the front entrance. "I'm here to see Gertie. She's expecting me."

"Not that way. Gertie's in by the pool." Lindstrom pointed to the back of the garage. "You can go through the breezeway," he said, wagging his finger. "Gertie'll be happy to see you." Em gave a mean-spirited cackle. "She's got nothin' better to do."

Brad frowned and Em averted his gaze.

Brad gave the car a wide berth as he walked alongside it

admiring the workmanship, especially the cream-colored leather seats that looked original. Em shouted to Brad. "Watch out for that extension cord. It's still a little chilly, but she insisted on opening the pool. Gertie never seems to get warm enough, so I got a heater fixed up for her."

Brad stepped over the yellow heavy-duty extension cord and followed it as it snaked its way out of the garage, past the breezeway and through the door to the enclosed pool, with excess cable coiled behind an electric space heater. Brad felt like he'd entered a tropical chlorine rain forest. Moisture condensed inside the glass walls surrounding the pool, and beads of perspiration gathered on his face. He quickly shed his fleece-lined coat.

Gertrude Lindstrom sat in her motorized wheelchair at the opposite end of the pool near double-doors that led into their home. A big smile crossed her face when she spotted Brad. She grabbed the joystick, swiveled the chair in his direction and propelled it along the tile surrounding the pool until the chair glided to a halt in front of Brad. She extended her left hand giving Brad's right hand a firm grip. Brad bent down and gave her a peck on the cheek.

"It's good to see you, Brad."

"I ran into Em on the way in."

"He's out there working on that old car, isn't he?"

Brad nodded.

"One of these days I'm gonna bury him in that car. I swear I will."

Brad smiled back at her. Thinking about his own model railroad, he couldn't begrudge a man's hobby.

Gertie wore a floral print bathing suit. She had draped a shawl over her shoulders, and covered her legs with a light blanket.

"You look a lot better than you did the night of the fire,"

132

Gertie said. "Did the police figure out what happened?"

"They suspect arson, but they're waiting for a report from the crime lab." Brad neglected to mention that the police suspected *him* of the arson. Any day now he expected them to return with a search warrant, seeking to find him in possession of the suspect accelerant.

"I would have been happy to come over and see you." Gertie's hand trembled as she gestured. "Em could have driven me. I like to get out once in a while," she said in a firm voice, giving careful attention to each word. Her dark eyes sparkled, but her face appeared waxy.

"I know you would have, Gertie, and I appreciate it. But I'm just as happy to visit you. Besides, I think this is my first opportunity to see your new pool."

"I love this pool. It makes me feel free again. I can almost forget about my paralysis when I float in the water and look up at the sky through the branches of the elm trees. My father planted those trees when I was a little girl, and now look at them." She let out a self-satisfied humph, as she stared up through the glass structure.

Reflections of the trees bounced off the serene surface of the water; their tight buds resisted the sun's prodding to open against the better advice of the spring chill.

Gertie spun her wheelchair ninety-degrees and pointed toward two lounge chairs at pool side. "Have a seat. I've already got mine."

The sun shone directly on her and Gertie squinted, then tried shielding her eyes with her good arm. "I'm gonna switch to the other side of you," she said, maneuvering her motorized chair.

"What can I do for you, Brad?"

"Gertie, I need you to think back to the time when my mother and sister were kidnapped."

Panic grew on her face. "Oh my. What's wrong?"

"Was there anything unusual going on with the business at that time?"

"Unusual?"

"I realize it's an open ended question, but I recently learned information that leads me to believe that my mother's and sister's deaths weren't a random act of violence. I think their kidnapping was an attack on my father."

She gasped. "Joe? How? I don't understand."

"I'm not sure I do myself, Gertie. I think it's possible someone was out to get my father by kidnapping my mother and sister. He was the real target and they were the bait."

"I see." Gertie pursed her lips as she digested Brad's assertion.

"I need you to think back. Were there any unusual contacts with my father in the days before the kidnapping? Anything you can remember? Anything."

Gertie tugged on her lower lip. "Not a thing. Everything was so normal and then the tragedy."

Her words echoed throughout the pool. The glass, hard tile floor, and the fan on the space heater amplified and distorted speech at the same time.

"The company did business with foreign governments. Were there any suspicious contacts related to foreign business?"

"Now that you mention it, I recall difficulties with a Central American country—Guatemala, I think. They wanted to purchase equipment that required a government waiver on technology transfer. The Iran-Contra scandal forced the government to be more thorough, which meant a lot more questions. Oh, and more paperwork. Nothing prevented the sale. Your brother handled most of the international business. You should talk with him."

"I will, Gertie," Brad said, "but I wanted to go straight to the horse's mouth. You knew everything that went on in the office." She blushed. "I don't want to alarm Andy with only wild theories."

She lifted her head up straight. "Andrew's not the kind to get alarmed. You know that. He knows how to take care of things."

Brad understood and nodded. "How about the business itself? Was there anything precarious about its financial position, cash flow, loans due, or creditors calling?"

She used her good arm to pull the shawl away from her shoulders. "Brad, can you help me into the pool? Em's been too busy this morning. We can continue our conversation as I swim."

"Sure, just tell me what I need to do."

At Gertie's instruction, Brad stood in front of her and grasped her arms. She lifted her feet from their mechanical rests and placed them on the floor, then Brad pulled her to an upright position, supporting her weight. At her signal he lowered her to a seated position on the tile edge at the shallow end of the pool, where her legs dangled in the water. With his help, Gertie donned a pair of plastic arm floats. She signaled Brad that he could let her go, and using her good arm and leg propelled herself into water three-feet deep. A few seconds later she floated in a stable position near the side of the pool.

Kneeling at the edge, Brad dipped his fingers into the water, which seemed cool compared to the heavy moist air in the enclosed space. Stripping to his boxers and joining her seemed, momentarily, like a sensible idea, but instead he tugged the lounge chair closer to the edge of the pool and sat down.

"We had excellent credit, and no cash flow problems,"

Gertie continued. "The biggest problem was coming up with $500,000 in cash to meet the ransom demand. They wanted it in non-sequential hundred dollar bills. You can't just walk into the bank and say, 'I'll take half-a-million in hundreds, oh, and make that non-sequential.' If we hadn't had a top credit rating I never could have managed to pull the money together. We'd been accumulating a limited amount of cash in CD's to purchase Diane's father's business, so the assets were there to back up loans for the funds. But I had to call in every chit I could think of just to get the money together for the kidnappers."

"Diane? You mean Andy's first wife?" Brad asked. He hadn't recalled any business deals involving Andy's wife, but it was a long time ago.

Gertie nodded. "Emerson got his bank to order more hundred dollar bills from the Federal Reserve. He told them he had investment customers who would be cashing in securities and wanted their returns in hundred dollar bills. Some of the people we borrowed the money from managed to get hundred dollar bills at their own banks. We were lucky to get the bills, any bills, and had no time to think about their sequence."

The answers to Brad's questions kept traveling to dead ends. "What about labor union troubles?"

Gertie shook her head. "None that I can recall. We had the usual hassles from our weekly meetings with the union stewards, but nothing serious enough to kidnap anyone over."

"You didn't mention the note." Em Lindstrom's voice came from the door near the garage.

Gertie splashed about in the pool as if she'd been caught off balance. Brad couldn't tell how long he'd been standing there or how much he'd heard.

136

"What note?" Brad asked.

"She got a note several days before the kidnapping." Em shouted at his wife, "Tell him!"

Gertie's complexion turned from an oatmeal shade to the whitish-gray color of grits, and her eyes glistened with tears.

"I didn't think it was important," she said, unconvincingly.

Brad got up from the lounge chair and stood staring down at Gertrude Lindstrom. He furrowed his brow and felt saddened that she had held back potentially valuable information.

"Tell me about the note," Brad barked. "Let me decide if it's important."

"There was a note on Joe's—your dad's—desk one morning. It happened at least a week, maybe ten days, before your mother and sister were kidnapped. The words were pasted from letters cut out of a newspaper on a plain sheet of paper. It said, *You can't get away with it.*"

"Dad never mentioned any note."

"He never mentioned it to anybody. I saw the note the morning it turned up on his desk. I always arrived at the office before him. I went in his office to lay a report on his desk and there it was. You know how he used to keep his desk filled with piles of paper?" Brad nodded. "Well, he always tried to clear his leather desk pad by the end of the day. The note was the only thing there. I couldn't help but see it." Brad pictured the desk, the one his dad and Gertie had shared when they first started their business, and now at the furniture refinisher's as he hoped to salvage it from fire damage.

Brad imagined the desk blotter with the kind of note Gertie described and her version of events. "If you left a report for him, he would have known you had seen the note."

Gertie moved toward the side of the pool, bracing herself against the lip with her good arm. "That's why I decided *not* to leave my report. When he came in that day, he never said a word."

"Brad!" A distant voice shouted his name.

Sharon rushed in from the garage past Em Lindstrom and almost tripped over the space heater at the edge of the pool. She wore a pained expression as she approached Brad.

"It's your dad," she began. "The nursing home called. They need you right away."

CHAPTER 15

Brad heard a tap on his bedroom door. "The limousine's here," his brother Andy announced.

"I'll be right down," Brad called out.

Brad looked in the full-length mirror, adjusting the Windsor knot on his maroon tie. Maroon was his dad's favorite color—for ties and sweaters at least—and Brad wore a matching handkerchief in the pocket of his charcoal suit with subtle pinstripes. On top of the dresser stood a photograph from his parents' wedding in a gilded frame. He glanced between the picture and his own image in the mirror, and he could see why so many people commented, during the two days of viewing at the funeral home, that he looked like his dad.

Today he had to say farewell, promising to deliver a eulogy at his dad's service. He didn't know if he could. Brad felt he could keep his emotions in check; realizing that, in small ways, he'd already been saying goodbye for the last ten years. But his strongest memories of his dad were from childhood. Like most sons and fathers, their relationship strained during his late teen and college years. In the decade before the kidnapping he'd been an absent son, playing while others in the family worked, living off his father's generosity and a trust fund his grandmother had left him. A self-indulgent journey, he realized now, in which he'd lost more than he'd found. Unfortunately, the only way he had become reacquainted with his father was in a caldron of sorrow.

Brad pulled 3" x 5" cards, on which he'd scribbled a few

notes, out of his coat pocket.

He heard a hard rap on the door. "You can be late for your own funeral, but not for Dad's."

"I'm coming, Andy."

A few minutes later, Brad descended to the foyer, where he found his Aunt Harriet sitting on the same Empire-style settee where ten days earlier she had waited for a taxi. She looked forlorn in her dark gray suit with black velvet lapels and a lacy veil over her gray hair. "Where's Andy?" Brad asked.

"They're waiting for us in the car." She sighed. "You know how your brother is—always afraid he's going to miss something."

Around them, caterers busily arranged cocktail tables and folding chairs for the reception that would follow services. Brad offered his arm and escorted his aunt to the limo. They climbed into the plush seat, the one facing backward, and sat next to Byron, Brad's teenage nephew from Andy's first marriage. Opposite them sat Andrew, his wife Barbara, and their two children, Chad and Erica. Andy adjusted his tight vest and greeted his brother with an icy stare, which didn't bother Brad since, on this particular morning, he treasured the silence.

The limousine took them to the funeral home for a brief private service, and then they followed the hearse to St. Matthew's Episcopal Church for the public ceremony. Once there the hearse drove to the front of the cathedral, while the limousine deposited family members at the north transept entrance. The Dean, in full ceremonial vestments, greeted them. Walking across the stone floor, past the intricately carved baptismal font, Brad stared up at the rustic ceiling beams. It all seemed so familiar and comforting, even though he hadn't visited St. Matthew's in years. He recognized the Frame Memorial over the north door. His dad had commissioned the stained-glass window to honor his father, a first-generation Scotch immigrant who settled in Philadelphia in 1925. Dominated by blue glass, it offered an impressionistic depiction of Daniel in the lion's den, and below it a passage from Daniel 6:16 carved in stone: *May your God, whom you serve continually, deliver you!* Gazing at the window, Brad thought he knew how Daniel felt.

Approaching his seat, Brad noticed Paula Thompson sitting on the aisle, a few rows back in the rapidly filling church. He acknowledged the reporter's nod with one of his own, and as he sank into the velvet-cushioned pew Brad prayed that his decision to contact her and reveal what he knew about the eighteen words in Wilkie's Bible wouldn't backfire. He promised her updates when he knew more, and would have to make good on that pledge when this day was behind him.

Brad and Aunt Harriet sat directly behind Andy and his family. Brad noticed for the first time that his brother, only five years older, had plenty of scalp shining through at his crown.

He felt a comforting hand on his shoulder and turned around to see Sharon smiling at him from a tear-stained face, clutching a damp handkerchief. Mark Bertolet sat next to her, looking uncomfortable in a black suit that might have dated from his high school graduation.

Mourners sat in silence, skimming the printed funeral program, awaiting the start of the service. The organist, joined by a flute soloist, performed a melancholy prelude by Ravel.

Shortly before 10 o'clock ushers admitted a couple through the south door of the sanctuary. Sharon tapped Brad's arm, but he had already noticed. The woman was statuesque, stunningly beautiful with blue eyes and blonde hair, and wore a bright peach-colored dress that made her all the more noticeable in the sea of dark-clothed mourners.

The musical prelude reached the end of a movement just as Harriet blurted out, "What is that bitch doing here?"

Brad heard a few gasps behind him, followed by shocked silence. Then murmurs swept Harriet's remark back through the rows of prestigious onlookers. Prim and proper social bees shared the buzz. At a less solemn occasion, Brad wouldn't have been able to contain his laughter.

Sharon leaned forward and quietly asked, "Who's that woman?"

Brad grabbed a pencil from the visitor's cardholder on the pew in front of him and scribbled a note on a card, passing it back to Sharon. It read: *Diane Panella-Frame, Andy's first wife.* Next to him, Harriet mumbled about the propriety of the outfit Diane wore.

Diane's escort—Ronald Allessi, Esq.—caused Brad more consternation than the color of her outfit. He wondered about their connection, and whether she had precipitated Allessi's interest in representing Wilkie.

Sharon whispered to Brad, "Did you see who—"

Brad nodded.

The prelude ended, replaced by the quiet rustling of parishioners consulting their programs. The cast iron bell in the church's steeple tolled ten. At the rear of the church the narthex doors creaked open and a lone bagpiper, in full dress tartan, led the procession playing *Amazing Grace.* Twelve men and three women served as honorary pallbearers, including the Governor, a former United States Senator, the Philadelphia Eagles' coach, the conductor of the Philadelphia Orchestra, and three Fortune 500 CEOs. As they rolled the solid bronze casket past his pew, Brad lowered his head into his hands, his shoulders trembling.

The coffin, topped with a spray of dozens of white roses, sat in front of the pews. A minister offered a prayer, and a soloist sang *The Lord's Prayer*. Andrew went to the lectern, struggling for composure as he read a passage of scripture from Corinthians.

The two brothers passed at the base of the chancel steps, offering each other a slight bow that belied that morning's tension between them. Brad approached the lectern and stared for a moment at the packed pews, then took a deep breath.

"On behalf of my family, thank you all for coming. Dad's been out of circulation for about ten years now, and this show of affection for him is a bit overwhelming. But I think it speaks, in ways more eloquent than I will be able, of the impact of his life on this community. For the last several days I've been in reflection, trying to summon to my mind the good times and ease out the painful memories of tragedy and illness that—unfortunately—marred the last decade or so of Dad's life. When people asked him what made him successful, my dad, with a twinkle in his eye, used to say, 'I studied to be an electrical engineer, and I married well.' "

Appreciative laughter rippled through the congregation.

"My strongest memories of him are as a different kind of engineer. When I was a kid, my parents gave my brother and me an electric train set. I always liked to load lots of cars behind the engine, with the result that the train barely moved—the speed I'd hoped for was impossible. My dad used to join us, wearing a railroad engineer's cap, and saw my predicament. Uncoupling all but a few cars, he explained that as I got older, he'd get more powerful transformers so the locomotive could pull more weight. From him I learned that the equipment on a train is known as the *consist*. The consist for a passenger train, for example, might be four coaches, a diner, a couple of sleepers, an observation coach, a baggage car, and, of course, the engine. It occurred to me that Dad was like a very powerful locomotive . . ." A lump formed in Brad's throat. "Dad managed to keeping adding lots of cars to the consist of his life—family, friends, a successful business, civic projects, government commissions, leadership in numerous professional associations, his church, and dozens of worthy charitable causes. For him, success brought higher expectations, and that's the proudest legacy I can take from his life."

Brad sank into his pew when the eulogy was over, feeling drained. He went through the motions during the rest of the church service, and at the short graveside committal. But he'd already said goodbye to his dad the best way he knew how.

CHAPTER 16

The limousine returned Brad and his family to the Bryn Mawr mansion after their trip to the cemetery. He retreated to his bedroom to freshen up for the noontime reception they'd announced, but Brad didn't feel like mingling with people. Finding the real killer—the person responsible for turning his world upside down—was what he preferred to do. Besides, with Philadelphia's social elite attending, he'd likely have to endure a gauntlet of requests for political contributions, honorary chairmanships of fundraising dinners, and investment opportunities.

Brad left his bedroom and stood at the top of the stairs. The odor of steamed salmon mingled with the aroma of steamship round of beef, wafted up to him as he leaned on the railing observing the chaotic scene in the foyer below.

Unlike Brad, Andy seemed energized by all the activity, backslapping with a couple of his buddies, bellowing, "Did you hear my aunt when Diane came in?" How differently, Brad thought, people react at a time of grief.

They roared with laughter. The black and white marble floor echoed the sound, while the room's crystal chandelier tinkled from the movement of people and the opening and closing of the front door as more guests arrived.

One of Andrew's friends snidely asked, "Who was that stud she was with?"

"I don't know, and I don't care," Andrew replied. "Getting rid of her was the best thing I ever did."

Brad knew what stud she was with, and wanted to know why. Diane and her escort weren't invited to the reception, but Brad could wait to contact her for answers.

Sharon's boyfriend, Mark, ambled through the foyer wearing his black suit, and Andy mistook him for a waiter—thrusting a half-filled glass of wine in Mark's hand and barking, "Get me a Dewars and water on the rocks." Poor Mark, Brad thought, figuring it was time he made his appearance, if only to make up for his brother's boorish behavior.

As he descended the stairs, Brad spotted Em Lindstrom engaged in an animated conversation with the Eagles' coach. Em kept bouncing his finger off the coach's chest. Through the archway to the drawing room Brad saw Aunt Harriet ensconced with the wives of Philadelphia's old money barons.

He watched as Mark returned to the foyer, smartly balancing Andy's Scotch on a silver platter with a white napkin draped over his arm. Brad smiled at Mark's sense of humor, realizing how well Mark's laissez faire attitude balanced Sharon's intensity. For her sake, he hoped their relationship would endure when she'd be working an erratic schedule on less desirable shifts as a rookie cop.

When Brad reached the bottom step, he noticed that his nephew Byron had Sharon cornered, and unless he misread the signs, Byron was hitting on her. Apparently his nineteen-year-old nephew fancied older women!

Brad approached Byron, and in a serious tone said, "Would you excuse me. I need a few minutes to consult with my associate."

Byron shrugged. "Whatever," he grumbled, as he grabbed a glass of red wine from one of the roving waiters and walked away.

Sharon gripped Brad's arm, her eyelids fluttering wildly, and mouthed the words, "Thank you."

"No problem," Brad said.

"Don't take this the wrong way," Sharon whispered. "But I'll be glad when the gathering of the Frame clan is over. I'm looking forward to getting back to work."

Brad nodded. "That makes two of us."

"How are you doing?" she asked.

"I'm fine." He sighed. "It's been an emotionally charged day, but I'm numb right now. All of this will hit me in a day or two. I'm glad Dad is finally at peace."

"It was a nice service, Brad, and your eulogy was very touching," Sharon said.

"Thanks." Brad blinked away a tear he felt forming in his eye. "I forgot to ask you yesterday. How did the physical endurance test for the police academy go on Monday?"

Sharon crinkled her lips and shook her head. "I postponed taking the test. I've been busy here, fielding lots of calls in the last few days. I left a stack of messages for you in the office."

Brad wished he had known. He valued her help, and knew how much she had pitched in to help organize his dad's funeral service. Sharon sounded stoic about it, but he didn't want to be responsible for any delay in her achieving her dream.

Sharon plucked a mini-quiche from a passing tray of hors d'oeuvres, and popped it in her mouth.

"I'll be tied up with family most of the day," Brad said. "Let's plan to get together in the office at nine in the morning. We've got a lot of work to do."

Brad felt a tap on his shoulder. "Excuse me, Mr. Frame." He turned and recognized Hiram Gibbons. A close-cropped Afro surrounded his head, with a swath of shiny cocoa-colored skin on top. Hiram wore a brown pin-stripe double-breasted suit and carried a briefcase. "Please accept my condolences on your loss," he said.

147

"Thanks, Hiram." Brad gripped his offered hand. "Thanks for coming. Have you met my associate Sharon Porter? Sharon, this is Hiram Gibbons, my dad's attorney." She shook his hand.

"Nice to meet you," Hiram said, before turning back to Brad. "I understand your aunt is returning to New York City in the morning?"

"Yes. I'm not sure what time her train leaves."

"Then I'd like to see you, Andrew, and your aunt alone for a few minutes. It's about your father's Last will and Testament."

Brad wasn't prepared for that request. "Why so soon? Can't it wait?"

"Your father asked me to read the will when all three of you were present."

Brad frowned in annoyance. "Dad hasn't spoken for the last five years."

"I know, Brad," the lawyer said in somber tones. "It was seven years ago when Joseph met with me and last updated his will."

"I guess we can meet in the library." Brad looked around to see if he could locate his brother and aunt. "I'll go find the others."

"Just the three of you," the lawyer reminded him. "A pleasure meeting you, Sharon."

Brad took a deep breath and watched as the lawyer headed for the library.

"Sharon, excuse me," Brad said, "while I round up my brother and aunt."

Spotting Andy first, Brad whispered the lawyer's request in his brother's ear. Andy looked first at his watch then the contents of his highball glass. "Give me ten more minutes."

"Fine," Brad said. "I'll get Harriet."

Brad passed Gertie Lindstrom sitting in her motorized chair and chatting with one of their neighbors, as he entered the drawing room. She reached out and patted him on the arm. He looked back at her and smiled ruefully. Brad approached his aunt as she held court with her septuagenarian friends, hoping to pull Harriet away quietly.

"Oh, Bradford, we were just talking about you," Aunt Harriet said when she spotted him. "There's someone I'd like you to meet."

Brad smiled at the ladies in her company as Harriet rose from the sofa, seized him by the arm and led him to where a young woman sat chatting with a small group. "Elizabeth," Harriet said, interrupting their conversation, "this is my nephew, Bradford Frame." Turning to him, she said, "Bradford, this is Elizabeth Montgomery."

"Excuse me," Elizabeth said to her friends, in a show of manners, before standing to greet him. Her nutmeg brown shoulder-length hair surrounded a cheerful face, and he caught a whiff of Lily of the Valley perfume.

She extended her hand. "Hi, I'm Beth Montgomery."

"I'm Brad," he said at the same time.

They both laughed. She eyed him carefully with a so-this-is-who-Harriet's-been-wanting-me-to-meet look. Brad took her offered hand in his, daring to hold it longer than polite, as he cocked his head in Harriet's direction and winked at Beth. He gazed into her dusky eyes and sensed compassion, or perhaps that's what he wanted to see.

"Do you live in Philadelphia?" he asked.

"No, New York. I'm a structural engineer with Oring-Whitman." Brad recognized the world-famous design firm and nodded. "I'm here visiting with my dad, Leland Montgomery," she added. He also recognized the name of one of his father's old golfing buddies.

"It's a pleasure to meet you," Brad said, glancing at his matchmaking-aunt as she stood next to them rubbing her palms together and beaming.

"Will you be in Philadelphia long?" Brad inquired.

"I go back tomorrow," Beth said.

That news felt like a cloud intruding on a sunny day, and produced a lull as he pondered where to take their conversation.

Beth added, "I'm sorry for your loss."

Brad stole another look into her eyes, like deepening twilight, before she blinked.

"There's a lovely buffet lunch in the dining room," Harriet began, linking arms with both of them. "Why don't you both fix a plate and find a quiet corner to talk?"

"I've already eaten." Beth demurred, gracefully disengaging from Harriet's clutch. "And besides, my dad started looking impatiently in my direction about twenty minutes ago. I think he's ready to leave." She smiled at Brad.

Brad spoke, "When you're back in the area . . ."

"If you're ever in New York . . ." she started to say.

Once again they shared a laugh.

Brad reversed the way his arm linked with Aunt Harriet's, and guided her toward the library. "Hiram Gibbons wants to see you, me and Andrew. About Dad's will," he explained.

"Well, what do you think?" Harriet asked.

Brad pretended not to know what she meant. "About what?"

Impatiently, she said, "About Elizabeth?"

Brad glanced back in Beth's direction, as she bid goodbye to her friends; he felt a warm glow deep inside him and couldn't remember how long it had been since he'd felt such stirrings.

Turning back to his aunt, he said, "Do you really think she's my type?" Then added, "She doesn't seem a bit like you, Aunt Harriet, and I think I need to find me a gal just like you." He put his finger on the tip of her nose.

"Oh, stop it." She blushed.

As Brad and his aunt entered the library, Hiram Gibbons rose from behind the desk, where his briefcase sat propped open in front of him. Hiram had made himself at home, having arranged a semi-circle of three chairs in front of the desk. Brad helped his aunt into the middle chair, taking the seat to her right.

"I hope this doesn't take all afternoon," Andy announced, as he entered behind them and sat in the open chair. "I've got a three o'clock tee time."

Hiram closed the library door. "I will only need a few minutes of your time," he said, reaching into his briefcase and extracting an ivory colored envelope. "First, I have a letter that Joe asked me to read to his son Andrew."

"Excuse me," Andy said. "If it's personal, why can't I just read it myself."

"I'll provide you with the signed original of the letter, but your father asked that I read it in the presence of your brother and aunt."

Andy folded his arms across his chest and slouched in his chair.

Extracting the folded sheet of paper from the envelope, Hiram explained, "This letter was dictated by Mr. Frame to a stenographer, in my presence, seven years ago on February 7th. It subsequently was transcribed and I read it to Joe before he affixed his signature."

Hiram unfolded the letter and began to read: "Dear Andrew. First, please know that your mother and I loved you very much. But we kept a secret from you that I regret. You were adopted. It was a private adoption arranged by our attorney, Mr. Latham." Brad noticed Andy straighten in his seat. "You were only a few days old when Mr. Latham brought you to us. We named you, as you know, after your great-grandfather on the Frame family side. Your mother swore everyone to secrecy on the subject of the adoption. She always promised me that we would tell you when you were old enough, which should have been thirty years ago. I always regretted that we didn't. You were our first son, and we loved you as much as our other children. Love, Dad."

Brad could hear his aunt sniffling in the silence that followed Hiram's reading of the letter.

Andy turned to his aunt, demanding, angrily, "You knew about this?"

"Yes. It was just like your father said." Harriet's hands trembled.

Andy glared at her.

Hiram handed Andy the letter, which he jerked from the attorney's hand. Brad could see it was printed on Hiram's law office stationery with his dad's signature. He wondered if there was another letter coming announcing his adoption, except that he looked too much like his father. But then everyone always said that Andy looked like Uncle Carl on his mother's side of the family.

"Now to Joseph Frame's will," Hiram announced. "It was executed at the same time as the letter I just read. I have copies for each of you, and without reading the entire testament, I would like to summarize the pertinent provisions:

"To each of my surviving grandchildren, I leave in trust the sum of $250,000 to be used for their education.

"To my sister, Harriet Frame-Beecham, I have established a trust to provide the sum of $50,000 annually for the remainder of her life, with the balance of the trust reverting to my estate at the time of her death." Harriet brought her hands to her mouth, in apparent surprise.

"To support the charitable endeavors I aided during my lifetime, I provide $500,000 to each of the fourteen charities listed in Schedule A.

"To advance the future of several Philadelphia cultural organizations, I have established endowments in the sum of $3,000,000 to each of the four organizations listed in Schedule B.

"To my son, Andrew Frame, I offer my thanks for his management of Joedco, Inc. and provide the sum of $1.

"To my son, Bradford Frame, I leave my Bryn Mawr estate and its contents, and additional properties detailed in Schedule C, along with the balance of my estate, including: cash, certificates of deposits, mutual funds, investments, and all of my holdings in Joedco, Inc."

Brad sat in shock. Why had his father made him the heir? A dozen thoughts flitted through his brain at once, the most prominent among them were how Andy would react and would this news further divide the only family he had left?

Andy jumped up from his chair and flung open the library door so hard it splintered the jamb as he charged out of the room shouting, "Barbara . . . Barbara . . ."

Brad rushed after him, fearing the worst.

Andy's wife, hearing the commotion, got up from her seat in the drawing room and rushed to the foyer. "What is it?" she said, panic in her eyes.

"Get packed. Let's get out of here before we have to hitch a ride back to Houston."

"Andy, wait," Brad shouted, inviting more stares from guests gathered in his foyer. "I don't know what to say."

Andy turned back to him and snarled. "The hell you don't. You probably dictated the damn thing."

CHAPTER 17

Brad spotted Sharon as she exited the kitchen, carrying an insulated travel mug. She looked flushed, but she wore a jogging outfit, so he attributed her pink glow to her morning run.

Sharon gestured with her thumb over her shoulder. "I made a fresh pot about fifteen minutes ago. The caterers arranged breakfast in the dining room."

Reversing course and heading that direction, Brad said, "Have you eaten? Want to join me?"

Sharon rolled her eyeballs. "I wouldn't go in there if I were you."

Brad stared at her quizzically.

"I've already visited the dining room. Andrew and Harriet are in there, just the two of them. It's a bit frosty."

"Oh." It didn't sound like a night's rest had improved Andy's disposition. Brad had tried to talk with him after Hiram and the other guests left, but Andy had cut him off.

"You've been officially warned," she said, exiting through the front door of the mansion and heading toward her suite above the garage.

"Good morning, everybody," Brad said, cheerfully, as he entered the dining room.

His brother and aunt sat opposite each other at the end of the table nearest the sideboard, where the caterers had arranged food. Harriet looked majestic in her pink chenille sweater and coordinated pants, absently stirring a half-empty cup, her pinky poised delicately above her hand. Andy, in running shorts, T-shirt and Nikes, sat hunched over the table riffling through the pages of *The Wall Street Journal*, looking like a dormant volcano that could erupt at any minute.

Spooning a generous helping of scrambled eggs onto his plate from one of the Sterno-heated chafing dishes, Brad selected two strips of bacon and fresh fruit to go with it. Opting not to aggravate his older brother, Brad skipped the open chair at the head of the table and instead left his plate at a place next to Aunt Harriet. In spite of the emotional impact of the funeral and the contretemps caused by the reading of his dad's will, Brad had enjoyed a good night's rest, and for the first time in weeks—though he wasn't sure why—he felt upbeat. Being the principal beneficiary of his father's will had surprised him; he'd expected to share equally with his brother. His lifestyle wouldn't change, he already led a comfortable life, but perhaps he'd carry a heavier burden of living up to his dad's legacy in the community—the one his eulogy had praised.

Returning to the sideboard, Brad filled his cup and carried the carafe with him to the table. "Can I give anybody a warm up?"

Two cups were speechlessly shoved in his direction, and he filled them, determined to act the gracious host. Brad noticed a gray squirrel scampering along the ledge outside the dining room window. The squirrel paused to peer through the window, seemingly checking out what everyone ate for breakfast.

Andy folded the newspaper and slapped it on the table. "I hope you've got somebody in mind to run the company."

"I *do*, as a matter of fact," Brad said, realizing he might have to endure a few tirades from Andy before sharing his ideas.

"Good." Andy barely opened his teeth as he said it.

"Bradford!" Harriet put her hand on Brad's arm. "Don't be hasty."

"Dad had no idea what I've done for the company the last eleven years," Andy said. "I've sunk my whole life into Joedco, turned it around, and what happens? The prodigal son inherits it all."

Harriet reached across the table to pat Andy's arm, but he pulled it away.

Brad slid his chair back. "And what does that mean?"

Andy took off his reading glasses and flung them at the table. "You know *exactly* what I mean," he said, jabbing the air with his index finger. "Where were *you* all those years? Off to Europe, South America, Japan—finding yourself! Ha! More like getting laid on seven continents while I kept turning profits. All that work—just so you could inherit it all."

Harriet drew herself up in her chair and put the palms of her hands on the edge of the table. "Andrew! Bradford!" she said in a strong but emotional voice. "Stop this squabbling!"

There was a lull, but not a truce. Andy looked at Harriet, caught her glance and then looked away.

Andy spoke again, the words tumbling out of his mouth in a torrent of emotion. "Why didn't Mom ever tell me I was adopted?"

Andy rubbed his eyes.

"Soon after they were married a doctor told your mother she would not likely have children," Harriet explained. "They arranged a private adoption expecting you would be their only child. Then a few years later Bradford came along, quite unexpectedly, and Lucy a few years after that. They were very happy with all of their children. They certainly didn't love you any less."

Andrew exhaled and stared toward the window.

Brad bit his lower lip. "Aunt Harriet, I don't understand why Mom didn't tell Andy about his adoption when he was old enough?"

"There is no good explanation," Harriet said, holding her palms face up in front of her. "By the time you were old enough, Andrew, your mother was afraid to tell you. It was against my advice, and even your dad admitted they should have said something. If you had remained an only child, she probably would have told you, but after Bradford and Lucy came along, I think your mother feared that if you knew, you would somehow feel different. She never wanted you to feel different."

"And how am I supposed to feel now? Huh? Having this information dumped on me at the age of forty-eight, on the same night I'm disinherited? Oh, yeah. I feel great." Andy pushed his chair back and paced the dining room, staring at walls, floors and ceiling, and occasionally muttering. Aunt Harriet started to get up from her seat to go to him, but Brad stopped her.

Andy turned and faced his aunt. "Did Mom ever say anything about my real parents?"

"Nothing specific, Andrew. She implied things . . . I mean. I picked up impressions, more than any details. My sense was that your birth mother was a young girl from a good Main Line family. Her parents probably sent her away to a boarding school so the pregnancy would not be known locally, and through their attorney everything was arranged. It's the way things were done back then. I never heard anything said about the father."

Andy's cell phone let out a muffled ring. He reached under his newspaper and fumbled for the phone, finally grabbing it and flipping it open. Andy picked up his glasses

157

from where he'd thrown them and studied the phone's display screen before answering. "Yes, Doris." His tone was all business, Brad noted, with no hint of family turmoil. "I should be back in the office on Friday. No, don't reschedule the meeting. I'll see Gordon at 10:30 before the others . . . Just have Ken send me an e-mail. I'll review it this afternoon and get right back to him. Anything else? Okay, good. Oh, tell Hank he better stick around Friday night, and not to make any early weekend plans. Thanks, Doris."

Andy laid his phone back on the table, then jumped back into their discussion. "If everything you said is true, it still doesn't explain Dad cutting me out of his will."

"I think I know," Brad said.

"I'm sure you do," Andrew said derisively. "I don't want to hear anything from you other than your plans to run the company. You'll control about 35 percent of the stock after the will is probated. It'll be a damn shame when it loses 40 percent of its value."

"What are you talking about?" Brad asked. "Why should the stock's value drop?"

"Because people don't invest in earthquakes. If they did, the Red Cross would sell stock." Andy's arms flailed as he paced and talked. "Investors don't like uncertainty. When a Fortune 100 company loses a CEO with a proven track record, the stock will naturally drop in value—five, ten, maybe as much as twenty percent—until investors feel confident with new management. But when they hear that a guy who's been playing cops and robbers for the last ten years is taking over the company, the stock's gonna go straight through the crust of the earth. No telling where it's gonna land. Hell, maybe some Aussie'll find cheap stock in his backyard."

"It's a solid company, and I expect it to stay that way," Brad said.

Harriet nodded, while wringing her hands.

"And who made it solid?" Andrew tapped his own chest with his finger. "But it's only solid as long as the public thinks its solid. Christ!" He brought his fist down on the table, rattling the cups, plates, and Aunt Harriet, who jumped in fear. "When Mom and Lucy were kidnapped Joedco stock dropped more than 50 percent. It was selling at 12¾ before the news broke, and hit bottom at 5½ in less than two weeks. We've had three stock splits since then. You know what a share is selling for today—eighty-seven goddamn dollars. When you're done, buddy, we'll be lucky if it's at 50. Give me a fu . . ." Andy eyed his aunt. ". . . break!"

Harriet glared at him.

"And don't give me any prudish looks, like you're gonna wash my mouth out with soap! It wasn't *me* that announced to a whole church full of people that Diane's a bitch."

Harriet blushed and tugged at the cowl neck of her sweater. "I'm sorry. I didn't realize I'd be overheard. The organ music was a lot louder just before I said it."

Andy snickered. "It was kind of funny though. Dad would have laughed if he could've heard it." He walked over to the sideboard and tried to fill his juice glass from a now empty pitcher. "Shit," he muttered.

Brad stood and walked over to his brother, grasping his shoulder. "Andy, I've been the Chair of the Board for the last ten years. I see no reason to make a management change. You're still the President and CEO as far as I'm concerned."

"Apparently, Dad thought differently."

The phone rang, echoing from its table in the foyer.

"If that's my stockbroker," Harriet said with a straight face, "I think I'd like to sell some stock."

Brad laughed.

"Go ahead and laugh, smart-ass," Andrew said. "I'll probably be cashing in my stock options by the end of the week. Before any news of this gets out."

"Andy, I know why he cut you out of the will," Brad said before picking up a portable phone extension from the top of the mahogany silver caddy in the dining room. "Hello."

"I'm glad somebody does," Andrew responded at full voice.

Brad thought he heard Paula Thompson's voice on the phone, as he covered the receiver and gestured for his brother to be quiet.

Andy plopped back into his seat, and stretched his legs.

"I'm sorry," Brad said, avoiding saying her name within earshot of his family. "It was a little noisy here, and I didn't catch what you said." Brad turned and walked over to the window, where he continued his conversation.

"Could we get together for a follow-up meeting?" Thompson asked. "I'd like an update on what you've learned."

"Sure," he said hesitantly. "I've got a nine o'clock meeting, but we could meet for lunch downtown by twelve-thirty."

"Did you have a place in mind?" she asked.

"How about Susannah Foo's?"

"Sounds good. I'll meet you there—twelve-thirty." He imagined the reporter scribbling the location and time in the notebook she always carried with her.

Brad replaced the portable phone in its cradle. Thompson's call prompted him to wonder how much he should share with his aunt and Andy about Wilkie's message and its implications. Andy already had dismissed Brad's skills as a detective, so he would barely listen, while telling his aunt would give her another family detail to fret about. He decided to wait until he had more information. Besides, he thought, neither of them would have paid Wilkie and Baker to kill his mother and sister.

"Everything all right?" Harriet asked.

Brad realized a worried expression had crept onto his face. He smiled and said, "Yeah, I'm fine."

Andrew said, "We're still waiting for your theory about why Dad cut me out of his will."

"It's not a theory," Brad said. "I talked to Hiram after you ran out yesterday."

"Oh, I'm sure Hiram had great things to say about me," Andrew said snidely.

"What are you talking about?" Brad asked.

"Skip it." Andrew batted the air with his hand. "Hiram's not one of my favorite people and I'm sure he feels the same way about me."

"Why?" Brad inquired.

"I pay lawyers to figure out how I can do what I want to do without landing in jail. Hiram was too conservative for me, always telling me what we *couldn't* do. I tried for years to get Dad to change law firms."

"I see." Brad sighed. "Hiram said Dad changed his will seven years ago, right after you moved the corporate headquarters to Houston. According to Hiram, Dad wasn't happy with your decision to move the company out of Philadelphia. It was an emotional issue for him. He summoned Hiram to the nursing home and told him he wanted to change his will."

Andrew glared at Brad in disbelief.

"I remember the move upset your father," Harriet offered. "But he never said anything to me about changing his will because of it. His roots were here in Philadelphia and the city was very important to him—just like his business. You know how the people around here are about this city; you could live here forty years but unless you were born here you aren't considered a Philadelphian. Joe got angry with me fifty years ago when I first moved to New York. I told him I could stay here and be an old maid, or move to New York and have a life."

Once again, Andy looked ready to explode. "I bet Hiram didn't mention that Dad's will was changed at about the same time that I yanked his $80,000 retainer as the corporation's legal counsel?"

"No . . . he didn't." Brad quickly replayed his conversation with Hiram in his mind, seeing if what Andy said about the yanked retainer were true, would it alter his impressions. He decided not. "Hiram said he tried to talk Dad out of changing his will," Brad explained, "and even threatened to contact the family, but Dad swore him to secrecy. I asked Hiram if there was anything *we* could do to contest the will. He said that anyone can contest a will, but it would be difficult to make a successful case in these circumstances. I reminded him that Dad was almost seventy-one when he changed his will and had had a paralyzing stroke. Hiram said the overwhelming medical evidence at the time documented that he was still of sound mind. The stroke paralyzing his speech happened two years later."

Brad's explanation was met with silence.

"I'd be happy to get a second legal opinion," Brad offered. "I didn't know you had personal run-ins with him."

"Hiram's right," Andy said. "I never said he wasn't an honest lawyer, just too damned cautious. Besides, there's

another downside. It'd be a very public fight. I'd get a reputation as litigious and lose out on eight-figure salary opportunities."

"I have no interest in losing you as the CEO of Joedco,"
Brad said. "What can we do to keep you?"

Andy propped his elbows on the table.

Brad continued, "Most of Dad's estate is tied up in the
company or in real estate. He owned a couple of office
buildings in downtown Philadelphia, and of course this
property. It's valued at just over three and a half million."

"I have no interest in this old place," Andy said. "It's
yours. Enjoy. I just built a twelve thousand square foot contemporary house on Clear Lake. There's a reason I'm not
living in Philadelphia. I prefer the smell of new money to
old wood, and fresh shrimp on the grill to pretzels from a
street vendor."

Harriet, who had kept her peace for a while, got up from
the table and toddled over to the sideboard eyeing a tray of
pastries. With her back to them, she said, "You're not exactly a pauper, Andrew. You've still got the trust that your
mother set up for you."

Andy seethed. "And so does *he!*"

Harriet turned, holding a mini-cheese Danish between
her fingers, and floundered for a way to soothe Andrew. "I
didn't mean that. Well, what I'm trying to say . . . You
can't . . ." She finally sat back down.

"I thought you had a train to catch," Andy said con-
temptuously.

Harriet looked hurt. "I changed my reservation to 12:45
so we'd have more time to visit."

"You haven't answered my question yet," Brad said.
"What can we do to keep you as CEO of Joedco?"

Andy drew in a breath. "Make me the *Chairman* and

CEO, and be prepared to offer a salary that puts me in the top 15 percent of Fortune 100 executives. You'll remain as Chair of the Executive Committee—it'll be a nice touch of family unity." Andy displayed the same take-charge demeanor he had demonstrated on the cell phone. "We're in talks right now to acquire a competing satellite technology company. I'll be able to sweeten the deal by offering the presidency to their exec."

"Done," Brad said. "I'm sure it's on my calendar, but remind me when is the next stockholder's meeting?"

"Next Tuesday, at the Marriott Marquis in midtown-Manhattan. You'll have to be there to show the flag. But . . ." Andy raised a finger in the air. "We'll need to issue a press release to signal these developments by Friday at the latest. The Street will be looking for signs of stability at Joedco, and they aren't going to wait for its founder to get cold. Tokyo investors will start testing the resilience of our stock while we're sleeping on Sunday night."

Brad smiled, remembering another reason why he'd enjoy making a trip to New York—a chance to spend more time with Beth Montgomery.

"I'll be there," Brad said. "If you send the corporate jet."

Andrew scoffed. "You just inherited four billion dollars. Go buy an airline."

CHAPTER 18

Andy had always intimidated Brad. His brother's dominant personality had helped shape his own formative years. The five-year difference in their ages provided Andy an advantage in size when they were kids, though Brad grew three inches taller than his brother during high school and had managed to keep the spare tire off his waist in his forties. Part of the cleverness Brad had developed was attributable to observing his brother's moods and methods and learning to counter his physical advantage. As volatile as his brother had been during the last twenty-four hours, Andy now seemed pleased with the arrangement to become Chairman and CEO of Joedco, and Brad figured it was as good a time as any to pull him aside for a serious chat.

"Let's take a walk," Brad said, holding open the front door. The two of them strolled under the portico and down the steps. Morning sun shone through the trees, leaving a dappled light pattern on the cobblestone drive.

"What's up?" Andy asked.

"Wanna grab your sweat pants or a jacket?" Brad asked, realizing how chilly the morning was compared with what Andy was accustomed to in Houston.

Andy shook his head. "I'm fine."

Brad turned left, intending to circle around behind the office and into the backyard. "I went to Wilkie's execution two weeks ago," he began.

"Yeah, I know."

"Afterward the prison's chaplain handed me Wilkie's Bible—the one he'd carried with him to the execution. He'd written words in the margins."

"When are you gonna tell me something I can't read in the papers?" Andy asked.

"There were eighteen words, in no particular order. It seemed like Wilkie was trying to send me a message, but I couldn't make any sense of it. I contacted the superintendent at the prison and found out that he had a list of scripture references that might act as a key to put Wilkie's eighteen words in order," Brad explained. "But someone made a stink—I'm sure you read that in the paper too . . ."

Andy nodded.

They crossed the patio, and Brad stole a glance through the windows into his office before they walked into the backyard.

"And the prison placed a lid on releasing any more information to me," Brad continued. "Then a couple days after the execution someone set fire to my office and the Bible was stolen."

"Aunt Harriet told me about the fire," Andy said.

"What you don't know is that I copied the pages with words from Wilkie's Bible, and using a few connections managed to get the list of scripture verses and figured out what Frank Wilkie was trying to tell me."

Andy's eyes widened, and he stared at his brother waiting for the news.

"Wilkie said he and Baker were paid to kill—*paid money kill* were his exact words."

Andy gave a low whistle.

"I knew seeing Wilkie executed wouldn't give me any closure, but I can't turn my back on his message."

Andy grunted. "I moved on a long time ago."

Brad nodded. "You could. I can't. With this new information, I'm determined to find out who paid the killers. I could use your help."

"How?" Andy asked, tentatively.

"The other day Gertrude Lindstrom—"

"Ah, yes, good old Gertie," Andy interrupted. "I'm her favorite member of the family, maybe that's why when I saw her after the funeral she just rolled right by me." He threw his head back yelling, "Ha."

After Andy's show of pique had subsided, Brad said, "I asked Gertie about foreign competitors and whether they had any reason to threaten Dad eleven years ago. She said *you* were responsible for international business and might know."

Andy rubbed his chin. "Nothing I can recall."

"And Gertie said Dad received a threatening note about a week before the kidnapping."

The lines tightened between Andy's eyebrows. "What kind of a note? I don't remember any note."

"She said the message was pasted from letters cut out of newsprint."

"What did it say?" Andrew asked urgently.

"It said, 'You can't get away with it.' "

The two of them had finished walking around the yard on the east side of the mansion and were back on the cobblestone drive. Andy looked off in the distance, as if he hadn't heard the answer to his question. "What's wrong?" Brad asked.

"There were other notes."

"No," Brad explained. "That's the only one Gertie talked about."

"No. No," Andy repeated, excitedly. "You don't understand. There *were* other notes. But they happened two years before the kidnapping. I never made the connection with

Mom or Dad at the time of the kidnapping because the other notes were sent to me."

"Really? What did they say?"

"I can't recall the exact wording, but very similar to the note Gertie described. It might have been, 'you won't get away with it,' or 'you'll never get away with it.' "

"Did you save any of them?"

Andy shook his head, and Brad eyed him warily. Threatening notes—albeit several years ahead of the kidnapping—could alter his working premise about the motivation for the crime.

"Did you conduct an investigation when you received them?" Brad asked, but he already knew the answer.

"No."

"I'll need your help in researching stock transactions from the time of the kidnapping," Brad said, as they returned to the front portico. "You gave me a good idea earlier when you were talking about the value of the company stock." It never hurt to flatter his brother, Brad had learned.

Andy smiled. "Sure. Call my office. Whatever you need. But let me give you a bit of advice. Wilkie's a scumbag. How do you know he isn't jerking you around with this message? You're the guy who caught him. Then for eleven years the scumbag waits for his chance to get even. He wants to play your fiddle one last time so he makes up a mysterious note—doo do doo do," Andy hummed the *Twilight Zone* theme.

Brad smiled.

"Think about it," Andy said. "I'm gonna jog for a couple miles. I'll catch you later."

Andy took off running, while Brad gazed after him. Andy had always intimidated Brad.

A three-person cleaning crew busily tidied up the mansion as Brad passed through the foyer on the way to his nine o'clock meeting. Rags squeaked on the windows, a heavy-duty vacuum cleaner noisily whirred in the drawing room, and mops renewed the shine on the marble floor of the entry hall.

Barbara Frame, her two children in tow, descended the curved grand staircase from the second floor. Barbara was about Sharon's age, and looked younger with blonde hair falling to her shoulders rather than twisted into a French braid like it was for the funeral. Amazing, Brad thought, how much Andy's trophy wife looked like Diane.

Barbara smiled when she saw Brad and said, "Are we too late for breakfast?"

Chad, age seven, who shared his dad's eyes and intensity of spirit, tugged at the sleeve of her jacket. "I'm hungry," he yelled.

"Check in the dining room. The caterers had a pretty big spread laid out." He checked his watch. "But that was about an hour and a half ago. You can find cereal and juice in the kitchen, I'm sure."

Erica, age three, and a miniature version of her mother began to cry.

"You'll excuse us," Barbara said, picking up her daughter and carrying her. "I better get them something to eat."

Sharon was already waiting when Brad entered his newly refurbished office. The smell of fresh paint replaced the odor of smoke from the fire, and his feet plunged a little deeper into new beige wool carpeting laid on a thick bed of padding. All the furniture was new, except for the oak partner's desk, which would remain at the furniture refinishing shop for at least another week. A plywood board placed across two wooden saw horses formed a temporary replacement.

Brad eased into the leather executive chair behind his makeshift desk and gazed at two stacks of papers.

"All the notes of condolence that have come in over the past several days are in the big pile," Sharon explained. "And the smaller stack is letters from potential clients."

Brad pushed the papers aside and opened his laptop.

"There's an interesting letter from the Police Chief in Wilkes-Barre," Sharon said. "He'd like your help with an internal affairs' investigation of two police officers implicated in the shooting of a third officer."

Brad raised his eyebrows as he peered at Sharon over the top of his computer.

"He's offering you carte blanche to run the investigation however you'd like," Sharon added.

Brad shook his head. "I think we have enough to keep us busy. Give the chief a call for me, will you, and tell him we'll pass; besides, it's not exactly the kind of case I usually handle."

Sharon looked disappointed, but she nodded.

"Hey, here's an e-mail from Nick," Brad said, scanning his computer screen. "He's developed information about Eddie Baker from his contact at Graterford. Are you free if I invite him to stop over around 6 o'clock?

"Sure. I'm taking the written section of the police exam this afternoon at two, but I should be back here by five at the latest."

Using the two-fingered hunt and peck method that he'd developed to type term papers in college, Brad dashed off a response to Nick Argostino.

"Any luck on getting a copy of Wilkie and Baker's trial transcript?" Brad asked.

"Oh, I completely forgot to tell you. The clerk's office said there was no way that we could get a transcript for at least six to eight weeks. But I had another idea. At the local library I could review microfiche of the *Inquirer* from the time of the kidnapping, the arrest, and the trial. Since I wasn't involved back then, any interesting detail is likely to jump out at me. And I can print copies if I need them directly from the microfiche."

Once more Brad realized what a loss Sharon would be to his agency.

"Are you okay?" she asked.

"Sure," he said, realizing he had to do a better job of maintaining his poker face. "Reviewing the *Inquirer* sounds like a great idea. Check the business section, too, and track items related to Joedco." He paused, debating whether to ask her. "Sharon, when you have time, could you develop a job description? I mean, if I have to replace you, you have the best sense of what my associate does."

Lacking enthusiasm, Sharon said, "Yeah, I'll take care of it. What's on your schedule for today?"

Brad left out his plans to contact Beth Montgomery to see if they could get together during his trip to New York City the following Tuesday. "I'm meeting Paula Thompson for lunch. I promised Aunt Harriet I would drive her to 30th Street Station, then I'll meet Paula in the city. We've got our meeting with Nick early this evening, and I'm going to call and schedule an appointment with Diane Panella-Frame," Brad said, looking at his watch. "But she's probably not up yet."

Sharon rolled her eyes.

"Oh, don't forget to add that."

"Add what?" Sharon asked.

Brad waggled a finger at her. "What you just did."

"Huh?" Sharon shook her head. "I don't know what you're talking about."

"Add it to the job description—what you just did." He winked. "You know, 'Roll eyes at boss, regularly, to signal astonishment'."

CHAPTER 19

Brad arrived at Susannah Foo's fifteen minutes before his scheduled lunch with Paula Thompson. He had called for a reservation earlier that morning only to learn the restaurant was booked solid at lunchtime, but they agreed to put his name on a wait list. Within seconds of his arrival, the manager recognized him.

"Ah, Mr. Frame," she said, beckoning him forward from the reservation queue. "I have a table for you." She escorted him to a table for two, and Brad slipped into the banquette leaving the chair for Thompson. A waitress promptly arrived asking if he'd like a drink, and Brad ordered iced tea.

Awaiting her arrival, Brad studied the menu and watched the other patrons. The best advice he'd ever gotten from a criminology professor was to study human behavior most keenly when there was no urgent need, since it would only sharpen perceptions for those times when people are wearing their emotional masks. He glanced from table to table, eyeing customers, deciding if they were engaged in a business meeting, enjoying a cozy midday rendezvous, or just relaxing after a harrowing morning. How many others in the restaurant, he wondered, laughing to himself, would be swapping notes about a murder case.

Thompson arrived precisely at twelve-thirty. She exhaled as she plopped down across from him, juggling a blue vinyl portfolio and wearing a green corduroy jumper over a tan blouse. "I'm here," she announced, sounding out of breath. "I don't have that many luncheon meetings and it threw off my morning routine. And then I took the wrong exit from the City Hall subway and had to walk a couple of extra blocks."

"I'm glad you made it," Brad said.

The waitress came by to tell them about the luncheon special—scallops and prawns in a lime-ginger sauce—and to take Thompson's drink order.

"Thanks for coming to my dad's funeral," Brad said when the waitress had left.

"What do you have for me?" Thompson asked, getting down to business.

"Our conversation still on background?"

She nodded, looking annoyed. Brad scrutinized her face. She seemed easy to read, he thought. Guileless. The passion for her work oozed from her pores.

Brad extracted a sheet of paper from his jacket pocket and handed it to her. She studied it as he explained, "That is Wilkie's final message to me."

"The superintendent sent you the list of Bible verses he found."

"No." When Thompson looked perplexed, Brad explained, "In a tribute to our state's great bureaucracy, he was ordered not to share that information. I can't tell you how it came into my possession."

The waitress returned and they both ordered the lunch special, with Thompson selecting hot and sour while Brad chose wonton soup.

Eyeing the paper Brad had given her, Thompson said, "Clearly you'd like to know who paid for the kidnapping?"

A diner at the next table flashed Brad a look when Thompson said *kidnapping*.

Circumspect in his response, Brad said, "I'm always anxious to find the truth."

Thompson frowned. "I'm not sure if my editor will let me use this."

"Why?"

"I don't have independent confirmation of what you've told me. I need a second source." Her eyes brightened. "I could request the list from the Department of Corrections under the state's Freedom of Information Act," Thompson said.

"You'll probably receive it in a couple months," Brad said, knowing how slowly bureaucracy grinds. "But it's only half of the information required to piece the message together—the rest are the pages from the Bible."

Studying her face, it looked to Brad like the wheels were turning in her brain.

"I may hold off using this for a while," she said, folding the note Brad had given her and sticking it into her portfolio.

"I won't mind," Brad said. "I shared information with you like I promised. If what Wilkie's message suggests is true—and this morning I was reminded he might only be jerking my chain—then I'll keep working to find the person responsible. If you delay telling the world, it will give me more time."

"My editor agreed to let me do a series on the death penalty in Pennsylvania," Thompson said.

"With a pro slant, I'm sure." Brad smiled.

The waitress delivered their meals on sizzling metal serving dishes, the citrus and ginger aromas floating to their nostrils.

After she'd taken a few bites of food, Thompson stared across the table. "I know we disagree on the death penalty. I think it's a barbaric ritual unworthy of people who call themselves civilized."

Brad shook his head. "Don't assume we disagree. Sometimes I think the only one who got any peace of mind from Wilkie's execution was Frank Wilkie. Lethal injection is one form of punishment—irreversible to be sure—but is the alternative of another forty-five or fifty years locked away in a forty-five square foot cell any less barbaric? Unless you don't believe in punishment for crime, in which case we definitely disagree."

"Would you agree that sometimes the innocent are executed?" Thompson asked.

"You're not suggesting Wilkie was innocent?"

Brushing droopy curls away from her eyes, Thompson said, "Let me ask you a question for an on-the-record response?"

"Sure, as long as *no comment* can count as my response."

"Can you ever forgive Frank Wilkie?" she asked.

The question stung, like merthiolate applied to an open wound. Brad had asked himself the same question, too often. "My spiritual and family upbringing taught me forgiveness, and I never knew anyone more forgiving than my mother," Brad said. "I guess it's the left side of my brain that can understand the warped behavior of a sociopath or even a psychopath and forgive him." Brad paused. Knowing she would quote him, he wanted to make sure the words came out right. "Honestly, there are places inside of me untouched by any left-brain logic or my mother's spirit of forgiveness—the unforgiving shadows of my soul."

Brad smiled. He'd just hung up the phone from talking with Beth Montgomery, and had arranged a lunch meeting with her during his trip to New York City the following Tuesday for the Joedco annual stockholder's meeting. Brad had wished for more time with her, initially offering Beth dinner and a Broadway show, but her work took her on a trip to Cleveland later that day so he had to settle for lunch. He'd just entered her cell phone number into his PDA from the scribbled notation on his desktop when Sharon dashed into the office.

"How did your test go?" he asked.

"Okay, I guess," she replied, hurriedly, before changing the subject. "Earlier today, after you left, I came over here to do a workout." Sharon pointed toward the spiral staircase in the office that led to a fully equipped gym on the second floor. "I'd just finished on the treadmill and started using free weights when I heard a noise down here in the office."

Brad sat forward in his chair.

"Then I heard your brother on the phone."

"Yeah, I told him he could use the office. Not a problem."

"But I think he was talking with Ron Allessi," Sharon said, concern etched on her face.

Brad digested the information, sensing that it muddied an already cloudy picture forming in his mind.

"Your brother wasn't talking very much," Sharon continued. "I heard him say, 'Yes, Mr. Allessi,' twice. And he definitely mentioned 'Diane' a couple of times. After that conversation, he made a bunch of calls—five or six—a couple to his office, I think."

Brad pulled the phone in front of him, studied the digital display screen, and said, "Let's find out."

CHAPTER 20

Brad lit paper and kindling in the fireplace, enough to set a sturdy oak log ablaze and take the chill out of the office before their scheduled meeting with Nick Argostino. He gazed out the patio door at the sapphire blue sky in the last moments of twilight. Decorative outdoor lighting illuminated the edge of the patio and low-voltage spotlights brought the trees that edged his backyard into focus against the deep blue sky.

He heard a rustling in the hallway and turned, expecting to see Sharon. Instead, Andy swaggered into the office, and thrust a sheet of paper into his hands. "The corporate communications office e-mailed me this. Let me know what you think."

Andy rocked on his heels with his hands clasped behind his back. Brad knew he didn't enjoy waiting on other people.

Brad glanced at the paper and said, "That looks fine."

"But you didn't even read it."

"Yes, I did. It's the press release announcing our intention to seek Board approval to name you Chairman and CEO of Joedco. It works for me. I have papers I'd like you to read." Brad reached into a nearby box and retrieved a brown accordion portfolio. After untying the string from the bulging folder, he extracted a document several pages thick attached to a blue cover. "It's from Mother's will." Brad handed the yellowed pages to his brother, pointing to a section near the end of the document. "What do you make of that?"

Andy read silently, pulling his suit coat back and tucking his thumb inside his belt. "I never knew about any of this. According to this, if Mom predeceases Dad—which she did—then Gertrude Cole becomes her sole beneficiary. Is that Gertie Lindstrom?"

Brad sat at his makeshift desk. "I believe it is."

Andy snickered, and Brad scowled.

"Take a look at codicil number one of the will," Brad said. "When she established trust funds for each of us, it replaced the earlier provision."

Andy flipped through his mother's will, nodding as his eyes moved methodically across the page while his index finger marked progress down the length of the document. "It must have something to do with Gertie lending them the money to start the business."

"Do you have a copy of their agreement at the office?" Brad asked.

"I'm sure the legal department can locate one."

"Send it to me."

As Andy took out a small appointment book from his inside coat pocket and scribbled a note of reminder, Brad continued, "I need additional information."

"Shoot," Andy said, pencil still poised above the book.

"Get me a list of all the Joedco stock transactions for ten days before Mom and Lucy were kidnapped and ten days afterward."

"Why?"

"I'm following up on a lead you gave me this morning when you talked about how much Joedco stock had dropped after news of Mom's kidnapping and death."

"Yeah, that's a hell of a good idea." Andy folded the press release, returning it to his coat pocket along with the appointment book, then turned to leave. "Well, I'm off to a meeting. Barbara and the kids are visiting *her* parents tonight."

Brad stopped him. "Why do you have such a low opinion of Gertie Lindstrom?"

Andy turned back to him and scowled. "Because she was an anachronistic old fusspot. She made my work twice as difficult. I don't know how Dad could stand her all those years. He should've just bought out her interest and let her go. Gertie would write three-page memos asking for detailed justification on travel expenditures. She questioned every sole-source contract I ever wanted to write, in spite of the fact that because of patent restrictions on technology, most of the suppliers we dealt with were the only source available for our satellite components. She even demanded receipts for items that cost less than two bucks. The company was paying me to do far more important things than jump through her hoops."

Brad pushed back his chair and swiveled to watch Andy. "I'd like to hear more about those threatening notes you mentioned this morning."

Andy froze in mid-step. "What?"

"You heard me. What were you doing fifteen years ago that would make an anonymous person warn you that you wouldn't get away with it?"

Andy made eye contact with Brad.

"I was building a successful company, that's what I was doing. Fifteen years ago we weren't even on the Fortune 1000 list." Andy drew in a breath. "That's what I was doing."

"Did you fire somebody?" Brad asked.

"What's going on?"

"Did you fire anybody that might then send you threatening notes?"

"No. Not that I can recall." Andy threw his hands up in the air.

Brad folded his arms across his chest. "Were you fooling around with somebody's wife? Or, maybe somebody's wife was fooling around with you. Is that a better way to ask it?"

Andy erupted. "That's none of your damn business." His right hand curled into a fist.

"Your marriage to Diane was on the rocks long before Mom and Lucy were killed, wasn't it?"

"I plead my rights under the Fifth Amendment."

The phone rang. Brad let it ring three times before answering, then recognized his detective mentor on the other end of the line. "Hey, Nick."

"About our meeting tonight," he heard Nick Argostino say.

"Yeah, we're expecting you."

"There's a small glitch. I'm on-call tonight, and can't leave the city. Any chance you could come over here?"

"Oh, sure. I'm in the middle of a meeting right now," Brad said, noticing that Andy had loosened his tie. "I expect Sharon any minute and we'll be on the road within a half-hour. See you later."

Andy looked at his watch.

Brad cradled the phone. "How did you receive the notes?"

"My secretary brought them to me."

"Consuelo?"

"No. Ah . . . Roslyn."

"Roslyn Hunter?" Brad asked.

Andy bobbed his head. "Yes."

"I remember her," Brad said. "Did you ask where she'd gotten them?"

Andy developed a rhythm to his responses—flat and un-

181

emotional, belying his tense body language. "The first time, I didn't bother the second time."

"And her answer was?" Brad prompted him.

"She found it when she came into the office."

"I see," Brad said. "What's going on with you and Diane right now?"

"I don't know what you're talking about." Andy's voice seemed to go to a higher pitch.

"Let me be a little more specific," Brad said, suspicion in his voice. "You were talking about her on the phone this afternoon."

Andy flashed an angry look. Glancing around the room, he added, "You got this place bugged?"

"You made five calls from here this afternoon. One to my cell phone, three to your office in Houston, and one local call to the law firm of Blankenship, Trawler and Ivanic."

Andy laughed and threw his hands in the air. "You're making this up."

"Hardly. The desk phone displays a digital readout of the last ten calls made from it. Unless I'm mistaken you talked with Ronald Allessi, an associate with that law firm—your ex-wife's escort to Dad's funeral. And I'd be willing to bet that Diane figured prominently in that phone call. What's going on?"

"We have nothing more to talk about," Andy said coldly, apparently ready to exit the battlefield. "We're leaving early in the morning—Barbara, the kids, and me. I've already put in an order for a cab. No use inconveniencing anybody around here. We've got a 6:30 a.m. flight."

Brad got up from the desk and walked over to his brother. "Walk out if you want. This morning at the break-fast table *you* were the one talking about how important

182

perceptions are to the value of the company. Something isn't right and unless you tell me what's going on you can forget about issuing any press release on Friday."

Andy twisted his neck, as if trying to loosen the kinks, before saying, "Diane's threatening an exposé."

"Why? What did you do?"

Brad saw Sharon enter the office just as he and his brother stood nose to nose. Andy scowled in her direction.

"I didn't do anything." Andy sounded exasperated, adding, "Well, I take that back. She had enough dirt on me ten years ago that I agreed to a generous divorce settlement. She got child support for Byron until he's finished with college—even graduate school. And she got alimony for ten years, which is almost over. But I know her; that bitch's not satisfied. Now that Dad is gone, she thinks I'm rich," he pointed at Brad, "like you. She doesn't know I got cut out of the will, and believe me I have no interest in bragging about it. Diane's coming after me for everything she can get her hands on."

"You're meeting with her tonight?"

"No. Allessi."

Sharon spoke up, "Why don't you contact the attorney that handled your divorce? If it was a legal agreement, it would be binding on both parties." Her suggestion surprised Brad, since he knew Sharon had gotten the short end of the stick on her own divorce settlement.

Andy shook his head. "That would be too simple. I've got a bigger fleet of lawyers back in Houston than I have cars. But this is extortion. Diane's threatening to publish a tell-all-book that'll ruin me." Poking his brother on the shoulder, Andy added, "And you can sure as shit bet her book ain't gonna make you smell like roses either. Allessi made it sound like an overnight best-seller. He promised it would have everything—murder, sex, adultery, bastard kids, greed, betrayal . . . Did I mention sex?"

"What about libel laws?" Sharon directed her question to Brad.

Andy exhaled. "There'll be enough truth in it to prevent it from being libelous. Hell, you don't run a twelve billion dollar business without having a pile of shit accumulate at your back door." An apt metaphor, Brad thought, for his brother. "Anybody who even thinks they were treated unfairly will be happy to be quoted in the book. They'll cite newspaper clippings, legal filings, divorce papers; hell, they can do an Internet search and get enough material."

"An exposé might not be all that bad," Sharon suggested. "There've been enough trashy articles and books written about politicians, but the garbage doesn't stick."

Andy laughed. "That's one area where government is behind the corporate world. The leader of a Fortune 100 company has seldom survived a personal scandal. Oh, there'll be a few early calls of support, but then the phone lines will buzz among the Board members. My demise as CEO won't necessarily be quick—death by a thousand cuts. And in the end, I'll be expected to fall on my own sword."

Brad sank into the freshly tanned leather of the sofa and closed his eyes. "A book," he repeated. "Have you talked directly with Diane about any of this?"

Andy grimaced. "I haven't talked with Diane in ten and a half years. Why would I want to start now?"

"What about your son?" Sharon asked.

"I don't talk with Byron about *her* either." Andy flailed his arms. "Which is more than I can say about her and what she's told him about me. My secretary arranges visitations, and lawyers talk with lawyers about alimony and child support."

"Your lawyers have dealt with Allessi before?" Brad asked.

"No." He shook his head. "Her attorneys are in Haverford, not the city."

"What time is your meeting?" Brad asked, glancing at the clock on his office wall.

"Nine at the Rosemont Country Club."

Brad stood up. "Go see Mr. Allessi. Find out what he wants. Just don't agree to anything."

Andy buttoned his shirt and repositioned his tie.

Patting Andy on the back, Brad reminded him, "Stopping extortion is my line of work. Let me handle this. Call me when you're back in Houston to let me know how the meeting went."

Andy grabbed his wool overcoat and threw it over his arm preparing to head out the door.

"And another thing," Brad called after him, "I'd recommend sticking with the club soda. Don't have any liquor, even if he buys."

Andy nodded and flashed thumbs up.

CHAPTER 21

He and Sharon left the office, walking the short distance to Brad's car, as a brisk wind blew across the driveway. When Brad unlocked the car's doors with the remote, Sharon pulled her coat tightly about her and raced to the passenger seat. Brad paused by the driver's door, gazing at the star-filled sky and found Orion, his compass to the universe. He'd had his first joyful encounter with constellations at summer camp when he was twelve years old, learning to spot Perseus, Andromeda, Ursa Major and Minor. Orion was his favorite; so easy to find Orion's belt, even on a murky night. Thinking of the stars and their distance in terms of light-years always gave him a sense of unease, overwhelming his brain, like static spoiling a broadcast tune. He took one last look at Orion's belt before getting behind the wheel, realizing once more how tiny his role was in God's unfathomable plan.

The car made good time in the post-rush-hour traffic, and Brad punched up the soundtrack to *Shakespeare in Love* on his CD changer. Noticing that Sharon hadn't spoken for a few minutes, Brad said, "You're quiet this evening."

"Just thinking," she said.

"Worried about how you did on the test?"

Sharon shrugged. "Yes and no."

Sharon stretched out in her seat, leaning her head back. Brad planned to ask another question but glanced over and saw that she had closed her eyes. He smiled as he remembered that's exactly how she looked at the end of the first case they'd worked together—reclining in a first-class seat on US Airways on the way home to Philadelphia.

Hired by a woman in Bucks County, Pennsylvania, to find out what her husband had done with $40,000 in a joint savings account, that case took a different tack when the woman was found stabbed to death. Brad immediately suspected the husband, a traveling salesman who spent two weeks of every month on the road. But he had an alibi from a hotel in Pittsburgh. The police arrested the woman's seventeen-year-old son, Lon, already on probation for stealing a car. Though the boy denied having anything to do with the murder, investigators had found droplets on a pair of his jeans that matched his mother's blood.

Sharon Porter had been his probation officer, and thought the young man incapable of murder. At the time, Brad was still getting used to having an associate in his agency. But Nick Argostino had convinced him, with the double-barreled argument that she was homeless and needed a place to live and would be a competent addition. Brad had misgivings on the latter. Sharon finally persuaded Brad to find holes in the father's alibi. They traveled to Pittsburgh and examined hotel records and receipts—discovering that three of the husband's room service receipts were never signed for. Interviewing wait staff, they learned that in each instance—dinner, a midnight order of beer, and breakfast the following morning—a man's voice had asked for the deliveries to be left outside the door, saying he wasn't dressed. A five-dollar tip had been slipped under the door each time, which only succeeded in improving the memory of the hotel's staff. A maid, who said she'd seen two different men coming and going from the room, ID'd a photo of the husband and helped produce a composite picture of the second man. Hotel security recognized the man from his picture, a two-bit local con man. When questioned, the man said he'd been paid $20,000 just to hang out and order room service. The husband was subsequently arrested and convicted of his wife's murder. Brad, impressed with Sharon's passion for justice, promptly offered her a job.

Brad pulled into the driveway outside of Nick's two-story Dutch colonial on Ardleigh Street in the Mt. Airy section of Philadelphia, triggering security lights mounted on the gable end of the detached garage. Emerging from the car, he heard a dog barking furiously, and the barking continued until Brad rang the doorbell—then intensified.

"Randy, come and get this dog." Brad heard Nick's muffled shout behind the door.

The door opened and Nick stood, slightly out of breath, holding his black and white Border collie on a short leash. "Thanks for coming over." The dog stopped barking, but gave both of them a good sniff and sat panting as Nick closed the door.

"It's about time." Nick grumbled to his teenage son, a gangly lad with his dad's coloring and freckles—but no purple hair, eyebrow piercings, or other overt signs of rebellion against a father who served as captain of detectives with the Philadelphia police force. Randy was only five or six years old when Brad had last seen him, and now stood nearly as tall as his father.

"Wait a minute, Randy," Nick said, as his son led the dog away. "Don't dash off. I want you to meet Brad Frame and Sharon Porter."

"Hey," his son said softly, flashing a wave before hurrying out of the room.

Nick shook his head, but also wore fatherly pride as he watched his son disappear.

Brad smiled. "He's workin' on developing quiet strength. Just like his dad."

Nick sighed. "I hope so. Right now I'm just praying he lives until his eighteenth birthday. It's tough raising a teenager." Nick led them into a spacious living room, pointing to a colonial-style rocker where they could drape their coats. Brad spotted the natural stone fireplace with its raised hearth and timber mantel, recalling how many times he and Nick had conferred there during the investigation of the murders of his mother and sister. The furnishings hadn't changed much in the last decade; Brad noticed a fresh slipcover added to the sofa, and the same drop-leaf maple coffee table sitting on a now faded braided rug.

Nick wrapped his arm around Brad's shoulder in an after-the-gridiron-game-clinch, asking, "How you doin'?"

"Fine." Brad realized it was the first he'd seen Nick since the detective and Sharon had confronted him. "I'm trying to stay focused. I appreciate what you did for me last week." Turning to Sharon, he added, "What you both did."

"I'm sorry I couldn't get to your dad's funeral. I had to work," Nick explained. "Can I get you anything . . . beer, soda?"

Brad shook his head and settled into a seat on the sofa as Nick glanced at Sharon.

"Hey, congratulations," Nick said. "You got the highest raw score on the police exam they've seen in the last two years. I'd flagged your application and they called me late this afternoon with the good news. There might be guys with veteran's preference who'll show up higher on the list, but we won't have any trouble reaching your name."

Sharon beamed. "Wow," she said.

"Yeah, that's great," Brad said, trying to disguise how conflicted he felt at Sharon's good news.

"I assume you already met the physical requirements," Nick said.

"I had to reschedule," she said, then after sitting next to Brad on the sofa, Sharon abruptly changed the subject. "What kind of information have you got for us?"

Nick flashed Brad a suspicious look, as if Brad had managed to curb Sharon's enthusiasm for the police job. Brad shrugged. He knew Sharon's test was rescheduled for the following day, and was surprised she hadn't provided the details, as well as by her generally tepid response.

"I've learned a few things that might interest you," Nick began, sitting in a nearby armchair. "Wilkie's partner, Eddie Baker, was incarcerated at Graterford. The Department of Corrections likes to keep guys separated that were convicted of the same crime, and Wilkie did *his* time at SCI Pittsburgh before the execution. I talked to an old Marine buddy of mine who works at Graterford and asked him to see what he could find out. Seems like Wilkie must've been the brains of the pair, if you can imagine that. Eddie got the nickname *'Snail'* because he was slow." Nick tapped the side of his head. "Elevator barely made it to the second floor. My buddy reported that because of his mental capacity and size—Baker stood five foot four and weighed about a hundred pounds with his clothes on—he was easy prey. Baker got protection for his first three and a half years in prison from a big oaf outta Germantown—in exchange for you know what. But then that guy got released, and Snail was fair game again. I'm sure somebody was after his skinny ass every time he turned around. The story inside the prison is that he couldn't take being fucked over all the time—literally. Eddie killed himself. He wasn't done in by anybody."

Nick's Border collie ran into the room trailing his leash behind him. Nick yelled for his son, "Randy, the dog got loose again. Come and get him." The dog crouched contentedly next to Nick wagging his white-tipped tail. Nick frowned and shook his head. "You know who the master is around here, don't you? Aloysius!" Nick said, pointing at the dog.

"That's a funny name for a dog," Brad said. "Where'd you come up with that?"

"We got the dog about eight years ago, back when I worked for a Captain who used to drive me crazy—all the time sending reports back to me asking for a redo. A stickler for details, the Captain always wanted *more* information. As a puppy, the dog used to bring me anything that wasn't nailed down, a newspaper, socks, it didn't have to be a bone for him to fetch it. My wife heard me complaining about Captain Aloysius returning paperwork to me all the time, and she suggested naming the dog after him. Then anytime I had a bad day at work I could come home, call out his name, look that dog in the eye, and say whatever I wanted. He never minded, and he still loves me. Don't you, boy?" Aloysius barked when Nick reached down and patted him on the head. "After I got promoted to Captain, I wondered how many of my officers named *their* dogs Nick." He threw his head back and roared.

Brad and Sharon joined in the laughter. Refocusing on the case, Brad asked, "Did the autopsy results support the conclusion of suicide in Eddie Baker's case?"

"My buddy reviewed his entire file. The autopsy showed no evidence of foul play," Nick said. "But something happened shortly before his death that may help explain Baker's actions. The prison got their first official notice of execution for Baker after the routine appeals process was concluded. Prison officials had to go through a formal notification to the prisoner that the Governor had set an execution date. How was Baker to know the Governor we had back then wasn't in a hurry to execute anybody? But the Governor's office still went through the motions; issuing more press releases about death warrants than actual warrants, so the public would think he was tough on crime."

"Baker hung himself, right?" Brad inquired.

"More like strangled." Nick looked grim. "Official cause of death was asphyxiation due to strangulation. According to the prison's internal report—my friend saw the file—Baker claimed to be sick and they let him stay in his bunk when most of the inmates were taken out for time in the exercise yard. Apparently Baker had the top bunk. When they found him, the bed was up against the right side of the cell, and pulled away from the rear wall by about eighteen inches." Nick's hands moved as he talked, demonstrating the location of the bunk bed and the gap at the rear of the bed. "Baker stuffed clothes and pillows in his top bunk and draped a towel over the back of the bunk so he couldn't be seen. Then he tore a pillowcase into strips and tied those together to form a noose." Nick spread his arms wide indicating a strip of about four feet in length. "One end was tied to the top bunk rail and the other around his neck. He probably would've just gone limp so the noose tightened around his neck and cut off his air. Not a pretty way to die. He was bare-naked when they found him, too. Maybe he was trying to send a message to all those guys who had their way with him."

Brad closed his eyes, trying to picture the scene, then found himself shaking his head.

"You don't buy it?" Nick asked.

Brad opened his eyes. "I'm remembering Wilkie's note and what it said about Eddie talking and getting killed. Doesn't seem like that part is true."

"Wilkie may have *believed* it was true. Word of a death in

another prison would spread fast. It's possible a guard made a smart-ass remark to Wilkie about it. Guards—and cops—do shit like that. Not that it ever happens on the Philadelphia police force." Nick winked.

Three short tones sounded.

"Hold on," Nick said, reaching for his beeper and examined the message. "I have to take this call. I don't know where my son went, but I'll take the dog with me."

Nick left the room with Aloysius reluctantly in tow. "Let me see if Ruth can get us some refreshments." As he passed through the entry hall he shouted up the stairs to his wife, "Honey, can you take care of our guests a minute?"

Nick disappeared before Brad could object.

A few minutes later Ruth Argostino entered the living room. She'd added a few pounds since he'd last seen her, but had the same expressive eyes and olive skin. Brad stood up. "Hi, Ruth. Nick didn't need to trouble you."

They hugged.

"It's not a bother," she said, sizing him up. "Welcome, stranger. Nick told me you'd be visiting. I wasn't being anti-social, but I've been studying for a re-certification test at work."

"We don't want to hold you up," Brad said.

Ruth Argostino shook her head. "I needed a break."

"I'd like you to meet my associate, Sharon Porter."

Ruth extended her hand. "Hi. I feel like I already know you. My husband talks about you all the time and what a great addition you'll be to the department."

Sharon blushed, while Brad felt emptiness and knew he would soon have to re-group at his detective agency.

They heard a low rumbling noise approaching, sounding like low flying aircraft, but passing quickly. "What was that?" Sharon asked.

"Oh," Ruth said, after a moment, "that's the Chestnut Hill train. The tracks are right behind our property. It runs about every fifty minutes this time of night. I'm so used to them, I barely notice any more."

Nick returned, apologized for his absence and thanked his wife for being a gracious hostess. Ruth hugged Brad tightly, whispering in his ear, "Come back soon."

After they resumed their seats in the living room, Nick continued, "I found out Wilkie and Baker met at Bensalem Heights' YDC."

"YDC?" Brad asked.

"Youth development center," Sharon explained, "a juvenile institution north of Philly. I recommended a lot of kids for placement there."

"Wilkie had a juvenile record as long as your arm," Nick explained. "He was a city kid, grew up on the West Side, never had much adult supervision. His record included burglaries, car thefts—mostly property crimes. On the other hand, Baker came from the mining country of northeast Pennsylvania—product of a broken home. His mother couldn't control him, and his rap sheet started with drugs, assaults, and graduated to a whole series of violent crimes including rape. Baker had a sick sadistic streak in him, and I'm sure he was the one who committed the brutalities in the kidnapping case. How those two paired up is a mystery to me."

"Maybe Wilkie became Baker's protector at the YDC," Sharon said.

Nick nodded.

"Odd that the sadistic one needed protection," Brad said.

"I'm no shrink, but he probably got off hurting his victims—a way of getting back for his own victimization. When they got out of Bensalem Heights, those two stuck together," Nick explained. "Before they were nabbed for the murders, they both worked downtown near Penn Station—night shift cleaning crew—within a block of your dad's office."

"Was there any contact between them when they were in prison?" Brad asked.

Nick shook his head. "I can't imagine how, with them three hundred miles apart."

Brad moved forward in his seat. "I appreciate the information, Nick."

"Wait," Nick said, holding up his hand. "According to his case file, when asked why he was in prison, Baker claimed he was too greedy. When the intake officer wanted a better explanation, Baker said he made a '$5,000 mistake'."

"Hmmm," Brad stroked his chin as he digested the information. "Wilkie said they were paid. They probably split $10,000 and spent most of it before they were caught. That means someone else netted $490,000 in ransom money."

"And," Nick said, leaning forward with his hands on his knees, "I learned who instructed Superintendent Dolewski not to send you a copy of Wilkie's list of scripture references." Nick wore a wide grin. "The directions came from the Deputy Director for Public Affairs at the Department of Corrections."

"Jeez, a guy like that would have to take his feet off the desk long enough to butt in to the Superintendent's business?" Brad commented.

Nick lowered his voice. "You didn't hear this from me, but it's just possible that it *might* have been because of a call he got from State Senator Violet Wesley's office."

Flash bulbs popped in Brad's brain, and the grin on

Nick's face confirmed his suspicions.

"From the Senator's office, not the Senator directly?" Brad asked.

"Gotta turn up the volume on this hearing aid." Nick fiddled with an imaginary amplifier behind his ear. "I could've sworn I heard you say Senator's office, and I know we weren't having any conversations about any Senator." Nick's belly rippled as he suppressed a guffaw.

"Right," Brad said, playing along with Nick's confidential tone. "Let's see, what were we talking about? Ah, Herb Trawler at Blankenship, Trawler and Ivanic, has a sister, doesn't he?"

Nick nodded. "Uh huh."

Brad connected the dots. "I think her married name is Wesley. One more reason why we're gonna have another visit with Ron Allessi."

CHAPTER 22

Brad was saving a document on his computer when Sharon descended into the office from the second-floor gym sipping from a 20-oz. bottled water. From her damp T-shirt, it looked like she'd had quite a workout.

"Did I hear you talking with your brother?" she asked.

"You do some of your best spying from up there, don't you?" Brad said, and then caught Sharon rolling her eyes. As her face reddened he clicked the computer into sleep mode. "Yup, Andy's back in Houston, but I got an update on his meeting last night with Ron Allessi."

Sharon pulled a wooden side chair up to Brad's make-shift desk and straddled it, then glanced at her watch before saying, "Do tell."

"Andy said they puffed on a few cigars together in the Tack Room of the Rosewood Country Club. Allessi was charming and undemanding, but arrived with a manila envelope, which lay in front of him the whole time. Apparently the attorney was very low key, and kept talking about how difficult things had been for Diane; how she hoped Andrew would understand her needs, etcetera."

"Sounds like he had your brother on the hook and was reeling him in," Sharon said.

"Yeah, Andy's not a good poker player," Brad said. "I would have never asked what was in the envelope, but when Andy did, Allessi slid it in his direction and invited him to open it. It contained the outline and chapter of a book entitled *Demons of Bryn Mawr*."

"I can hardly wait to see the movie."

Brad laughed. "My brother swore he hadn't had anything to drink. But when I asked how bad it was, Andy's response was, 'I swallowed the olive.' As you can guess, Andy and I are the demons. The synopsis portrayed him as a corporate climber who doesn't care who he steps on or climbs over to get to the top."

"Dare I ask?" Sharon said.

"I'm the brother coasting through life on good looks and family money."

A devilish grin came to Sharon's face.

"What are you thinking?" Brad asked.

"Nothing," she said, coyly. "I'm just wondering who'll play you in the movie."

"Oh, stop. There won't be any movie. Not if I can do anything about it."

"Did Andy read chapter one?" Sharon asked.

"He could only stand reading a couple of pages, before he threw it back at Allessi. Apparently it started off with him abandoning his wife and seven-year-old son."

"Can he fax you a copy?" Sharon inquired. Brad noticed she glanced at her watch again.

"No. Allessi kept it. I asked Andy if there was an author's name on the synopsis or chapter, and he said no."

"Interesting."

"Yeah, that's what I thought." Brad pushed back from his seat and walked over to the French doors. "According to my brother, Allessi never said anything explicit. He used phrases like 'generous offer' and 'reasonable settlement.' He told Andy that he'd gladly assist in drafting a new alimony agreement."

Brad's fax machine began to whir.

"What time is your physical endurance test?" Brad asked.

"One o'clock," Sharon said. "I can't believe Allessi actually mentioned alimony."

"He didn't. Andy admitted he had used the word first, so that the lawyer only had to respond, 'If you need help drafting a new one . . .' Andy figured Allessi was worried that I'd wired him up for the meeting."

"Maybe you should have," Sharon said.

"He may not be the world's smartest lawyer, but Allessi knows he'd be disbarred if he were caught in any extortion scheme."

Brad walked over to the fax machine, as it finished spewing out three pages.

Brad studied the document. "Hmm. Interesting."

"What is it?" Sharon asked.

"It's the list I requested of major trading in Joedco stock—five thousand shares or more—during the period from ten days before Mom and Lucy's kidnapping until ten days after their death became public. There are a couple of interesting names on this list. Diane Panella-Frame sold 65,000 shares of stock a week before the kidnapping. Hiram Gibbons bought 32,000 shares." Brad flipped through to the back of the list as he walked back over to his desk. "Four days after my mom's funeral Gertrude Lindstrom bought 40,000 shares."

"How much money are we talking about?" Sharon inquired.

"Andy said the stock was selling at 12 and ¾ before the news." Brad circled back around to his desk top, reactivated his computer, and clicked on a calculator program. He punched in a few numbers, then announced, "Diane sold $830,000 worth of stock."

Sharon mouthed the word "wow," then added, "I wonder what prompted her to do that?"

"Gertie mentioned that Joedco was getting ready to purchase Diane's father's company," Brad explained. "Maybe Diane figured Joedco stock was headed downward after the acquisition. But I'll ask her about it this afternoon. I called Diane and told her I wanted to meet with her, and she invited me for tea."

His ex-sister-in-law, Diane Panella-Frame, lived in Haverford, another moneyed enclave along Philadelphia's Main Line. It had been a long time since Brad had been to the home that she once shared with his brother, located on the crest of a hill at the end of a long winding driveway. But he found it easily enough, recognizing the English Tudor–style design with brick facing on the lower level and rough stucco and dark wooden timbers on the second floor, dormers, and gables.

Brad parked his car in the driveway and walked to the front door where a maid in black uniform, and with ample cleavage, received him.

"Monsieur Frame, Madame is expecting you," she said, in a thick accent.

Brad chuckled to himself. He'd known Diane for more than twenty-five years, and no French maid or other ostentatious displays could alter the indelible impression she'd made on his family years earlier. For all of the house's old country charm, the interior was contemporary. The maid escorted him across a white tile floor, past white walls adorned only with minimalist prints, down a short flight of white carpeted steps leading to an all-white living room, framed on one side with a glass-walled view of an English country garden with tulips just coming into bud. Amidst the plush white furniture, white-enameled light fixtures, and white drapes, the only splash of color in the room was

Diane Panella-Frame wearing a smartly tailored teal suit and ivory blouse and seated at the end of an L-shaped sectional sofa. She stood to welcome him.

"Brad, how nice of you to come to tea," she said, extending her hand. "It's been too long." Her eyes studied the length of him. "You look like you're taking care of yourself."

"I am, thank you, Diane," Brad said, clasping her hand with both of his.

Brad marveled again at the similarities between Diane and Andrew's second wife, Barbara. Diane stood with her feet in the second position, and Brad remembered how she used to brag about her ballet training. Her blonde hair, meticulously arranged in curls and waves, seemed lacquered in place, and since she looked no older than when he'd last stood that close to her more than a decade earlier, Brad imagined she might have had a few cosmetic surgeries. She pointed to the sofa, inviting him to sit.

"What would you like to drink?"

Before he could respond, she said, "Let me order something special for you, Brad." Diane summoned her maid with a crystal bell. "I know what you like," she purred.

The maid quickly appeared, and Diane said, "Marie, two flutes of Champagne et Framboise."

The maid nodded. "Oui, Madame."

Brad smiled. He'd first met Diane at a Philadelphia area frat party that a buddy invited him to when he was back home from Princeton during spring break. A bring-your-own-bottle affair, most of the partygoers brought six-packs of beer or fifths of rum to lace their Cokes, but Diane had a picnic basket filled with raspberry-flavored Champagne. She was stunningly beautiful, and he didn't mind sharing a few glasses of Champagne with her over a few hours in a dimly lit lounge of the frat house. Later, after she'd met and married Andy, Brad had learned that she kept embellishing the story of the one and only evening she'd spent with him.

Brad winked at her. "You remembered."

"Of course, how could I forget? I always said that I married the wrong brother." She sighed. "How is Andrew? I saw him at the funeral. He looked well."

"The business keeps him very busy."

"Andrew always was a workaholic. Particularly when some young secretary could be persuaded to stay late at the office." The sweetness in her voice disguised the barb.

"Don't go there, Diane," Brad said firmly. "He is my brother, and . . ."

She held a finger up to her glossy lips painted a peachy-pink. "Shhh. I promise I'll be kind. I don't want to spoil such a nice visit."

Marie returned pushing a fancy silver cart containing the drinks and tea sandwiches. The maid draped a napkin on Brad's lap before handing him the flute, then Brad chose a white-bread triangular-shaped sandwich from an offered plate of goodies.

Diane waited until Brad had eaten his sandwich before resuming their conversation. "You know Andy and I don't speak to each other."

"That's what I understand," Brad said off-handedly, signaling his intention not to follow her further on the subject of his brother.

Diane wasn't done. "I really won't complain about Andrew. After all, he gave me Byron, the light of my life. He is the sweetest, most considerate young man. A good student. Not out chasing skirts all the time like his father. Every mother should be so lucky to have a son like Byron."

After watching Byron chasing Sharon, Brad suspected he

had a few more of his dad's chromosomes than Diane was aware.

"What can I do for you today, Brad?" Diane asked.

"I'm looking at some company transactions from eleven years ago."

"Let's see," Diane said, dimpling her cheek with a finger, "I would have been in junior high school back then." She giggled and sipped her raspberry-flavored Champagne.

"Specifically, Joedco bought your dad's business," Brad explained. "What can you tell me about that?"

"Daddy was getting ready to retire. For some reason, I can't explain why, Daddy always liked Andrew."

"Diane!" Brad raised his arms in exasperation.

"All right, Brad," she said, demurely. "One night they— Daddy and Andrew—got to talking and the subject of Joedco buying Daddy's business came up. Then Andrew talked to the Professor and he liked the idea.

"The Professor?" Brad looked puzzled.

"Your dad. That's what everyone called him."

"I knew he taught at Penn," Brad said, "but I didn't know the title had stuck." The revelation reminded Brad how detached he had been from the family business. In the decade before his father's stroke, he hadn't visited the corporate headquarters once. His strong memories of visits dated to childhood, before he would have grasped the significance of the nickname *professor*.

"Daddy's company wasn't worth very much," Diane continued. "They weren't on the cutting edge of technology, but Andrew felt that they had some talented engineers. I think they paid $30 million, which was quite a bit of money back then. Daddy was happy with the agreement. He was ready to retire to Florida."

"Is he still in Florida?" Brad walked over to the serving

cart, selecting two more bite-sized sandwiches.

"Yes. My parents have a place in St. Petersburg."

"At about the same time, you sold 65,000 shares of Joedco stock. What was the reason for the sale?" Brad asked.

Diane shrugged her shoulders. "You'll have to talk with Andrew. I'm sure if we sold stock it was something Andrew wanted to do."

Brad set his Champagne glass on the coffee table and turned toward her. "But the stock was in your name."

"All the stock was in my name. Andrew wanted it that way," she explained. "We still had to file all the disclosure forms on any trade, but he thought it caused less commotion if everything was in my name. Actually that worked to my advantage during the divorce, giving me leverage."

Brad leaned back in his seat. "How well did you know Gertrude Lindstrom?"

"Quite well. I still see Gertie and Em every six months or so." Diane looked worried. "It's a shame what's happened to them."

Brad said, optimistically, "Gertie seems to be able to maneuver quite well in her wheelchair."

She shook her head. "I think medical bills are the cause of it all."

Perplexed, Brad asked, "The cause of what?"

"The bankruptcy. The Lindstroms are filing for bankruptcy."

"I haven't heard anything about it," Brad said. "I talked with them last week."

"It just happened yesterday. Gertie called me, poor thing, and I told her we would have to get together soon."

"What can you tell me about Andy's relationship with Gertie?" Brad asked.

"She may have been the only woman in the office that wasn't his girlfriend at one time or another." Diane raised her hands in front of her face, looking like a damsel-in-distress from an old silent movie. "I'll stop with the digs at Andrew. Really I will. I know there was a lot of tension between them. After the Professor—your dad—made Andrew the Chief Operating Officer, he and Gertie butted heads all the time."

"When was that? I wasn't very engaged in the business back then." Brad added, "I'm still not."

"I think Byron was about four . . . maybe fourteen or fifteen years ago. Gertie was the only person who would stand up to him, but he gradually froze her out of the business. Em once told me that Andrew would frequently call her into his office at seven o'clock at night, just as she was getting ready to leave for the evening and tell her that he needed a report by nine o'clock the next morning. According to Em, she would sometimes stay at the office until midnight to finish the work. Gertie didn't know how to say no. Gradually, Andrew put more layers of management between the two of them. Finally, when he moved the business to Houston, she retired. It's funny. She doesn't seem to be bitter about it. When we get together and I make barbs about Andrew, she makes it clear she doesn't like me criticizing him. Just like you, Brad."

"Honey, the hot tub is ready." Brad heard the voice before seeing its owner. Ronald Allessi sauntered into the room wearing only a white terry cloth towel around his waist—at least he didn't clash with the room decor. His body was toned and his chest wore a thick matte of black hair. "I'm sorry, I didn't realize you had company."

"Ron, come here sugar," she said, beckoning him to her. "I want you to meet Brad Frame, my ex-brother-in-law."

She grabbed his elbow and played with the dark fur on his arm.

"I'm not exactly dressed for meeting important people," he said, showing no embarrassment nor any sign of recognition from their previous meeting.

Brad stared at him, but Allessi never flinched.

"Don't be silly, Ron." Diane put one arm around his waist and pulled him closer. "Brad isn't important." Correcting herself, she said, "Well, I mean he's almost like family."

"Exactly," Brad quickly agreed.

Diane gazed adoringly at Ron, while her manicured hands seductively stroked his thigh through the terry cloth. Soon the outline of an erection became visible under the towel.

"I'm sorry to interrupt your meeting," Allessi said as he broke free of Diane's grasp, and tightened the towel around his hips. "I'll see you in a little bit, honey." Her eyes followed his every move until he had disappeared at the end of the hall.

"Isn't he just scrumptious?" Diane gushed.

Scrumptious wasn't the word Brad was thinking. He stood up. "I don't want to keep you from the hot tub, Diane. I appreciate your hospitality."

"Anytime, Brad. I've got some girlfriends at the country club I'd love to introduce you to sometime. You've got so much going for you."

Brad winced. "Thanks. I'll keep that in mind."

CHAPTER 23

Andy's voice boomed over the speakerphone in Brad's office. "In Tokyo, the Nikkei's got us up two points. On the New York exchange we're up a half, but we'll do better later today."

"Uh huh," Brad responded as he positioned the leather desk pad on top of his newly restored oak partner's desk. The refinishing company had delivered it early that morning, and he could hardly tell the restored panels from the original desk. Excited to have the desk back, it was his father's legacy that he prized the most.

The treadmill in the gym above him silenced as Sharon finished her morning workout, and it dawned on him that a health club membership would make a great gift to congratulate her on the new job with the Philadelphia police department. He scribbled a note of reminder.

"Our communications department leaked word of today's press release," Andy continued. "*The Houston Chronicle* noted it yesterday in its business section, but *The Wall Street Journal* gave it a front-page blurb this morning. I checked the early edition of *The Philadelphia Inquirer* on its Web site, but there was no mention of it. The press conference is at 11 a.m. Eastern Time. You can watch a Web broadcast of it on the Joedco site." Nothing enthused his brother more than announcing deals.

Brad stared at the phone impatiently.

"Yeah, Andy that's great. I hope it goes well. Thanks, by the way, for the list you sent me of stock transactions, but I've got a couple of questions I need to ask you, and I'm still waiting for a copy of the legal agreement Dad had with Gertie Lindstrom."

"Hold on," Andy said, barely covering the mouthpiece on his end, as Brad heard him bellow orders for a copy of the agreement. "They'll fax it to you within twenty minutes."

"Thanks." Brad continued, "Diane said *you* were the one responsible for the sale of 65,000 shares of Joedco stock. It was in her name, but you ordered it sold in the week before the kidnapping. Why?"

There was a pause on the other end of the line.

"I don't like the tone in your voice," Andrew said.

"Let me try again." Brad repeated his question in a monotone. "Why did you sell 65,000 shares—"

"Don't be cute," Andy said. "I heard you the first time. Look, I had another investment opportunity. A buddy of mine was starting an alternative energy company, and he needed investors. He had promising research on a chemical-based electrical cell. His stock opened at a buck fifty a share and I figured I'd get in on the ground floor. It went bust a couple years later. Nothing more to it. No sinister plot, since I know that's where your mind was heading."

Sharon descended the spiral staircase, pulling a cotton robe on over her shorts and T-shirt. Brad mouthed the word "Andy" and pointed toward the speakerphone. He got up from his desk and paced around the room, raising his voice so he could be heard. Sharon stood listening to their conversation.

"I'll tell you what I was thinking, Andy," Brad said. "The other day you talked about the impact of the kidnapping and murder on the value of Joedco stock, but I'm wondering if the market wouldn't be just as affected by word that one of its officers was selling a large block of stock."

"Don't get a hard-on brother, it wasn't that big a trade."

Brad folded his arms across his chest and shook his head. "Maybe not by today's standards, but eleven years ago?"

"Nah, no big deal." Andrew changed the subject. "What about Ron Allessi? Did you find out anything more when you met with Diane?"

"Let's just say that Ron is probably in somebody's hot tub right now."

"What?" Andy said. "I don't understand."

"Relax. I'll handle this. One chapter does not a book make."

Andy replied, "Huh?" just as Brad lifted and then replaced the handset terminating the speakerphone call.

Sharon mopped her brow with a towel.

"You get any more toned," Brad said, "and they'll have you doing all the heavy lifting down at the police department."

Sharon tossed her hair at him and headed for the door.

"Make sure you're ready by noon," Brad said, "the Lindstroms are coming over. Oh, how's that job description coming?"

"There's a draft on the computer. It's titled *Irreplaceable*."

Brad glanced back at her and smiled. "I already know that."

Sharon turned back to him. "Your brother . . ." she began, haltingly. "He's so different from you. I'm surprised you never suspected he was adopted."

"I never did," Brad said. "He looks like cousins on my mother's side of the family. I remember thinking *I* was adopted—or wishing I was."

"Why?" she asked.

"I'm not sure. Maybe because I was the kid in the middle. As the oldest, Andy demanded a lot of attention—"

Sharon interrupted. "I can see that."

"By the time Lucy came along—first girl in the family and all—my parents spent all their time doting on her. I used to imagine my *real* parents showing up and taking me off to a cabin in the woods."

"Funny," Sharon said. "I practically grew up in a cabin in the woods. I never thought about being adopted, but my daydream was always to someday be spirited away to a mansion like this."

The deli delivered lunch at 11:45. Sharon helped Brad set silverware, dishes and napkins on the table in the solarium, at the northwest corner of the house. Promptly at noon he heard the Lindstrom's van in his driveway. He helped Em set up a portable ramp so Gertie's wheelchair could negotiate the two steps from his driveway to the entrance porch.

"I appreciate you coming over on such short notice, Gertie," Brad said as he led the way to their luncheon spot. "Our last meeting over at your place was interrupted with the news of Dad's death."

Gertie abruptly stopped her wheelchair. "A meeting," she said, "I thought this was just a social occasion."

"Of course. Think of it as a social occasion with a few questions," Brad said in a reassuring tone.

Gertie resumed forward motion in her wheelchair, with Em hovering protectively behind her. She wore a floral print blouse and black slacks. A knit shawl covered her shoulders and paralyzed right arm.

The gazebo-shaped solarium was attached to the northeast corner of the mansion. Brad remembered when his father had hired architects to incorporate the solarium into their Georgian-style home. Construction started the same fall that Andy left for a private school in Virginia. Brad had watched the workman building the octagonal-shaped structure, with wide windows separated by teak mullions, and cushioned window seats ringing the interior. Brad hoped the sun would warm the room to Gertie's satisfaction, even as he noticed colorful patterns of light on the white tablecloth, cast by the stained glass windows in the solarium's cupola. Brad removed one of the four chairs so Gertrude's wheelchair would fit at the table.

"You've both met Sharon before," Brad said, gesturing to his assistant.

"Yes," Gertie said, as she and Em nodded in Sharon's direction. "It was nice of you to invite us, Brad."

Em lifted the napkin from his wife's plate and placed it in her lap.

"This is such a beautiful room," Gertie continued, "I remember your mother used to sit here to do her needlepoint. It's such a sunny place in the afternoon."

Brad dished up salad and quiche, while Sharon poured glasses of iced tea. Brad agreed the room was warm and cheerful. He watched the sun filtering through the limbs of the beech trees, whose buds had just opened to reveal the delicate green of spring.

"You should get married, Brad." She added, "A wife would appreciate you so much."

Brad laughed. "You've been talking to Aunt Harriet."

"Just like you appreciate me, right dear?" Em asked, the pink of his face contrasting with his white hair. Dark capillaries near the surface of his cheeks matched his burgundy-colored tie.

Gertie looked at Em adoringly, smiling on the left side of

her mouth. "This is just like when we used to meet for lunch downtown. Once a week," she explained, "we'd get together for salad at one of the underground restaurants at Suburban Station."

"Penn Station," Em corrected her.

"It wasn't fancy, mind you, but it was nice to visit with each other in the middle of the day. When I could steal some extra time we'd walk underground and come up on the other side of City Hall and visit the old Wanamaker's store."

Brad nodded. Wanamaker's was a Philadelphia tradition, and he recalled the annual holiday pilgrimage when his parents took him to their toy department.

Gertrude sighed, and rubbed her leg with her good hand. "I know Em appreciated the chance to get out of the house today. I'm a little hard to manage for long distance trips."

"She's not that difficult," Em said. "It takes time to load and unload the van. When she's rolling on her own, I have to work to keep up." He laughed.

Brad noticed the grime under his fingernails and around his cuticles, and asked, "Is your car almost ready for the road?"

Em shook his head. "I don't know if I'll ever get it ready."

"I think Mort slipped one over on you when he sold you that Hudson," Gertie said.

"Who's Mort?" Sharon asked.

"A co-worker from Third National Bank," Em replied. "He was an antique auto dealer on the side. I always wanted a Hudson when I was younger, but couldn't afford it."

"Was Third National taken over by Mellon Bank?" Brad

asked, preferring to make small talk while they ate.

"No. A New York bank bought it and cannibalized it," Em said. "They sold off various parts. Investments—my old department—got sold to Dean Witter. I think they've already sold it to another company. I'm just as glad to be retired."

Brad poured more iced tea. "Last week you told me about a note that Dad received within a week of the kidnapping. Do you recall how the note was addressed?"

Gertie put her fork down and thought for a minute. "It just said Mr. Frame, as I recall. That was a long time ago."

"You told me the note consisted of letters or words cut out of newspapers."

"Yes, that's right."

"Was the envelope addressed the same way?"

"I never saw the envelope, just the note on the top of his desk."

"Did Dad work late the night before?" Brad asked.

Em Lindstrom nudged her. "You don't have to stop eating."

"No need to ask such a foolish question," Gertie said, picking up her fork. "Your dad always worked late."

"Do you recall how late *you* worked on the night before you saw the note?"

"I didn't work at all that day," Gertie said, taking a bite of her food.

"I see," Brad said. "Then you don't know for sure that he worked late?"

Em's silverware clanged onto his plate. "She answered your question."

Gertie stared at Em, and he finally helped himself to more salad. The quiche remained untouched on his plate.

Brad relaxed in his chair. "Yes, she did, Em. I'm sorry. I

was just trying to get an idea who might have been around to find the note." Turning back to Gertie, Brad asked, "Was Roslyn Hunter working in the front office at that time?"

Birds chirped noisily outside the window. Brad noticed that each time he asked Gertie a question she would glance at Em before answering.

"Roslyn was on maternity leave," Gertie said. "Gretchen was the only secretary in the front office."

Turning to Em, Brad said, "Last week at your pool, you were the one who first mentioned the note. It's obvious the two of you have discussed it. Why did you think it was worth mentioning?"

Em dabbed his mouth with the napkin. "She first told me about it a couple of years ago, when she was in the hospital recovering from her surgery. We had a lot of time to talk back then. The whole thing sounded like a threat to me. When you came over, asking questions, I figured you needed to know about the note. Wasn't sure she was gonna tell you about it. Actually, I don't think she would have if I hadn't spoke up."

"Gertie, remember what the note said. What was it that my dad wasn't going to get away with?" Brad asked.

Her face was flushed. "I . . . I don't know."

"But you have an idea, don't you?"

Gertie sliced into the quiche with the fork in her left hand and speared a small bite. She brought it to her mouth slowly and chewed for a long time before swallowing.

Brad tried again. "Was Dad having an affair?"

Gertie and Em exchanged glances. "No," she said firmly. "If I'd seen the note on Andrew's desk then I might have suspected an affair was the reason."

"Then what do you think it was?"

Gertie remained silent.

"Tell him," Em ordered. His face flushed.

"They had a big shouting match," Gertie said, "two days before I saw the note."

"Who?"

"Hiram Gibbons and your father," Gertie explained. "Andrew put out the word with a few of the big law firms in the city that he was looking for a new General Counsel. Hiram didn't know about it until a friend of his from law school called to inquire about the job. Of course, at first, Hiram didn't know what he was talking about." Only the left side of Gertie's mouth moved as she spoke. "When he finally figured out what Andrew was doing, Hiram was embarrassed and furious. He marched into Joe's office and slammed the door. There was so much shouting. You could practically hear everything they said. The secretaries were scared; I was scared. I left work early that afternoon and walked over to Em's office. It was only a couple of blocks. I'm afraid I made quite a scene." Gertie glanced apologetically at Em. "But he managed to calm me down."

Sharon reached over and patted Gertie on the arm.

Em spoke up. "It wasn't right what Andrew was doing with the company. All the changes he made—it was hell for everybody."

Brad propped his elbows on the table, clasped his hands together and leaned forward until his hands supported his chin. "I'm meeting with Hiram later this afternoon."

Alarmed, Gertie said, "Oh, please don't tell him I told you."

"Don't worry. He won't need to know."

Em downed the rest of his iced tea, and pushed back his chair, saying, "We appreciate your hospitality Brad."

"Actually, there's something else I'd like to talk with you

about. I understand you've filed for bankruptcy."

"And what if we have?" Em said, defensively.

"It's no shame, Em," Gertie commented.

"I guess what I'd really like to know is what I can do to help."

"We don't need your charity," Em said, rising from his chair. "Come on, Gertie, let's go."

Gertie raised her left hand, trying to stop him. "We appreciate your concern, Brad," she said. "Really, we do. There have been a lot of medical bills, and I'm afraid it's gotten us overextended. Em seems to feel that bankruptcy is the best solution."

"I could buy back your Joedco stock," Brad said. "I understand you bought 40,000 shares the week after my mother and sister were killed."

"The timing was unfortunate," Em said, fiddling with the napkin beside his plate. "We had a deadline to exercise a stock option. We took money out of savings—left over from the sale of all of the original farmland around our property—and used it to buy the stock."

"Em handled the purchase at the bank," Gertie explained.

Em looked perturbed.

"I could buy back your stock," Brad said again. "Perhaps that would eliminate the need for the bankruptcy."

"I . . . maybe it—" Gertie began, but Em cut her off.

"Brad, I don't think you fully understand. My wife is a profligate spender." Em punctuated every syllable. "A few years ago we used the stock as collateral for extensive renovation work done on our house. The stock is not *ours* to sell at the moment. If you gave us a million dollars it would be gone next week. Two million the week after that. Three million by the first of the month. If you're offering charity, we don't *need* it."

Gertie's chin dropped onto her chest. Her jaw quivered.

"Let's go, Gertie." Turning to Brad, Em said, "I know the way out."

Em Lindstrom grasped the handles on the back of the wheelchair and started pushing her out of the room.

"Never mind all the money he's sunk into that old car over the years," Gertie said as he rolled the chair around the corner.

"Shut up, you old windbag." Brad could hear Em barking at her in the hallway.

After a few moments of silence, Sharon said, "Well, that was a pleasant lunch."

"There's still an apricot torte in the refrigerator," Brad said. "Would you like some?"

"Nah, maybe later," Sharon said. "Em complained that Gertie was a spendthrift, but didn't Andy tell you how she drove people crazy at work accounting for every penny?"

Brad nodded. "She was certainly the latter at work. Dad spoke of it, too. Gertie was very fastidious. But I don't think it's uncommon for people to apply different standards to their personal and work lives. Em is probably right. They were always traveling and having parties. Gertie's wealth was inherited. She grew up learning how to spend it, but not necessarily to manage it."

CHAPTER 24

Brad fingered the business card Ron Allessi had given him, then laid it on his desk. He dialed the phone number on the card, but voice mail answered. He didn't bother to leave a message. Besides, he thought, Allessi probably had caller ID and would know he'd tried to reach him.

Turning his attention to the fax his brother's office had sent, Brad studied the agreement between his dad and Gertrude Cole, made when he was barely two years old. She had loaned a million dollars to help his parents start Joedco—an abbreviated version of Joe and Edith's Company—which didn't seem like too large a sum given what he knew of her family's wealth. The loan was to be repaid at seven percent interest, slightly higher than mortgage rates at that time, Brad thought. It took ten pages of legal jargon to lay out the fairly simple terms, hidden between plenty of whereas' and parties of the first part. He stuck a copy of the document in his jacket pocket, intending to ask his father's attorney if he could shed any additional light on the arrangement.

Sharon was waiting for him beside his car, and they headed for Hiram Gibbons' office. Clouds moved over the area from an approaching cold front, but blue sky was still visible on the horizon as he sped down the Schuylkill Expressway into center city Philadelphia. Inbound traffic was light, but backups were forming on the outbound lanes from commuters hoping to beat the worst of the rush hour traffic. Once they reached the grid of city streets it all seemed a tangled mess of late afternoon traffic.

Brad pointed to a contemporary glass and steel building. "Dad's office used to be right over there," he explained, "on the northwest corner of 18th and Market Streets. Dad had a great view to the north. When I was a kid I loved staring out his office window and watching the Amtrak and SEPTA trains as they traveled between 30th Street and Penn Stations."

Brad pulled into a parking garage.

Hiram Gibbons' office was on the 27th floor of the "clothespin building" in downtown Philadelphia, directly across from City Hall. Claes Oldenburg's sculpture of a gigantic clothespin stood in front of the building. Most people couldn't remember the official name or address of the building, but everyone knew the landmark piece of art.

The receptionist, a petite African-American with her hair pulled back on her head, greeted them as soon as they stepped off the elevator, inviting them to have a seat while she notified the attorney. Brad caught a whiff of her exotic perfume, and noticed her long fingers were accented with ebony polished nails. She punched a few buttons at the console on her mahogany desk and spoke into a headset announcing their arrival.

Brad sat on a plush rust-colored sofa arranged with several chairs on an intricately designed Persian rug in the lobby, while Sharon stood staring out the window.

A few moments later, Hiram Gibbons came striding across the lobby. He was the kind of guy for whom a $1200 suit was made—gracious, unflappable, circumspect. Hiram spoke in a deep bass voice. "Brad, Ms. Porter, welcome. Thank you so much for coming. I would gladly have driven out to see you."

"I won't take much of your time," Brad began.

Hiram grabbed Brad by the elbow and guided him to his

office, with Sharon several steps behind. "I hope the traffic wasn't too bad," the lawyer said.

Hiram paused briefly at his secretary's desk. "Kristin, hold my calls."

Gibbons' corner office overlooked Philadelphia's ornate City Hall with the famous statue of William Penn on top. The lawyer sat with his back to the window, which shadowed his face, but accorded his visitors spectacular vistas past the business district to the Delaware River, with New Jersey barely visible through the distant haze. Sharon stood for a few more seconds, gawking at the view.

"What can I do for you?" Hiram asked, when they'd settled into their seats.

"I need information," Brad began. "In the week before my mother and sister were murdered you bought 32,000 shares of Joedco stock. Why?"

Hiram laughed quietly. "I believe in the free enterprise system. Is there anything wrong with buying stock?"

"You're avoiding my question," Brad said with a smile.

Hiram leaned forward. His dark skin shined and his eyes were wide and penetrating as he looked at Brad. "First, I'm not sure I remember the reason. Second, you should have told me *why* you wanted to see me, in advance. Then I could have checked my records. That was a long time ago."

Brad inched forward in his seat. "I understand that during that same week you had a confrontation with my father in his office regarding an advertisement for a new General Counsel."

Hiram leaned back, his hands laced together in front of him, and thumbs tapping against each other. "Yes. I remember it very well. We had words on that subject, the first and *only* time your father and I ever exchanged harsh words. In the end we both discovered that our beef was

220

with Andrew, since your father didn't know any more about the proposed changes than I did. Joseph finally got Andrew to reverse course. If you're suggesting a causal relationship between my stock purchase and the altercation I had with your father, let me assure you that there wasn't one."

"There's another subject I'd like to pursue with you," Brad said. "When Dad and Mom started Joedco they borrowed a million dollars from Gertrude Lindstrom; she was Gertrude Cole then. This afternoon I received a faxed copy of the terms under which the money was borrowed." He reached in his coat pocket and handed Hiram a copy. The attorney studied the document as Brad continued. "They were to make a full repayment of the loan over twenty years, with no penalty if repaid sooner. As collateral, Mom and Dad had to name Gertie as a beneficiary in their wills in an amount equal to the outstanding principal and interest on the loan. In addition, Gertie retained options to purchase stock in Joedco at one-half the market value for a period of thirty years. Can you shed any more light on this arrangement?"

Sharon withdrew a small notebook from her purse, along with a pen, prepared to take notes.

Hiram leafed through the document for the next several minutes, occasionally nodding. Then Hiram sat up straight in his chair; his legs were set wide apart, and his large hands grasped his kneecaps as if he were picking up a grapefruit. Smooth and articulate, Brad imagined him as a Supreme Court justice. "Another firm drafted this agreement," he began. "It pre-dates my work with your father. I don't think this type of agreement was unusual given the circumstances. Your father started the business with a promising—and as it turned out—a very lucrative idea. He came out of the academic world but without a lot of business acumen; I think it would have been a challenge for him to arrange financing through conventional sources, back in the days when a banker grilled you in the hot seat across from his desk. Your mother came from a wealthy family, but until your grandfather died she didn't have an independent source of money. I recall asking Joe why he didn't get his father-in-law to bankroll his idea. It was a question of pride for him, not wanting to rely on family, to make it on his own. Having Gertie named a beneficiary in both of their wills was good protection for her. I don't know, maybe your parents offered that kind of guarantee, without her asking for it. As far as stock options, they're fairly common in business deals. I don't see anything unusual. I recall reviewing this agreement in the files when I was general counsel."

Brad stared out the window.

"Is there something else?" he heard Hiram ask.

"There's no mention in the agreement for Gertie's involvement in the company. Yet I know that she served as Joedco's chief financial officer for quite a few years."

Hiram scanned the legal papers again. "This is strictly a loan documentation. There may have been other reasons why she and your dad chose to work together."

"Yes," Brad said, after awhile.

Brad stood to leave, then turned to Sharon, asking, "Could you wait for me in the lobby? I'd like to speak with Hiram privately."

"Sure," Sharon said, hurriedly gathering her purse—nonplussed by his request.

"What is it?" Hiram asked, after the door had clicked shut behind her.

"About my father's will," Brad began.

"Yes, what would you like to know?" Hiram spread his

arms in front of him. "We don't have any secrets from each other."

"Taking my brother out of the will," Brad said, hesitantly, "was that really Dad's idea or yours?"

Hiram sighed deeply and clasped his hands. "If you had asked me that question a few minutes ago, I might have thrown you out. But I can see that something is troubling you. I'll be honest. I don't care much for your brother, and I've made no secret of it. But I worked for your *father*. He found me fresh out of law school at Penn, and gave me the opportunity of a lifetime to be the general counsel for his promising new enterprise. When Joe suggested taking Andrew out of his will I honestly tried to talk him out of it, not because of any warm feelings for Andrew, but because I thought I knew your father well enough to realize he might regret his decision later. In the back of my mind I imagined revisiting the issue with him, six months or a year later, but after his physical condition deteriorated I decided not to raise the subject," Hiram said, with a wave of his hand. "Am I sorry your brother lost out on the fortune of a lifetime? Not. One. Bit. Your brother is the kind of man for whom the phrase 'blood is thicker than water' is a crutch. He stands behind your family name like it's a shield that will protect him. Your Dad spent thirty years developing a solid business reputation. In my opinion, your brother's already managed to squander that. Quite frankly, if he weren't your brother I doubt you would care one iota about his inheritance."

Brad knew his brother's faults, just as well as Andy knew his. They seldom expressed an inclination to walk a mile in the other's shoes. But Andy was still his brother, and he loved him.

"The company has done very well under Andy's leadership," Brad said.

"That may be, but is success just about the bottom line?" Hiram asked rhetorically. "Back to your point, Brad, the ethical question for me regarding your father's will is: Did I act in your father's interest and at his direction? The answer is, I did."

Brad digested Hiram's comments, then stood up. He clasped the attorney's hand and grasped his shoulder. "Thanks for your candor. I think you're right about my father regretting his decision to disinherit Andy. I don't want to challenge the will, but I'd like you to draft an agreement that would share half of my inheritance with him. I haven't discussed this with my brother, so please keep it confidential."

Hiram exhaled. "It could take awhile. I'll have to get a tax attorney involved."

"There's no rush. Work up a draft and we'll talk again."

Hiram nodded.

Brad found Sharon standing next to the lobby windows gazing at the Philadelphia skyline.

He retrieved his car from the garage and they drove one block north before heading west on JFK Boulevard toward the Expressway.

Pointing to his right, after they'd passed City Hall, Brad said, "There's Penn Station."

"Is that the back of your dad's old office building on the left?" Sharon asked.

"Yup," Brad said.

"You were talking about Andrew, right?" Sharon asked, as they inched their way onto the expressway.

Brad didn't respond at first. He thought about what Hiram Gibbons had said about success and the bottom line. What was the real bottom line in business, or life for that matter? The simple answer eluded him. When he spoke, it was to reminisce. "I remember playing baseball in the backyard when we were kids, just the two of us. Andy would pitch, and if I'd hit the ball I would run toward the bases we set up, like a rock for first base, a piece of wood stomped into the dirt for second base. If I made it to second, I'd return to the plate to bat again, and we'd agree that an imaginary man was on second base. Then if I made it as far as first base on the next at bat, the imaginary runner would advance to third—I think we used an old burlap sack for our base marker there—and then there'd be another phantom runner on first. My brother liked to tag out these imaginary runners. Even if I safely got to a base, he'd chase down the ball and then claim to have tagged out the guy ahead of me. This was when I was eight or nine and he was thirteen or fourteen. He was bigger and older, and I could never successfully argue with him."

Sharon laughed. "I can just picture the two of you."

"Andy certainly showed his competitive spirit, even then." Brad continued, "I was eleven years old when he went off to a private school in Virginia for his junior and senior years. From there he went to Duke, and I'd only see him occasionally during the summer or at the holidays.

"It's funny," Brad mused, "when we were kids I looked up to him—wishing I could be just like him. I think I've spent more time with Andy this past week than at any time since the kidnapping. I see how different we've become."

CHAPTER 25

Brad felt like cheering as he hung up the phone from talking with Ralph Blankenship, the managing partner of *Blankenship, Trawler and Ivanic.* A productive conversation, Brad sensed a potential breakthrough with Ron Allessi. He tore off the half-sheet of paper on which he'd copied a West Philadelphia address, folded it, and placed it in his wallet.

Brad set up an easel with a flip chart next to his desk on which he wrote the words from Frank Wilkie's final message.

me and eddie not big guy
paid money kill
eddie talked he get killed
find real killer
i sorry

Out of the corner of his eye, Brad saw Sharon amble into the office, sipping through a straw from her travel mug, just as he finished writing the last line. "Good morning," he said.

Sharon looked first at him, waving hello, and then spotted the flip chart. Brad walked over to the French doors. Shielding his eyes from reflected glare he checked a thermometer just outside the window. "It's sixty-eight degrees, would you mind if I opened these doors?"

"Sounds like a good idea," Sharon said. The room needed airing out from the stale odor of Andy's cigars, Brad thought, as he propped open the door. Cool, fresh air drifted into the office.

Standing next to the flip chart, Brad said, "I'd like to talk about the case—sort of re-group—and get your thoughts."

Sharon noisily sucked up the last of her drink. "Go ahead."

Pointing to the chart, Brad said, "I'm gonna play devil's advocate and suggest that most of Wilkie's message isn't worth pursuing any more. The fact that Wilkie was sorry won't bring anyone back to life." Brad took a red felt-tipped marker and crossed out line five of Wilkie's note. "We also know that the part where he talked about Eddie Baker being killed is wrong. It was suicide, and an autopsy proved it." Brad scratched out the third line.

"Wait a minute. Call me a cynic," Sharon said, "but isn't it possible the system covered its ass for letting someone get away with hanging Baker inside the prison?"

Brad smiled. "Yeah, I'd say that's cynical. I thought *I* was the one playing devil's advocate this morning." Brad paced behind his desk. "It's like Nick suggested, that a prison guard—maybe even a fellow prisoner—fed Wilkie the story that Eddie had been killed. Emotional intimidation."

"Maybe our buddy Ron Allessi planted the idea in Wilkie's head about Eddie getting killed," Sharon said.

Brad met Sharon's gaze as he contemplated her suggestion, then wagged his index finger in her direction. "Yeah. You know, that would fit with other ideas I've had about Allessi."

Putting the cap back on the marker, Brad then used it to point at the chart. "Take a look at the second line of the note—*paid money kill*."

"Your brother delivered the $500,000 in ransom

money," Sharon said, "so someone got paid."

"The question," Brad said, "is who and how much? Baker made an off-hand remark about being paid $5,000. But who paid him? Wilkie? If so, how much did Wilkie get?"

Sharon shook her head. Brad knew the question of money was a blind alley at the moment.

"How would you explain the threatening notes your dad and brother received?"

"Good point, Sharon," Brad said. "Earlier this morning I spoke with Gretchen Morse. She was the receptionist who found the note that Gertie told us about. Gretchen said the envelope was addressed to 'Mr. Frame.' Now that's the same way my brother said his notes were addressed. Then I contacted Roslyn Hunter—Andy said she'd found the notes for him—but her husband said she was out grocery shopping. I think I should try again." Brad sat at the desk, pulling the phone closer to him.

Thumbing through the Rolodex he spotted her number, then dialed it.

After three rings, a woman's voice answered. "Hello, Roslyn, this is Brad Frame."

"Are you Andrew's brother?" she asked warily.

"Yes, I won't need much of your time," Brad said, trying to assure her.

Outside, the landscapers powered up their mowers.

"May I put you on hold for a second," Brad said. He covered the mouthpiece and got Sharon's attention as he pointed toward the open French doors. He caught a whiff of freshly mowed grass just as Sharon pulled the doors shut.

"I'd like to ask you about an incident that happened thirteen or fourteen years ago."

"Oh, my, that's a long time ago," she said, in a pleasant but thin voice.

"Yes, I know. Can I put you on speakerphone so I can make a few notes while we talk."

"That's fine," Roslyn responded.

Brad pushed the speakerphone button, and pulled a tablet closer to him with a pen poised in his hand. "I'm wondering if you remember receiving a couple of notes, which were addressed to Mr. Frame, and you delivered them to my brother, Andrew."

"Oh, yes," she said, sounding relieved. "I never thought I'd be able to help you with something that happened that long ago, but I remember those notes."

Sharon scooted closer on the sofa, cupping her ear.

"Do you remember how you found the notes?" Brad asked.

"I usually was the first person in the office. There were two notes, several weeks apart, with letters Scotch-taped on the outside of the envelope. I found them slid under the door when I entered the office."

"I see," Brad said, jotting the details on the tablet.

"How did you know to give the notes to Andrew rather than my father?"

"They were addressed to Mr. Frame, that's how Andrew insisted he be called. Material for your father was usually addressed to Joe, by those close to him, or to the Professor."

"I see," Brad said, nodding. "You've been very helpful, Roslyn. I just have one more question. Did my brother seem upset after he'd read the notes?"

"It was hard to tell," she said, adding, "To me he always seemed upset."

Brad suppressed a laugh. "I can understand why you

might say that. Thanks for your help, Roslyn, it was a pleasure talking with you."

He replaced the receiver as the antique clock behind his desk chimed the half-hour.

"It sounds like all three notes were intended for Andrew?" Sharon asked.

Brad nestled back in the cushioned leather of his desk chair and stared at the ceiling. "Yes, I think all three of the notes were meant for Andy, and the last one missed its mark."

Sharon kicked off her shoes, and pulled herself up on her knees on the leather sofa.

"For a working hypothesis," Brad continued, "let's assume that the person who sent the notes wanted my brother to receive them. Since they were slipped under the front door of the office, almost anyone passing down the hallway could have left them, including the last person out the night before."

Sharon looked like a fresh thought had crossed her mind. "Okay, I buy that," she said, a hesitant edge to her voice. "But if the notes were intended for your brother then they have nothing to do with the kidnapping."

"I'm not so sure," Brad said. "According to Gertie, the third note arrived just days before the kidnapping. The other two notes were several years earlier. The threats may have been directed to Andrew. But back then, only Dad— or the company he headed—could respond financially to the kidnapper's demand."

Sharon nodded.

"Think about how Dad and Andy responded to the notes. Andy never thought twice that the notes might have been for him; if he didn't anger three people before breakfast, he probably figured he'd had an unproductive day. He may not have known who sent the notes—a jealous husband, disgruntled secretary, or jilted mistress. But when somebody told him he wasn't going to get away with 'it,' he sure as hell had a long list of possibilities for what *it* was. On the other hand, according to Gertie, my dad left the note lying in the open on his desk overnight. I imagine he studied it, and with the benefit of a clear conscience threw it away."

"Okay, you've been the devil's advocate long enough," Sharon said. "Tell me what you're thinking."

Brad stood next to the flip chart, circling the fourth line with the marker—*Find real killer*. "That's what's troubling me. I can explain every other line. Eddie Baker wasn't a *big guy*. *Paid money kill* could have referred to money Wilkie gave Baker. But this," Brad said, tapping the fourth line of the message, "I don't have the answer yet. If somebody hired Wilkie and Baker to kidnap my mother and sister, then the notes could point to a long-festering motivation."

After a pause, Sharon asked, "Is there any chance your brother was involved in the kidnapping?"

Brad sighed then pursed his lips. "God, I hope not."

"Could those lawnmowers be any louder?" Brad commented, as a rumbling noise neared the front of his office, followed by a backfire.

"It's Mark!" Sharon shouted, jumping up from the sofa and running to the window. Brad saw Mark Bertolet's three-tone—counting the gray filler patches on the body—'67 Ford Fairlane roll across the cobblestones. The car backfired again as it rolled to a stop.

An idea percolated in Brad's brain as he heard the squeaky slam of Mark's car door.

A moment later Mark stuck his head in the office,

asking, "Am I interrupting?"

"Hi honey," Sharon said, racing to her boyfriend, throwing her arms around his neck.

"Hey, Mark," Brad said. "I was thinking about a road trip into West Philly this afternoon. What's the chance of you driving?"

"Cool," Mark uttered, and never noticed the are-you-out-of-your-freaking-mind look that Sharon flashed Brad.

"I should have mentioned I'll pay you $50," Brad said. "You can treat Sharon to dinner tonight to celebrate her new job with the Philadelphia Police Department."

Sharon unleashed another scowl at Brad, as Mark led the way to his car. Sharon sat next to Mark, while Brad climbed into the back seat and navigated the trip. Once in the city, they headed west on Market Street traveling well beyond the Penn and Drexel campuses before turning in to a maze of side streets. At Brad's direction, Mark circled one particular block.

"Pull up here, Mark," Brad announced. "The open spot behind that blue car."

Several shades of blue, Brad noticed, and—like Mark's car—covered with gray patches and primer.

"See the bald headed guy standing over there?" Brad asked, pointing out a man who looked like a bouncer at a sadomasochist's bar.

Sharon sat with her arms folded across her chest. "You mean the one with the lightning bolt tattooed on the side of his head?" she asked.

"Nah, I don't think that's a lightning bolt," Mark said, not realizing Sharon was directing a barb at Brad.

Brad slipped Mark a fifty dollar bill. "Give him this. Ask him to keep an eye on your car."

Two minutes later Mark rejoined them. He looked wide-eyed, as he exhaled. "I gave him the money. He said my car will be here."

"Good. You might as well come with us, Mark," Brad said. "If you're gonna date a cop, this will give you a little flavor for detective work."

Sharon punched Brad in the arm.

Brad led the way as the three of them traversed a narrow walkway between two row houses, then walked across a small litter-strewn yard to another set of row houses. There were two doors on the dilapidated back porch. Brad studied the hand-painted numbers before pounding on the right hand door, giving it six or seven hard raps.

Ron Allessi answered the door, shirtless and wearing a pair of faded jeans. He couldn't have looked any less happy if the IRS was on his doorstep.

CHAPTER 26

"You turned up at my place one day. I figured it was time I showed up at yours," Brad announced.

"Ah . . . ah," Allessi stammered. "How did you find out where I live?"

"That's not important." Pointing to Sharon, Brad said, "You remember my associate?"

"And this is Mark," Brad said, adding, "He's on special assignment." Brad noticed Sharon rolling her eyes.

"Aren't you gonna invite us in?" Sharon said.

Allessi staggered away from the door. As they entered the apartment through a galley kitchen, Brad noticed the old porcelain sink piled high with dirty dishes, which spilled over onto the speckled countertops. Plywood cabinets were missing doors, and the linoleum was worn through to the underlayment in a couple of spots. A single bare bulb in the ceiling lit the musty-smelling living room, with sparse furnishings and peeling paint on the walls. Toward the front of the house, visible through an open doorway, he glimpsed Allessi's unmade bed.

Allessi grabbed a T-shirt from the back of a chair and slipped it on, then stood in the middle of his living room facing them. The scar above his left eye, which Brad thought had looked so menacing, now seemed more like a benign flaw.

"What do you want?" Allessi asked.

"You're a moving target that I couldn't quite figure out," Brad said. "When I saw you at Diane's house the other day and you gave virtually no sign of recognition, that's when I realized you were freelancing."

"I don't know—"

"You know exactly what I mean. Everything you've done has been designed to line the pockets of Ron Allessi. I'm betting the idea of finding a stash of missing ransom money first led you to Frank Wilkie. When the Governor signed his death warrant a couple of years ago all the details of the case appeared in the newspaper. You probably read about the ransom money when you were in law school, and thought you'd see if you couldn't con Wilkie into telling you where he hid it."

"Wilkie claimed he didn't know anything about the money." Allessi showed his first hint of genuine passion, Brad thought.

"Maybe he didn't. But you kept after him, and kept him alive by filing appeals. Every time the sand was about to run through his hourglass you turned it over, delaying the inevitable. I'm sure the firm found it admirable that you were representing him pro bono. They didn't realize you had a tax-free $500,000 fee in mind for yourself. Then you gave up, and his time ran out. You didn't care anymore. You hadn't visited him for six weeks before his scheduled execution. I double-checked; you *were* the last minute cancellation as his execution witness.

"When you struck out finding the treasure map to the loot, you lost interest. That is, until you read Paula Thompson's article in *The Philadelphia Inquirer* stating that Wilkie had given me his Bible and mentioning that it might contain a message. Suddenly your light bulb was back on." Brad moved toward Allessi, who stepped back. "Maybe there was a treasure map after all. That's when you came to see me."

Brad leaned toward him. Allessi lost his balance, falling

backward onto the sofa, but not before Brad heard Allessi's head thud against the wall.

"Shit!" Allessi muttered, rubbing the back of his head.

"That's a good idea. Have a seat," Brad said. "You might as well get comfortable. We're gonna be here for a while."

Brad glanced over at Sharon's boyfriend, noting he stood with a wide-eyed gape taking in the scene.

Sharon laughed after Allessi tumbled on to the couch. Allessi seemed to take out his frustration by pounding the sofa with his fist while glaring at Brad.

"You claimed that your representation of Wilkie would result in a book deal," Brad said, "but the only book deal you seemed interested in was getting your hands on Wilkie's Bible."

"Wilkie made an agreement," Allessi explained, as a hint of desperation crept into his voice.

"Save it," Brad said. "Then—probably not coincidentally—less than twenty-four hours after your visit, someone broke in, stole the very Bible that *you* were looking for, and set fire to my office."

"Hey . . . wa . . . wait," Allessi stammered. "I didn't commit any arson."

In spite of Allessi's pathetic look, Brad had no pity. "Maybe some of your Camden friends."

"No . . . No . . . You've got it all wrong."

"Have I?" Brad said. "Why didn't we hear anything more from you after the Bible was stolen?"

Allessi squirmed in his seat, and Brad could tell he was unnerved.

"I figure you got what you came for. The next thing I know you crashed Dad's funeral with my ex-sister-in-law on your arm."

"Wait a minute. I don't know anything about the Bible. Let me explain," Allessi pleaded. "Diane called me. She saw my name in the paper, and called asking if we could get together. I suggested meeting her for a drink after I got off work, and we met at her country club."

"Uh huh," Brad mumbled matter-of-factly, while at the same time anxious to hear what prompted Diane's sudden interest in Allessi.

"Diane gave me an earful about your brother, like his attraction to thin, young, blonde secretaries. How he'd abandoned her and their seven-year-old son. What a struggle it was to live on the alimony he provided." Brad imagined Diane's diatribe against Andy, and knew that Allessi was giving him a sanitized version.

"Did Diane tell you all of this before or after you two shared the hot tub?" Brad asked.

"That was a bonus." A smile crept onto his face.

"After she confided in you about her deep and abiding feelings for my brother," Brad said, caustically, "you decided to extort money from him."

"She . . . I didn't—"

Brad cut him off. "Freelancing. Trying to find that treasure map again, weren't you? If you couldn't dig up $500,000 from Wilkie, you'd squeeze it out of my brother. Diane would have been a willing accomplice in that effort."

"Don't describe Diane as an accomplice," Allessi said, sounding tender toward her.

Aunt Harriet's one-word description of Diane came to Brad's mind—bitch!

"But my brother wasn't buying what you were selling. You made a tactical error. You raised the idea of a book deal again, this time with my brother. When Andy told me," Brad explained, "something began to smell. I figured you for a con man the first time I met you, but I underesti-mated how big a con."

Allessi scowled at him, then ran his hand through his black hair and folded his arms across his chest.

"I contacted Ralph Blankenship, the managing partner of your law firm," Brad said.

Allessi shot him an angry look, but Brad could tell he had his full attention.

"I found out that the folks at *Blankenship, Trawler and Ivanic* weren't happy to see their firm's name mentioned in the *Inquirer* in conjunction with Wilkie's execution. Mr. Blankenship told me a lot of their hard-nosed clients are in favor of bringing back the guillotine. He laughed when he said it, but I got the point. They didn't want clients think-ing their hefty retainers were aiding a prisoner on death row. Frankly, your employers are concerned that you've misrepresented yourself and the firm."

"I told them the newspaper makes mistakes all the time," Allessi said.

"Oh, I'm sure you did. Convincingly. But I found out that you're not exactly an associate at *Blankenship, Trawler and Ivanic*. You're working there as part of a legal assis-tant's program until you finish law school."

Brad reached into his wallet and pulled out the business card which Ron Allessi had given him. Brad tapped the card, right below the printed "Esq." Next to Allessi's name. "Esquire," he said. "This might be exhibit number one. When I spoke with Ralph, and sensed that they've had their own misgivings about you, I suggested their firm might want to hire me to investigate your background. Unfortu-nately, they don't get to see your tailored suits, Cashmere coat, and that natty silk scarf you wore to my office. I'm wondering where you got the Lexus?"

Allessi averted Brad's gaze.

Glancing around the cheap apartment, Brad said, "I'm betting Diane never visited you here. Where did you tell her you lived when you weren't playing with her in the hot tub?"

Defeated, Allessi replied, "Cherry Hill, New Jersey."

"Of course," Brad nodded. "A prestigious enough zip code, but far enough away that she wouldn't suggest swinging by to visit."

Allessi sank into the couch, getting smaller by the minute, Brad thought.

"I'm gonna give you some free advice," Brad said. "Don't show up at work again. I'm meeting with Ralph Blankenship on Monday morning. After he gets my report, you're gonna be too big of a liability for them to continue their association with you."

CHAPTER 27

Brad sank into his seat on Amtrak's southbound Acela Express and stretched, glad to be heading home. He'd had a long, but good, day.

It had begun when Sharon—in what Brad could only describe as an act of charity at that hour of the morning—agreed to drive him to the Bryn Mawr rail station at five-thirty a.m. so he could catch the first commuter train to 30th Street Station. After boarding the early-bird Acela Express to New York, Brad studied the agenda for Joedco's annual stockholders' meeting. He was still Chair of the corporation until the Board approved the plan to name Andy the Chair and CEO, and the Board wouldn't meet until late morning. Brad didn't want to disappoint his brother by looking unprepared, but he marveled at how anal the corporate briefing materials were. The communications department provided him with a two-inch thick binder on the intricacies of Parliamentary procedure, but also detailed instructions for directing stockholders to the restrooms, and an overblown, two-page introduction for his brother. *Ladies and Gentlemen, here's my brother, Andy Frame,* Brad had said to himself, rehearsing an abbreviated—and in his opinion more appropriate—version of the introduction.

An Amtrak attendant in the first-class coach asked Brad if he wanted something to drink. Planning to nap, Brad declined. But then he spied a copy of that morning's *Philadelphia Inquirer* on the empty seat next to him, and decided to read instead. He picked up the paper, and summoned the attendant so he could order a ginger ale.

Flipping to the local section, Brad spotted an article on the death penalty by Paula Thompson, the start of the series she had told him about.

DEATH ROW IN PENNSYLVANIA
by Paula Thompson

Who controls the property of a condemned killer? How about his story? It is generally recognized that a criminal cannot profit by his crime. But should anyone else profit from the actions of a killer at the expense of the victims of crime? Pennsylvania, according to key legislative leaders, may be a step closer to settling this issue, especially after what followed a recent execution.

Several years ago, victims' rights' advocates secured legislation denying criminals the right to sell their stories and profit from them. But criminals have found creative ways to capture the media spotlight, while others skim the profit from telling their stories—in the form of books, lectures, and movie rights. Only a small amount of what advocates describe as "blood money" ever makes it into the hands of victims' families. Key legislative leaders may now be ready to close those loopholes, and ensure more justice for crime victims.

Two weeks after Frank Wilkie was executed for the murder of Edith and Lucy Frame, the State Department of Corrections is still debating the fate of his personal belongings. Such items are usually given to next of kin, but Wilkie died without family ties. A few mementos belonging to a now-deceased prisoner wouldn't normally prompt so much discussion in the policy-making corridors of the Corrections Department, but on the night of his execution Frank Wilkie left a note for the family of his victims. The note was inside a Bible, which the condemned man carried to his death. Wilkie gave the prison's chaplain instructions that the items were to be given to L. Bradford Frame, the son and brother of the murdered women. Superintendent Henry Dolewski, of the Rockville State Correctional Institution, where Pennsylvania's executions are carried out, found the note on the floor of the lethal injection chamber. Since that time, Ron Allessi, with the law firm that represented Wilkie's appeals, has fought its release to anyone other than himself.

Last week the *Inquirer* reported that the prison chaplain had given Wilkie's Bible to Brad Frame, and that it may have contained a final message from the executed killer. We have since learned that the Bible was stolen from Frame's Bryn Mawr estate. The *Inquirer* has obtained an exclusive look at this note, which is still in the possession of prison officials. According to knowledgeable sources, it may point the way to others responsible for the tragic death of Edith and Lucy Frame.

When contacted, Brad Frame said he was "anxious to get a copy of the note from the prison's warden," but withheld comment on the substance . . .

Brad was grateful Paula hadn't blown his cover. His strategy to openly share information with her was paying off. Ron Allessi came off in a lesser light than in Thompson's earlier stories, and Brad smiled, realizing her article wouldn't help Allessi with an already bad week.

The article continued on the following page with quotes

from politicians and bureaucrats eager to be on the right side of victims' rights. Brad noticed that part two of Thompson's series on the death penalty would deal with a "botched execution and a cover-up."

Brad sipped his ginger ale, pulled the sports section onto his lap to see how the Phillies were faring at the beginning of the new baseball season, and occasionally peered out the window as the high-speed train rolled by the scenery.

Closing his eyes, Brad smiled as he replayed the lunch he shared with Beth Montgomery at Mancuso's, one of his favorite New York dining spots. Off the beaten path, in Chelsea, the location had worked perfectly. Brad caught a southbound cab on Broadway at 45th when his meeting at the Marriott Marquis concluded and Beth took the "A" train uptown from the subway station near her office in lower Manhattan. Coordinating their departures—in true 21st Century fashion—via cell phone, they arrived at the restaurant within minutes of each other.

Unlike other women he'd known, Beth seemed more self-assured—and correspondingly less fascinated with his lineage or finances—a fact Brad liked, but which, in a strange way, made him feel more self-conscious. Five years younger than him, Beth had worked in New York City for the past eight years since earning her Master's degree in Engineering. Over lunch-sized portions of linguini carbonari—Isabelle Mancuso's specialty—they talked about far flung topics like Broadway shows they enjoyed, the engineering challenges of rebuilding the World Trade Center, and favorite ice cream flavors—he made a mental note that she liked butter pecan.

Over dessert he noted that she had avoided playing twenty questions with him about his background.

"I have a confession to make," Beth said, smiling. "I

243

probably already know more about you than you'd like me to."

An attractive woman, Brad thought, who grew more intriguing as they talked. "Dare I ask what you know?"

"I know about the time you and your brother soaked your mother's flower beds with the garden hose and dared your sister into a mud wrestling contest."

Brad's mouth slacked open.

"I know that you can't stand Brussels sprouts," Beth continued, "and that you have a fantastic model train set."

"Okay," Brad said, "I'll bite. How do you know all this?"

"Lucy and I were roommates at Bryn Mawr College for three years. I spent a lot of time with her at your place. She showed me the trains, and told me the rest. Oh, and a lot more," she managed to say without sounding like a blackmailer.

Brad felt the blood rising in his cheeks, and when he saw the grin on Beth's face, he could tell she saw him blushing.

"You were always traveling," Beth added.

Brad hoped she hadn't heard of some of his youthful indiscretions. He thought of them and smiled to himself.

"Lucy and I were great friends and we stayed in touch after college. I attended her funeral, but I doubt you remember."

He gazed into her eyes. "I don't."

"About a month ago, I was staying with Dad for the weekend and decided to visit St. Matthew's cemetery where your sister is buried. I've thought about Lucy a lot since the . . ." She didn't say the word. "But that was my first visit. It was a cold cloudy day, and it looked like it might snow. I spotted a shiny flat stone at the edge of the road, near her grave, and I polished it with a handkerchief in my purse; then laid it on top of her gravestone."

"It's still there," Brad said. "I visited the cemetery just the other day."

"I'm glad," she said, as silence fell between them.

"I would enjoy showing you the model trains again," Brad said. "Or we could try the mud wrestling?" He laughed.

"I just might enjoy that." She winked at him.

Brad couldn't remember when he'd spent a faster two hours. He found her unpretentious, and yet there was something about her that fascinated him.

They promised to get together in Philadelphia, where Beth was scheduled to spend a week's vacation before Memorial Day. But Brad wasn't sure he could wait that long to see her again, and New York was only an hour and fifteen minutes away on a fast train.

Brad's cell phone rang, just as the Acela crossed the Delaware River at Trenton, New Jersey. He glanced at the phone's display screen and saw the call originated from HOME, answering, "Hi, Sharon."

"Brad, where are you?" she asked, urgently.

"Fifteen minutes from 30th—"

"Nick Argostino just called. Paula Thompson has been murdered. He wants you there."

Brad felt anger and anxiety swelling in his gut. "Give me the address," he said. "I'll catch a cab and meet you there."

Copying the South Philadelphia address in his notebook, Brad recognized it as a residential street, most likely Paula's home. Like a computer searching for information on its hard drive, Brad swept through his brain recalling his recent conversations with Thompson and her interest in the eleven-year-old murder case. Dread crept up his spine, as he thought about her latest *Inquirer* article and whether Paula's knowledge of Wilkie's note had led to her own death.

CHAPTER 28

The cab deposited Brad at the end of Paula Thompson's blocked-off street, already clogged with police and emergency vehicles. Red lights seemed to flash everywhere. Brad walked along a brick sidewalk to the address Sharon had supplied. A once prosperous neighborhood, it looked to Brad like it had fallen into disrepair, but was now in the midst of gentrification. Only a few houses remained boarded-up, while most had freshly cleaned and re-pointed brick, white-trimmed windows with flower boxes and black shutters.

Brad arrived at Thompson's two-story brick townhouse just as two coroner's assistants carried a stretcher with her body, zipped in a black vinyl bag, to the back of their van. Brad approached a uniformed officer at the base of the brick and concrete steps.

"I'm Brad Frame. Captain Argostino is expecting me."

"Just a minute," the officer said, before mounting three steps and entering the townhouse.

Seconds later Nick appeared in the doorway, beckoning Brad to join him.

As he climbed the steps, Brad noticed a man with three camera cases slung over his shoulder, and heard Nick ask, "Did you get all the shots I wanted?"

"Yeah," the photographer said. "I should have them developed and on your desk by the time you get back to the office."

Brad stepped into the living room and saw no evidence of a crime. But a female officer knelt next to a sobbing woman seated in a mission-style chair, covered in a fabric of Native-American design. The woman had dark spiked hair, and wore jeans and a baggy sweatshirt.

"Is that Lydia?" Brad asked, recalling that Paula had mentioned she and her partner had been together for six months. He sensed she'd shared that information to see how he would react, dropping Lydia's name as a litmus test. When Paula discovered Brad was okay with that aspect of her life, he felt she relaxed a bit more in his presence.

"Yes. Lydia Sanchez," Nick said. "She found the body. We've only gotten the bare facts from her. She's been too broken up. I've assigned the uniformed officer to stay with her."

"Where's the crime scene?" Brad asked, as he scanned the rest of the living room noting a stereo tape deck and neatly stacked CDs, which served as the focal point of the front wall.

"Kitchen," Nick whispered, adding, "Messy. Gunshot."

Nodding in Lydia's direction, Brad asked, "Do you mind if I try to talk with her?"

"Go ahead."

Brad cautiously approached, and knelt next to Lydia's chair, signaling to the police officer that she didn't have to move. In the most comforting voice he could muster, he said, "Lydia, I'm Brad Frame. I knew your friend Paula."

"Yes, I know who you are," she said, with a Hispanic accent. Tears streamed down her cheeks. "I didn't even get to spend the weekend with her." She moaned. "I was with my family in Baltimore. Why did this have to happen?"

"I don't know," Brad said. "But you might be able to help us find who did this."

Lydia sniffled.

"When did you last see Paula?" Brad asked.

"This morning. I left for work at five-thirty." Lydia's breath seemed to catch on nearly every word. "Paula was still sleeping."

"Where do you work?" Brad asked.

"Seidels—a package delivery service near the airport. I have to be there at six-thirty."

"What time did you get home?"

"Same time I usually get home, I think. About three-forty-five."

Brad glanced over at Nick. "The 9-1-1 call came in at three-fifty-five," Nick said, after consulting his notes.

"What did you do when you first entered the house?" Brad asked.

"The door was unlocked, and that made me worry a little bit. Paula usually left before I got home. She always locked the door."

Brad saw Nick scribble a note, probably about the unlocked door.

"Did you hear any noises when you came in?" Brad asked.

"No." Lydia shook her head. "I thought maybe she had trouble when she tried to lock it. I double-checked using my key, and it seemed okay. Then I went upstairs and changed my clothes."

"Did anything seem unusual when you were upstairs?" Brad asked.

Lydia stared, and Brad could tell she was still in shock—responding to his questions on autopilot. "I came down to the kitchen and that's when I found her." Lydia sobbed heavily. Brad pulled a clean handkerchief out of his pocket, offering it to her.

Lydia took a deep breath before continuing, "Everyday before she left for work, Paula got coffee ready so that . . .

so that, I'd have a fresh cup when I got home . . ."

"It's all right," Brad said, expecting another torrent of sobs. "Take all the time you need."

Lydia dabbed her eyes with the handkerchief. "When I went to the kitchen . . . I found her, and she . . . There was all that blood."

"You don't need to go into all that," Brad said, watching her face, hoping she would meet his gaze. "Where were you when you called the police?"

"I panicked and ran out screaming. I went to Juan and Raoul's next door, and they called the police. I stayed with Raoul, and Juan came over here and waited for the police."

She dissolved into tears as she finished her story. Brad started to stand, but Lydia grabbed his arm. "Paula liked you," Lydia said, adding, "Not at first. She said you got off to a bad start."

Brad smiled back at her, while recalling the confrontation with Paula at Wilkie's execution. "I liked her too."

"Paula said you were helpful with a story she wrote."

Brad stood. "Yes, it was in today's paper." He put a hand on her shoulder, saying, "I'm sorry, Lydia."

Brad thought he heard his name being called, then realized it was Sharon shouting from the street, and he suspected that the officer standing guard at the steps wouldn't let her pass.

Gesturing toward the door, Brad said, "Nick, I'll need your help to get your soon-to-be-rookie into this crime scene."

Nick poked his head out the door, got the officer's attention with a whistle, and seconds later Sharon stood with them in the townhouse's living room. A badge, with the proper amount of authority, can work miracles, Brad thought.

"Let me show you the kitchen," Nick said. Brad thought Nick's demeanor seemed unusually tense, and he acted less collegial. Brad wondered why Nick wanted him at the crime scene, since they already had a van-load of criminalists, photographers, and detectives present.

As they passed through the dining room, Brad noted the deep emerald green color of the walls and the way floral fabric had been stapled to the ceiling to produce a tent-like effect. The furnishings were sparse, of second-hand-store origin, he thought, and mismatched. But the sideboard looked like a valuable antique, maybe a family heirloom.

"Did Paula ever say anything about Lydia that would suggest this might be a crime of passion?" Nick asked.

Brad shook his head. "No. And Lydia's grief seems genuine enough to me."

"Just thought I'd ask," Nick said. "Covering the bases."

"What kind of hate crimes have you had in this neighborhood?" Sharon asked.

"I'm not sure," Nick said. "Which is a good sign. Because if I don't know about it, most likely the stats haven't been significant enough to flag in our monthly reports."

Nick stopped them as they arrived at the open doorway to the kitchen. Brad could see that the townhouses backing to Paula's property blocked the late afternoon sun from the kitchen window. Two fluorescent light fixtures in the suspended ceiling provided most of the light.

Nick pointed. "See the bullet hole in the refrigerator?"

Brad saw the dark spot in the refrigerator door, about four feet off the ground. His eyes darted around the scene, noting the kitchen sink's placement below the window, and recognizing new oak cupboards and vinyl countertops arranged in an L-shape on the right hand side of the room. On the left side, a two-person table sat in front of a bookshelf.

The smell of death lingered in the room. Brad thought he caught a whiff of gunpowder, but maybe it was his imagination. But there was no disguising the odor of the final elimination of human waste that can accompany death.

Brad noticed a mug on the counter, while a second broken mug was visible on the off-white vinyl tiled floor below the kitchen sink. Next to it was a dark red puddle. The rest of the floor looked a sloppy mess.

"It looks like she threw a pot of hot coffee on her assailant," Nick said. "The technicians are gonna collect the cups and the carafe to see if we can find any fingerprints or trace evidence, but I wanted you to see their placement first, Brad."

Brad inched his way forward into the room, taking in the entire scene. He studied the drip coffee maker, sitting on the edge of the counter, still plugged into the wall. The digital clock on its face showed 4:03. On the heating plate was a small now-dried brown stain.

"The time is wrong," Brad said, looking at his watch and noting that it was after 6:30 p.m.

"I used to have a coffee machine like that," Sharon said. "I never like to leave small appliances plugged in because of the possibility of a fire hazard. So every time you plug it in, the clock automatically resets to 12 o'clock. You even have to advance the time to at least 12:01 before the brew switch will operate. 4:03 probably means she plugged it in about four hours ago."

"Which would mean that she was alive at about two-thirty this afternoon, but dead by three forty-five," Brad said.

"That would fit with what we've learned so far," Nick said. "Neighbors heard what they thought was a backfire shortly before three. We've got an officer canvassing the neighborhood to see what anyone else noticed."

"What about the weapon?" Brad asked.

"The bullet was embedded in the refrigerator door. It's already on its way to the lab, but it looked like a .45 caliber to me," Nick said. "I'd say it was probably fired with a double-action revolver, but the gun hasn't been found on the premises. Criminals just never cooperate that much. We'd prefer to find the gun with the owner's name engraved on the handle. An address sticker on the barrel would help, too." Nick laughed. "It'd make our job a lot easier."

"Fired at what range?" Brad asked.

"I'd say about six feet. There weren't any powder burns that I could see on the body—medical examiner will tell us for sure. The shot was fired from over there." Nick pointed toward the doorway where they first entered the kitchen. "Finding the bullet in the refrigerator enabled us to quickly establish the trajectory," he explained.

"Where was she—"

"Just above the heart." Nick anticipated Brad's question. "There was a lot of blood, as you can see."

"What was she wearing, Nick?" Sharon asked.

"A denim jumper over a dark blue cotton blouse."

"Sounds like she was dressed to go to work," Sharon remarked.

"Yes. We already contacted the *Inquirer*. She was expected at their offices around three. It would have taken about fifteen minutes from here for her to get to work. So she made coffee for her girlfriend at about two-thirty, then should've left for work, but someone interfered with her routine."

Brad watched as Nick stood near the middle of the kitchen, hands on his hips, looking in all directions.

"Something's bothering you?" Brad said.

Nick shrugged. "Not really. Just confused that's all. Most of the coffee was spilled on that side of the room." Nick pointed toward the small table. "Since it wouldn't have been possible for her to throw a pot of hot coffee at her assailant after she was shot," he noted wryly, "I keep trying to picture the little dance that might have gone on here."

"Was this a robbery gone bad?" Brad asked.

Nick stared at Brad for a few seconds, almost as if to say you-tell-me. But then he shook his head. "I don't think so. Her purse wasn't touched. She had thirty bucks and four credit cards in her wallet. No evidence of any possessions disturbed in the house. As you can see they were immaculate housekeepers.

"Then it must have been somebody she knew," Sharon speculated. "Maybe she told him to have a seat. Then they had an argument and she let fly with the hot coffee."

"Yeah, it's possible," Nick said. Though from his expression, Brad figured he'd already discounted that possibility. "That'd sure make a guy mad. The water would have been hot, but not scalding. They make these coffeepots nowadays so you can almost drink the coffee as it comes out. It might have produced first degree burns, but it wouldn't have incapacitated anyone."

"Was any blood or coffee tracked back through the house?" Brad asked.

"Not that we could tell. There was a throw rug at the entrance to the kitchen," Nick explained. "We've sent that to the lab for analysis. There were a couple of footprints in the kitchen. They took photos, but I'm not prepared to say it wasn't from one of our men who arrived first at the scene. Lydia was out here too, as was the guy from next door."

"Excuse me, Captain." A uniformed officer stood in the doorway to the kitchen. "We've done a door-to-door canvas talking with neighbors. Only three of the residences were occupied this afternoon. The neighbor across the street saw a young man knocking on Ms. Thompson's door about three p.m., but never saw him enter the premises. She described the man as blonde and in his early-20s, but another neighbor reported a sixteen-year-old blonde kid was working the street selling magazine subscriptions for his school."

"Thanks, Ed, for the report," Nick said. "You can tag these other items and close up shop here, we're about done."

Nick led the three of them back into the dining room, then faced Brad. "In the *Inquirer* this morning, I noticed your name mentioned ahead of our esteemed elected officials."

It was now clear to Brad why Nick had invited him; Nick had read Thompson's article that morning, saw Brad's name in connection with Wilkie's note, and knew that the two of them had had conversations. Nick wanted the scoop.

"Everybody's a cynic," Brad said, glancing at Sharon. "I told Paula about Wilkie's message—showed her the phrases we came up with—since I was hoping to flush out a Camden con man who I figured had stolen Wilkie's Bible and probably torched my office. I've already put a crimp in Alessi's con. But if you're thinking there's a connection between her article and this crime, I agree with you. I'll gladly share his address so you can question him about Paula's murder."

Nick tightened his lips and nodded.

"I'm curious," Nick said. "Thompson mentioned a botched execution and cover up for the next article in her series. You know anything about that?"

"No, but I can tell you that Paula wasn't a fan of capital punishment. She was a passionate idealist."

"So was I, once," Nick said, "before I became a police officer."

"Where are you parked?" Brad asked Sharon when they had exited Thompson's townhouse.

"New Jersey," she quipped. "Nah, it's just around the corner and up a couple of blocks."

They only had walked a few hundred feet, when Sharon grabbed Brad's arm and said, "I'll be right back." She turned and ran toward Thompson's townhouse.

Brad didn't have a clue what she was up to, as he studied a neighborhood in the midst of renewal. Saddened by Thompson's death, and convinced of its connection to his family's murder eleven years earlier, Brad hoped he could find who was responsible before there were any more deaths.

Five minutes later Sharon returned, wiping tears from her eyes.

"What's wrong?" Brad asked.

She turned and looked at him, her eyes puffy. "Oh, Brad," she said, before throwing her arms around him. She spoke, the side of her face against his chest, which muffled her words, but Brad thought he heard her say: "I just told Nick I wasn't interested in the police job. I want to stay with you."

"It's okay," Brad said, returning her hug. He held her tight and patted her back as she cried for a few more seconds. Brad smiled. It was the best news he'd heard all day.

CHAPTER 29

Brad rode back to his estate in Sharon's car. They arrived at dusk to find a familiar looking blue Lexus parked in the driveway and lights ablaze inside the mansion.

"Did you leave the lights on when you left?" Brad asked.

"I wondered that myself," Sharon said. "No. It was daylight. I'd never turned on any lights."

Brad got out of the car and approached the house warily, opening the front door with his key as Sharon followed behind.

"Oh, there you are, Bradford," Harriet said, sounding relieved. Brad stared in disbelief as Harriet hurried over to him in a matronly gray suit and high heel shoes that clacked on the marble floor when she walked. "I was so worried about you. I even called the police. I was afraid something awful had happened."

"How did you get in?" Brad asked, pointing toward the door.

Innocently, she said, "I used my key. Joe gave me a key a long time ago."

"It would have been nice if you had let me know you were coming," Brad said, trying not to sound peeved. "Especially since I just saw you in New York City eight hours ago."

"I told you I'd be down to visit soon."

"Yes, but you didn't say it would be this evening." Brad glanced at Sharon and saw her chuckling. He wasn't amused.

"I didn't know myself." Harriet sounded flustered. "I

mentioned to Andrew that I wanted to come to Philadelphia and take care of getting a gravestone for your father, and he offered me a ride."

"On the corporate jet?" Brad asked. "But you don't like to fly."

"On those great big ones, heavens, no!" She shuddered. "Not crammed in with all those people. This was a nice cozy airplane, with only Andrew and me and a lovely stewardess.

Brad wondered which one of them had piloted the plane.

"I even had a Brandy Alexander at 23,000 feet," she continued. "I'm just glad to see you here." She threw her arms around him, talking in his ear as she said, "I even checked with Andrew to see if the two of you were having dinner together."

Brad pulled away. "In Houston? Aunt Harriet, you're not making any sense. You knew I was coming back to Philadelphia."

"Andrew's in Philadelphia," she announced. "He had business to take care of. He's staying at the Ritz Carlton."

Brad glanced at Sharon and could tell she shared his suspicions.

"Aunt Harriet, what time did you arrive in Philadelphia this afternoon?" Brad asked.

She paused, using her thumb and forefingers to figure the time.

"About one-forty-five," Harriet said, then misinterpreted the look of distress on Brad's face. "Oh, your brother said he would have offered you a ride, but that you were meeting a friend in New York for lunch and then taking the train back to Philadelphia."

"I wish Andy would have told me," Brad said to no one in particular.

"You're home," Harriet said, clasping her hands together. "That's the important thing. Oh," she said, spinning on her heels, "Diane's waiting for you. We've been having a nice chat in the drawing room."

Brad advanced several steps and peered through the archway, and saw Diane Panella-Frame seated demurely on the Chinese sedan in the living room. He frowned in Aunt Harriet's direction as he realized Diane had overheard their conversation about Andrew.

Brad summoned up his manners as he walked toward Diane, saying, "That must be *your* car in the driveway."

"Brad, thank you for seeing me." Diane remained seated, but extended her hand like she expected it to be kissed. Instead, Brad offered a polite handshake.

Diane cleared her throat. "Actually, the car is one of the reasons I came."

"How can I help?" he asked.

"You remember my friend, Ron? You met him at my house last week."

"Yes. I think I remember." Brad tried to keep a straight face. "The one with the hairy chest and the white towel around him, right?"

Diane gushed. "Well, that description does narrow the field. Yes, I can tell you remember him. Ron brought his car over to my place on Friday night, and I gave him a lift to the train station Saturday morning. I haven't seen him since. He told me to go ahead and drive it as much as I wanted. I've been thinking about buying a new car, so I thought I'd give it a whirl. Well, I kept expecting to see him over the weekend, but he never showed up. I think he's missing."

"Missing?" Brad repeated.

"I can't even reach him," Diane said, sounding distressed. "He gave me an office number and they said he's not there anymore. They wouldn't give me any more information. And the number where I used to leave him private voice messages has been disconnected."

Aunt Harriet, seated next to Diane, clucked her tongue.

"I'd like to hire you to find him," Diane finally announced.

"I see," Brad said, not anticipating her request. "Do you have the keys to the car?"

"Yes." Diane fumbled through her purse. "They're here someplace. Ah, here they are."

Ironic, Brad thought, when Diane produced keys on the end of a white rabbit's foot.

Brad whispered to Sharon, handing her the keys. Sharon excused herself.

"You don't suppose Ron was after you for your money, Diane," Brad said, "and now he's found someone richer and more beautiful?"

Diane put her finger on the dimple of her chin and glanced upward. "Richer, maybe," she said. That was apparently all her vanity would let her admit.

"We should have information in just a few minutes," Brad said. "You didn't need to come all the way over here. You could have called me."

"It wasn't out of my way. I was visiting Gertie Lindstrom, and I thought I would swing by. Besides, I saw the lights on."

Brad glanced at Harriet.

"Gertie's very depressed," Diane said, sounding dejected herself, as Harriet reached out to comfort her. "Their house is up for sale, and Gertie can't understand why. The bankruptcy came as such a shock to her and she's blaming herself because of all the medical bills and personal care she requires."

Harriet sat next to Diane shaking her head, acting like they were bosom buddies, but anyone who'd been at Joseph Frame's funeral knew how she really felt about Diane.

"I offered to help them," Brad said, "but Em was too proud to accept it."

Sharon returned carrying a sheaf of papers along with the car keys, which she handed to Diane. "The Lexus is a rental, at about $150 a day with all the insurance and extra coverage," Sharon said. "Ron was supposed to return it to the dealership by Saturday afternoon."

"Looks like Ron Allessi stuck you with a problem," Brad said.

Diane seemed momentarily flustered. "Well! Interesting. I'd better be going. Thank you for your time, Brad," she said, gathering her purse and heading for the front door.

"If you'd like me to see if I can locate him," Brad said.

"No," Diane said, firmly. "I don't think that will be necessary. You see, I only wanted to find him so that I could give him back his car. But thanks to you, now I know where to return it."

Brad closed the door behind her, and seconds later heard the rhythmic thumps of tires across his cobblestone drive. He watched as Harriet scooped up a packet of papers from a nearby table, handed them to him and announced, "I got your mail, Bradford."

Brad noticed that several letters had ragged edges, like they'd already been ripped open.

"You never told me an arsonist set fire to your office," Harriet said, matter-of-factly.

The anger rose in him as he glanced through the mail to see which items had been disturbed.

"Toluene is very dangerous," she continued. "Your Uncle Oscar, God rest his soul, owned several auto body shops. A fire destroyed one of them when someone smoked a cigarette near an open container of Toluene. Luckily no one was killed. You need to be more careful."

"You opened my mail?" Brad asked, sharply.

"Well, I . . . Yes. It was from the insurance company and I thought that maybe it had something to do with Joe. That's when I saw the arson report. I couldn't help it," she said, with an edge in her voice. "I worry about you, Bradford."

Brad held up two of the envelopes. "Did worry cause you to open sympathy cards addressed to me?"

Harriet babbled on. "One was from your cousin in St. Louis. I was anxious and curious to see if there was any word on the baby's arrival."

Brad exploded with anger. "Aunt Harriet, don't *ever* open my mail again. Do *you* understand me?"

She bowed her head, avoiding his belligerent stare.

Brad marched toward the grand staircase. Halfway up the steps he leaned over the railing and said, "If I don't see you in the morning, I hope you have a safe trip back to New York *tomorrow*."

Moments later, he slammed his bedroom door shut.

CHAPTER 30

Brad sat at the desk in his office. He'd just finished reading the account of Paula Thompson's murder in the *Inquirer*, when Sharon bounded into the room.

"Did you see Aunt Harriet this morning?" Sharon asked.

"Not yet," Brad snapped, at the mention of her name. He was still peeved at his aunt for snooping through his mail.

"Did you talk to your brother this morning?" she asked.

"I tried. I called the Ritz-Carlton at six-thirty, but Andy had already checked out."

"I've been thinking," Sharon said. "Two of Paula's *Inquirer* stories were followed by crimes—the fire in your office and her murder. In both instances the articles suggested information regarding a message from Frank Wilkie. *We* know what Wilkie's message was. But only one person is going to commit murder to find out what the message says. And that is the *real killer* mentioned in Wilkie's note."

Brad nodded. He'd already done a similar analysis. "Have I mentioned how glad I am that you're going to continue to work for me?"

"Only half-a-dozen times." Sharon shifted her weight as she stood.

Sensing her unease, Brad said, "There's something else you want to say?"

"You need to think about *all* possible suspects," Sharon said softly.

Brad nodded. "Tell me what *you're* thinking."

"Your brother made a point about reading *The Philadelphia Inquirer*'s Web page for business news," Sharon said. "If he regularly consulted its Web page he would have seen Paula's articles too. We know Andrew was in Philadelphia yesterday. Can we find out if he was in the vicinity on the night of the arson?"

Brad exhaled. He hated to admit it, but Andy's name had floated through his brain as a suspect more than a few times during the past week. Recalling the events of the kidnapping, it was Andy who had delivered the ransom money. Brad recognized Andy as a brilliant corporate strategist, but could hardly imagine him planning his own family's execution. The anguish they all shared during that horrible week eleven years ago was genuine, Brad knew. It had brought his dad, brother, and him closer than they had ever been, like planets pulled near by a powerful gravitational force before spinning away to their own distant orbits.

Aunt Harriet cleared her throat. Brad turned and spotted her standing in the doorway to his office, wearing black slacks and a violet sweater and looking embarrassed. "I don't want to bother you, Bradford, but I wanted to say that I'm sorry about last night." She sounded chastened. "I was wrong to open your mail."

"I'm the one who should apologize, Aunt Harriet," Brad said, getting up from his chair and walking over to hug her. "I was too harsh last night."

Their hug seemed to restore her effusiveness.

"There is one more thing," she said. "I was thinking about what Diane said last night about her meeting with Gertie. Joe always told me that Emerson Lindstrom still had the first dime he ever made, so I didn't understand about the bankruptcy. I hope you don't mind, Bradford," she said, talking rapidly as if she thought he might stop her, "but I called an old friend of mine who is in the real estate business locally. I pretended to be interested in buying the Lindstrom's house. They are asking $1.7 million, but Marge told me it likely would sell for $1.4 million—which would be a steal. I told her I'd heard a rumor the house might be tied up in bankruptcy, and I was interested in immediate possession. She assured me that wasn't the case, and said the owners were even willing to self-finance the deal. I didn't think you could do something like that if you were filing for bankruptcy. What do you think?" Aunt Harriet sounded out of breath.

Brad frowned. "You're not really thinking about moving next door, are you?" Harriet looked crestfallen until a big grin spread across Brad's face.

"I think I know which side of the family gave me my detective chromosomes." Brad winked at her.

Harriet beamed. "I'm going to pack my bag, now that I know my trip wasn't wasted. I'll call a cab to get to the station."

"I can drive you, Harriet," Brad said, glancing at his watch.

"No. No," she protested. "You've got work to do." Harriet disappeared down the hall.

"Andy should be back in Houston by now," Brad said. Picking up the receiver he dialed Joedco's corporate headquarters, recognizing the charming efficiency in Andy's secretary's voice.

"Hello, Doris. It's Brad Frame here."

"Mr. Frame, it's good to hear from you. My condolences on the death of your father."

"Thanks, Doris. If he's available, I'd like to speak with Andy."

"Just a minute, Mr. Frame. I'll check."

"I'll hold, but don't put me into his voice mail. I want to speak with him personally."

Brad swiveled in his chair, accessing the notebook computer on his desk. He launched his e-mail program and started typing while he waited for his brother to pick up the line.

"Mr. Frame, I'm sorry," Doris said. "The privacy light is on his phone and when that happens the only option I have is his voice mail."

"Doris, do me a favor," Brad said. "Go pound on his door and tell him to check his e-mail and respond to me A.S.A.P. or I'll be selling my shares in the company. Say it exactly the way I told you." Brad covered the receiver and told Sharon, "That should get his attention."

Resuming his conversation with Andy's secretary, Brad said, "I'll be waiting by the computer. Thanks, Doris."

Fifteen minutes later his computer played a short MIDI file of a vintage train whistle, the signal for incoming e-mail.

Brad opened his Outlook program.

"Let's see. Oh, it's from Andrew. What a surprise!" He glanced at Sharon and chuckled.

Brad stroked his chin as he read the message, occasionally leaning toward the computer screen. His mouth hung open and he wet his lips with his tongue. When he finished reading he leaned back.

Brad stood up, and motioned Sharon into his chair.

"Call Experian and do a credit check on Emerson Lindstrom, while I touch base with Nick."

He pulled out his cell phone and speed-dialed Nick Argostino's number.

CHAPTER 31

A Century 21 FOR SALE sign had been planted at the head of the Lindstrom's driveway, Brad noticed. Their house looked quiet. The wheelchair accessible van sat next to the garage and Brad pulled his Mercedes behind it. He and Sharon emerged from the car. April's changeable weather had brought a cold front, with a temperature twenty degrees cooler than the day before when they'd visited Paula Thompson's townhouse. A brisk wind stirred up dust, prompting Sharon to shield her eyes with a scarf. Brad found the garage door wide open and called out Em's name before walking past the two-toned green antique Hudson toward a set of shelves at the back of the garage. There he examined the labels on several containers of paint solvent. Brad unscrewed the cap on one and detected a familiar pungent odor. He let Sharon, who had followed him, have a whiff. She turned up her nose.

Brad then tried the door at the back of the garage, finding it unlocked. The two of them passed through the breezeway to the Lindstrom's glass enclosed pool. "Hello," he shouted as they entered.

Em Lindstrom did backstroke laps, but not like an Olympic swimmer. He kicked wildly, matching the erratic sweeping motion of his arms as he propelled himself the length of the pool. Water lapped at the small fringe of white hairs that grew from the middle of his chest, and a white potbelly rose above the surface of the water, causing the elastic band on his beige swim trunks to flip forward.

Brad didn't think Em realized they were there, as he

stood on the tile surround at the deep end of the lap lane. "Where's Gertie?" Brad shouted as Em got closer.

Em seemed nonchalant and continued doing laps. He bellowed, "She's taking her afternoon nap."

Sharon shed her jacket, tossing it on one of the poolside chairs. The atmosphere was stifling, even more so than it had been a week earlier. The humid chlorinated odor reminded Brad of his mother's laundry room when he was a kid. Light fog rose from the surface of the water as hot air from the space heater warmed the air.

"Please stay at this end," Brad shouted. Em took his time making a turn at the shallow end of the pool near the entrance to the house, and slowly glided back toward where Brad and Sharon stood. "Why don't you get out of the pool so we can talk?" Brad asked.

Lindstrom remained on his back and moved his arms just enough to keep his head above water. "I'm fine right here."

"I'd really like to talk with both of you." Brad turned to Sharon saying, "See if you can find Gertie." Sharon started around the pool toward the house's entrance at the opposite end.

"No," Emerson yelled, standing up in the water. Even in the deep end, the water only came up to his chest. "You don't need to talk with her."

Sharon glanced at Brad, who held up his hand stopping her.

"How much does Gertie know?" Brad asked.

"About what?" Em splashed water on his shoulders, and took a few steps to his left. He cupped his hand over his eyes shielding them from the sunlight.

"It'll be easier for us to talk up here," Brad said, squinting from the glare reflecting off the water's surface.

"We can see each other face-to-face."

Sharon returned and stood next to Brad.

"There's nothing to talk about." Em leaned back in the water and resumed paddling.

"Let's talk about bankruptcy," Brad said, impatient with Em's stalling tactics. He swiped the sweat from his brow before slipping off his sport jacket, and placed it around the back of one of the poolside chairs. "You've got a perfect credit rating; we checked. You're not filing for bankruptcy and you don't need to. I'm curious as to why you told me you were. I notice you've got the house up for sale, too."

"I don't recall that *I* ever told you we were filing for bankruptcy. Gertie may have."

"But where did she get an idea like that if it wasn't from you?"

"I hate nosey neighbors," Em said.

Probably as much as I hate liars for neighbors, Brad thought, turning his back on Em and looking plaintively at Sharon. Struggling to maintain his professional demeanor, as the bile rose in his throat, he wanted to back off and counted on Sharon to take over for him. Brad pulled out his handkerchief and wiped his face.

"I think I'll go find Gertie now," Sharon said to Brad, loud enough for Emerson to hear. She turned once again toward the house entrance.

"Wait," Em said, trying to stop her. "For her own good, I've got to get Gertie out of here. She's not doing well. She needs a warm climate. She can't continue to stay here."

"She can't or you can't?" Sharon pointedly asked.

Em closed his eyes, ignoring her.

Brad had regained his composure and tried a different approach. "Joedco stock looked good this morning," he said. "It opened at ninety-three dollars. Eleven years ago you bought 40,000 shares at half price. The stock sold then at $5.50 a share, but Gertie's agreement with my dad let you buy the stock at $2.75. Your original investment was $110,000."

A bell mounted on the wall at the shallow end of the pool clanged loudly. The phone. Emerson once again stood facing them, trying to find his footing on the bottom of the pool. On the second ring Em snapped his head in that direction. By the third ring, clearly agitated, he turned toward the clanging bell. Brad and Sharon exchanged glances as they spotted the pink pattern on his otherwise pale back, and Brad realized why Em hadn't wanted to get out of the pool. A large mottled area of sunburned skin extended from his right shoulder blade to the elastic band of his swim trunks.

"What happened to your back?" Brad asked.

The phone stopped ringing and Em calmly turned around in the water and faced Brad again. Em's eyes had lost their focus.

"I needed to know what that damned reporter knew, that's all." Pointing to his back, Em added, "She didn't have to do this to me."

"And when you came and stole the Bible Wilkie had given me, you had to know what I knew, right? Then you set fire to the office, hoping we'd never know the Bible had been taken."

"I was afraid Wilkie had implicated me in the kidnapping of your mother and sister," Em said. "He never knew my name, but a description would have been easy to figure out."

Brad and Sharon exchanged glances.

"That reporter wouldn't tell me anything until I finally flashed the gun at her. Then she said she'd cooperate and show me the message Frank Wilkie sent you. From a bookshelf in her kitchen she pulled out a notebook and then took a single sheet of paper out of it and laid it on the table. I bent over to look at the paper and it was blank. Before I could react she doused me with hot coffee."

Em calmly leaned back in the water and resumed his backstroke. "That's when she had to die," he said. "I . . . I couldn't let her get away with that."

"Every time you thought you were covering your tracks you only managed to build a trail back to yourself," Brad said, his own voice rising with emotion. The twisted reasoning in Lindstrom's confession had sparked his anger. "You lied and told Gertie you had to declare bankruptcy, but then offered to finance the sale of your own house. This morning I found Toluene in your garage, the same accelerant used to start the fire in my office, and I'm guessing the police will be able to match the chemical composition exactly. When I saw the burn on your back, I knew you had gone after Paula Thompson, and were responsible for my mother's and sister's death. What I'd like to know is why?"

Gertrude Lindstrom entered from the house; the whir from her motorized wheelchair prompted Emerson to turn around.

"Oh, Brad," Gertie said, her face brightening as she saw him. "A Captain Argostino from the Philadelphia police called and wanted you to know he's on his way. Em, you didn't tell me we were expecting company."

"I didn't know," he said flatly.

Emerson Lindstrom faced Brad. "She doesn't have to stay, does she?" Em pleaded with his eyes.

Gertie rolled her motorized wheelchair toward where Brad and Sharon stood. "It's hard to hear what you're talking about at the other end."

"Why did you do it?" Brad repeated his question.

"Not with her around," Em said.

"Let me guess," Brad said, the anger rising in his voice. "As an investment banker, you knew that a kidnapping and murder in the family of a company's executive would cause the stock to plummet. And then you could afford to buy even more."

Em glowered at Brad. "I said not with her around."

"What, Em?" Gertie asked. "What about our stock? Why are you so angry? Why don't you want me around? What did I do?"

"Nothing!" Em screamed at her. "You didn't do anything."

"Then what's going on? I want to know what's going on." She stared at Brad, asking, "Why are the police coming here?"

"Your husband needs to talk to—."

Em cut him off. "I only wanted Gertie to have what was rightfully coming to her," Em said. "I thought I could sweeten the deal, and the time was running out when she could exercise her stock option. I figured there'd be negative publicity and the stock price would drop on the uncertainty of everything. Then she could buy more of it. On my way to work, I always stopped at a shoeshine stand in Penn Station, next to my office building. That's where I first met Wilkie. He stood around seeing what he could bum off of people; he did janitorial work in the building overnight. One day I asked him if he'd like to make some serious money." Em lowered his voice. "I only wanted a kidnapping . . . get some headlines in the news. But I didn't know who I was dealing with, and everything went wrong." Em shook his head. "I paid them up front. That was my mistake. The whole thing got out of control."

"You made more than one mistake," Brad said. He glanced at Gertie who looked dazed and confused.

"Do you know what a son-of-a-bitch you've got for a brother?" Em asked. "He deprived Gertie of the one joy of her life. For twenty-five years, ten . . . twelve hours a day, she helped your dad with the business. It was her whole life. Then Andrew came along and made it a living hell." Em pointed at Gertie as she sat in her wheelchair listening intently. "She did everything she could to please him. And all Andrew ever did was try to drive her out of the business. He made her work until nine, ten . . . eleven o'clock at night. Gertie never complained to him. She wouldn't get home until midnight and then I'd get an earful."

"Em, what are you saying?" Gertie asked. "I didn't mind the work."

He turned and pointed at her, saying angrily, "Just shut up."

"If your gripe was with Andy," Brad asked, "why take it out on innocent people? Mom and Lucy never did anything to you. Why make my dad suffer?"

"He . . . He cou . . . could've done something about it, but he never did. The business was his responsibility. I tried to talk with Joe, but he never had time for me. I wanted to make him understand how Andrew was affecting Gertie's health. It wasn't right what Andrew did. It wasn't right. He had to pay. I was gonna make him pay. I wanted to teach him a lesson, but then things got out of hand," Em repeated, as his voice trailed off.

Em wrapped his arms around his chest and appeared chilled, in spite of the humid warmth.

Gertie looked to Brad for answers. "Edith and Lucy? What did he do to them? I know he was always jealous of

Joe," Gertie began quietly, seemingly talking to herself. "One time he accused me of having an affair with Joe. Em was jealous because I liked my work."

Em spoke, his ramblings overlapping his wife's. "I sent Andrew warnings. His treatment of her gradually made her sick. No doctor would ever tell me that her working conditions caused her tumor, but I knew better. She wouldn't be a cripple today if it wasn't for your brother."

"Em, no. You don't understand," Gertie said, shaking her head. She rolled her wheelchair another three or four feet along the tile floor and turned it to face the pool. "Em, look at me," she pleaded.

"And you wouldn't be a millionaire if it weren't for my brother. Andy reminded me that Joedco stock split three times in the last ten years. In response to a question from me, Andy e-mailed me this afternoon—the 40,000 shares you bought after my mother and sister were murdered are now 320,000 shares and worth about thirty million dollars. Unfortunately, where you're going, it won't do you much good."

"Hello! Brad?" He heard Nick Argostino holler from the garage.

"We're in here," Brad shouted back.

Nick walked through the doorway from the garage and surveyed the scene. He wore a gray suit and almost immediately loosened his tie and wiped his brow in the humid atmosphere of the pool. Brad was glad to see him, greeting Nick with a firm handshake. In hushed tones, he briefly recounted to Nick what they'd learned so far.

Nick gazed at the man in the pool, and in an authoritarian tone asked, "You're Emerson Lindstrom?"

Em nodded.

"Please get out of the pool," Nick said. "I'd like you to

come in for questioning in the death of Paula Thompson."

Emerson ducked his head under the water, bobbing up a few seconds later and resumed floating on his back, as if he didn't have a care in the world.

"Say something, you bastard," Brad shouted, his voice charged with eleven years of pent up anger. Sharon put her hand on his shoulder.

Gertrude peered over at Emerson from her wheelchair and pleaded, "Em, tell me what they're saying isn't true."

"You got your ransom money," Brad said, his voice quivering with emotion. "Why did you have my mother and Lucy killed?"

Gertie shrieked! "My God, you didn't kill anybody? Em, tell me you didn't kill anybody."

Em lifted his head and spoke softly. "It wasn't about money. I told you, things got out of control. I never wanted them to kill anybody. A couple of days after the kidnapping I spotted Wilkie at the shoeshine stand. I told him to call it off. He said it was too late, that his partner had a sadistic streak. That's all he said, but I knew . . . I could hardly live with myself. Believe me, I never expected anybody to die." Em sounded remorseful, but then he smashed his fist into the water and shouted, "But that damned brother of yours had ruined her life. He created a living hell for Gertie. I wanted Joe's attention, to make him realize what Andrew had done to *my* family."

With her good hand, Gertie tugged at the wisps of thin hair on her forehead as her husband talked. "Oh, Em . . . You don't understand." Gertie screamed at him from her wheelchair. "Andrew is my son."

Em stared over at her, marking the first time he seemed to pay any attention to what she had said. He took in her revelation with an expression of scorn and disbelief, then paddled around in the water turning his back to her.

Brad studied Gertie; her face flushed pink in anger, as she grasped the significance of her husband's confession. Gertie swiveled her wheelchair sharply away from the pool. Her good hand seized the controls and she would not let go. She clamped her jaw tightly and wore a contorted mask of wretched anger.

Gertie jammed the joystick-style control forward and her wheelchair careened down the tiled surface surrounding the pool. It rolled quickly. She turned sharply to the right, the wheels coming perilously close to the edge of the pool. She toggled the switch and lined up the chair, taking aim at the electric space heater.

"Gertie, NO!"

When he heard Brad shout, Em turned his head. His eyes widened in fear. Em struggled to plant his feet on the bottom of the pool. The water came mid-way up his chest once he got his footing. He scrambled toward the ladder at the side of the pool, but the mass of water impeded his efforts, as he appeared to run in slow motion.

Like a battering ram, Gertie struck the electric heater with a quick thrust of her motorized chair. The heater sailed airborne toward the water. Em raised his left arm in a parrying motion to deflect the heater away, but instead it toppled over his arm and landed on his chest where it first made contact with the water.

Emerson screamed.

His agonizing cry echoed off the glass of the pool enclosure. His arms flailed about. Sparks flashed inside the heater. He lost his balance and fell backward. The electric cord tightened around his arm, pulling the metal casing of the heater in sizzling contact with his chest. Emerson's body convulsed from the electric shock, and his mouth hung open but emitted no sound. Water churned around him from his struggle.

Sharon ran into the garage and unplugged the heater's extension cord, but it was too late.

Nick extracted his cell phone, and Brad saw him punch a few buttons before announcing an emergency at the Lindstrom's address.

Emerson Lindstrom's lifeless body slipped beneath the surface then bobbed back up. A pink and white denture dislodged from his mouth and spiraled to the bottom of the pool. He floated on his back, seemingly suspended with his arms outstretched, mouth gaping. The waters stilled around him, Em's violent encounter marked only by the ripple of the water against the sides of the pool in ever increasing rings.

CHAPTER 32

Brad turned away from the gruesome scene.

Gertrude Lindstrom sat transfixed in her wheelchair, gazing at Emerson's body as it floated in the pool. Her hands lay limp in her lap, and her body began to shake. Brad knelt beside her, and pulled the shawl more tightly around her shoulders. In the distance he heard warbling sirens. "It's over, Gertie," he said, then realized the words applied to him as well as to her. He reached behind the wheelchair and disconnected its battery, preventing any sudden decisions by Gertie to join her husband in a watery grave.

An ambulance arrived ahead of the police. Minutes later, a forensic photographer snapped pictures before the coroner's staff fished Em's limp body out of the pool.

Gertie, still in a state of shock, mumbled.

"What is it, Gertie?" Brad asked.

"The car," she said. "Look in the Hudson. Em never let me get near that car."

Brad stood and glanced at Sharon. She went to see Nick Argostino where he conferred with the officer in charge. Brad watched as the three of them headed for the garage.

Gertie reached out to Brad with her good arm, looking plaintively and signaling for him to come closer. In a hoarse whisper, she said, "Don't tell Andrew. I don't want him to know about me."

"Mom and Dad kept your secret. It'll be safe with me," Brad said.

She shook her head. "Your parents never knew. There

were so many times I wanted to tell Joe that Andrew was mine, but I never did. I was only seventeen when I got pregnant. My father sent me away, saying he would take care of everything. When I gave birth, they told me I had a son, but they whisked him away before I ever got to see him. Five years later, after my father died, I found a letter to him from the lawyer who handled the adoption. It mentioned your mother's maiden name and the section of Bryn Mawr where your parents used to live. The attorney assured my father that he'd been given a good home. But I just had to know how my baby was doing, to see him, if only once. From the information in the letter I was able to figure out where he was." Tears streamed down Gertie's face. "Soon afterward I read that your mother would be hosting a tea at the museum. I went, with the intention of befriending her. She was pregnant with you at the time. My heart leapt when she talked about her five-year-old son that she'd named Andrew. When she spoke of wanting to build a new house . . . Well, I offered to sell them the land from my property." Gertie seemed choked with emotion, her words came haltingly. "Then I knew I could watch my boy grow up. Becoming Joe's business partner enabled me to see even more of Andrew. As he got older, he reminded me more and more of my father. Intense. Yes, overbearing at times, but still my son."

An officer approached and announced, "We're going to drive you to the police station, Mrs. Lindstrom." She nodded.

The officer backed the wheelchair along the tiled-edge of the pool. Looking at Brad, Gertie lifted her now shaking left hand and put two fingers across her lips. Brad raised two fingers to his own lips in a signal of silence.

Sharon returned with Nick.

"We found the revolver used to kill Paula Thompson, along with the Bible that Wilkie left you, in the trunk of Lindstrom's car," Nick announced. "And there's a metal strong box with a lot of money in it. The local cops are counting it now, but based on what I saw—hundred dollar bills, and the age of the money—it's probably the $500,000 in ransom."

Brad's eyes glistened. He felt a growing sense of perspective, if not closure, on the events that had transformed his life.

Brad, Sharon and Nick stood outside the Lindstrom's house as the police drove their wheelchair accessible van to the base of the porch ramp. The cool temperatures and light breeze brought relief from the humid heat of the indoor pool.

"I'm guessing voluntary manslaughter will be the charge," Nick said, as they watched two strapping officers hoist Gertie's wheelchair into the van. "I doubt the DA will oppose bail. Besides they don't really have the facilities at the county jail to take care of her."

A persistent beep sounded, signaling reverse, as the van backed away from the Lindstrom's porch, then made a wide turn before heading up the gravel drive.

Nick Argostino put his hand on Brad's shoulder. "I'm gonna go. I don't have a case here anymore. She took care of my prime suspect in the Thompson murder. Now I've got to go back to the office and remember where I put that damned *case closed* rubber stamp." He winked.

"Thanks for all your help, Nick," Brad said.

Nick climbed into his government-issued sedan. Rolling down his window, Nick said, "You'll repay the favor for me someday."

"We're done here," Brad said, with a sigh, after Nick's car drove away.

Sharon pointed at Brad's Mercedes. "They've got your car hemmed in." The coroner's vehicle, two unmarked cars, and a police cruiser blocked the way.

"Let's walk," Brad said. "I could use the fresh air. I'll pick up the car later."

The amber tones of approaching sunset washed over the foliage along their path, giving bark, twigs and even the underbrush a rich warm glow, while the new green of spring sparkled in the gentle radiance. Brad felt healing as the fresh smells of spring wafted over him. He could hear the birds warming up for their evening calls as he and Sharon wound their way up the hillside between the Lindstrom's and his estate. Midway up the slope Brad stopped in front of a wooden bench at the side of the path.

"I'd almost forgotten about this," he said, plopping on the middle of the rough-hewn bench, and stretching his legs while his arms draped across the back. "Mother asked Dad to make this for her. From this spot you can't see any houses, only the trees. Mom wanted a place to escape. She even planted her favorite . . ."

Brad scrambled across the path, dropped to his knees and gently tore at the underbrush, which grew next to the trail. "I found one," he shouted. Sharon looked on as Brad pushed away debris and dead leaves revealing the stem of a daffodil pushing its way out of the soil. "My mom planted these," he said, delighting in his discovery.

Sharon knelt beside him, joining him as they raked away the moist flimsy-compost of last year's leaves with their fingers, uncovering more tender shoots. She nodded when Brad said, "I'm gonna come back here more often."

ABOUT THE AUTHOR

Ray Flynt is president/CEO of a national human services association based in Washington, DC. A native Pennsylvanian, he holds a BA in Social Sciences and a Master's Degree in Public Administration. Ray's career has spanned the fields of criminal justice, education, the arts, human services, and he has served as a strategic planning consultant to non-profit organizations. Ray is a member of Mystery Writers of America, and active in their Mid-Atlantic Chapter. He is also an avid amateur theatre performer and set designer. He lives near Annapolis, Maryland. For more information, visit www.rayflynt.com.